The
Janus Cycle

CW00551147

The
Janus Cycle

Tej Turner

Elsewhen Press

The Janus Cycle
First published in Great Britain by Elsewhen Press, 2015
An imprint of Alnpete Limited

Copyright © Tej Turner, 2015. All rights reserved
The right of Tej Turner to be identified as the author of this work has been asserted
in accordance with sections 77 and 78 of the Copyright, Designs and Patents Act
1988. No part of this publication may be reproduced, stored in a retrieval system
or transmitted in any form, or by any means (electronic, mechanical, telepathic, or
otherwise) without the prior written permission of the copyright owner. A version
of Chapter 3 *Bruises* previously appeared in the *Impossible Spaces* anthology edited by
Hannah Kate and published by Hic Dragones in 2013.

Elsewhen Press, PO Box 757, Dartford, Kent DA2 7TQ
www.elsewhen.co.uk

British Library Cataloguing in Publication Data.
A catalogue record for this book is available from the British Library.
ISBN 978-1-908168-46-7 Print edition
ISBN 978-1-908168-56-6 eBook edition

Condition of Sale
This book is sold subject to the condition that it shall not, by way of trade or
otherwise, be lent, re-sold, hired out or otherwise circulated in any form of binding
or cover other than that in which it is published and without a similar condition
including this condition being imposed on the subsequent purchaser.

This book is copyright under the Berne Convention.
Elsewhen Press & Planet-Clock Design are trademarks of Alnpete Limited

Printed and bound by CPI Group (UK) Ltd, Croydon, CR0 4YY

This book is a work of fiction. All names, characters, places, clubs, schools,
spiritual organisations and rock bands are either a product of the author's fertile
imagination or are used fictitiously. Any resemblance to actual popular beat
combos, cults, academies, entertainment establishments, sites or people (living,
dead, or time travelling) is purely coincidental.

Contents

1 Friday... 9

2 The Christmas Puppy 31

3 Bruises 59

4 Red Rivers.. 79

5 Shadow Sisters... 95

6 Going Back... 131

7 The Dog Man... 173

8 Blisters 181

This book is dedicated to mothers.

Barbara Turner, who left this world too soon. Sue Watterson, who in her love and care took on the (sometimes troublesome) responsibility of raising me.

Joyce Turner, Margaret Jackson, and Marjorie Jackson – my grandmothers. And also Dorf Jackson, who was like a grandmother to me.

And finally; Kate Beck, Jeanine Fox-Rioche, and Tracy Dixon. Mothers of my friends who have all been caring at certain points of my life.

Much thanks to you all.

1
Friday

I hate Sunday mornings. That moment when you open your eyes to cruel sunlight beaming through the window and igniting a whole orchestra of pain. Squirming, groaning, covering your face, closing your eyes – it takes a while for you to accept that nothing will stop it playing out. The weekend is over and your body is punishing you.

Like most Sundays, I told myself I was never going to do it again.

And, as usual, I wasn't fooling anyone.

Curled up on the couch, once again, because last night I didn't think stumbling into the bedroom was worth the risk of exciting my girlfriend's wrath. Throughout the last few months I have learnt through trial and error that it is much easier to just creep into the living room, sleep on the couch, and greet her in the morning when she is usually more agreeable.

It was now time to face the music. I stretched my aching limbs and crawled to my feet.

I knew she was in the bedroom because I could hear faint noises from the television. So I lightly pushed the door open and stumbled into the room.

Vanessa was lying under the duvet, tucking into a packet of crisps, and she managed to tear her eyes away from the TV for a brief moment to spare me a look of contempt.

"Nice waste of a weekend?" asked the girl who probably spent the whole time vegetating on the couch, watching soap operas and reality TV shows.

I shrugged, knowing that any reply, whether honest, sarcastic, defensive, or apologetic would simply incur more salty comments.

At this point you are probably noticing that something doesn't quite ring about our relationship. Well, let me tell you a few things about Vanessa and me...

For our relationship to be considered dead would imply that it was once thriving. The truth is we used to be fuck-buddies but at some point we both needed a new flat, and it just so happens that sharing is cheaper. The sex died down very quickly, and after I moved in she soon began to put on weight, almost as if to spite me. A face, which at one point could have been considered pretty, is now frequently soured by the expression one pulls having just sucked the juice out from a lemon. Neither of us is prepared to acknowledge the fact that we have reached a cul-de-sac because we are both too lazy to change gear into reverse and turn it around. I work Monday to Friday so I can spend the weekends in various degrees of intoxication, whereas she is so lazy she hasn't seen her parents who live five doors away for six months – now, where would either of us manage to find time for a breakup in that?

"Nothing to say?" she asked, as she turned back to some riveting TV show about home improvement. "I haven't seen you since Friday."

And that was when I remembered what happened on Friday.

My weekends are usually a blur of drink and drugs. I kill too many brain cells on the journey to remember it all, but this weekend something very unusual happened. Memories of Friday night replayed in my mind. The face of someone I met flashed before my eyes.

Was it a dream? Did it really happen?

Didn't she give me something to remember her by? I reached into my pockets. One packet of fags; three matches; my phone; a thimble, (where the hell did *that* come from?); one Rubik's cube: not quite solved.

No wallet – that was where I put it.

"What's the matter?" she asked. "Lost something?"

I ignored her and held back a curse. Where in my distorted haze of a weekend had I lost my wallet?

"Kev's house," I realised. "I left my wallet at Kev's!"

I refrained from referring to him by his usual term of endearment – K-Hole-Kev – for obvious reasons. Vanessa is like a spider and this flat is her web. I am a fly she has caught hold of – a vile, disgusting one – but one she, for some reason I don't think even *she* knows, wants to keep in her grasp. She has learned over the last few months that drugs have a way of untangling me from her strings.

"Oh no," she shook her head. "You are *not* going there today!"

"Why not?" I asked. "I need my fucking wallet!"

"Fine!" she screamed, and then pointed one of her long red fingernails at me. "But no drugs!"

"I don't want to take drugs. I want my fucking wallet!"

"Promise me you won't take drugs," she commanded.

I rolled my eyes. It was a Sunday, why would I want to take drugs?

"I promise I won't take any drugs."

I popped a couple of aspirin and a few minutes later I was walking up the driveway of the marvel which is K-Hole-Kev's house.

This isn't the sort of place that you bother to knock before you enter, the door doesn't even have a working latch. I swung it open and entered the familiar scene of his rundown kitchen.

This place hasn't seen much cooking, but the counters were scattered with their usual assortment of empty cans, wrappers, ashtrays and pizza boxes. There were a few bottles of beer left over from the weekend on the side, I couldn't recall Vanessa forcing me to make any promises about not drinking and she is one of those people who claim that alcohol is not a drug, so I – rather smugly – cracked the lid off with my lighter.

But just as I brought it to my lips and took my first swig, K-Hole-Kev emerged from the hallway with a baseball bat in his hands.

If he was trying to surprise a burglar, he's lucky I'm not one because his sneaking advance was about as subtle as nails on a blackboard, he was holding the bat in his scrawny arms with the grace a young child brandishes a toy and, with scruffy hair and tired eyes, he had his usual just-got-out-of-bed look – which is ironic because he doesn't sleep much.

"You're not taking my TV!" he screamed.

"Kev, your TV is broken," I reminded him.

He had thrown a table at it a few weeks ago because he thought that the kid on the cereal advert was trying to eat him. He is probably better off without it.

"I might have a TV!"

"Kev, I was there when you broke it! It's me, *Pikel*."

He leaned in closer and narrowed his eyes for a few moments, eventually recognising me and dropping the bat on the floor.

"Pikel! Man, you came back!" he exclaimed, as if it had been longer than six hours since I last saw him. He put an arm around my shoulder and guided me into the living room.

We sat down on the couch and on the coffee table in front of us was a pile of white powder that I guessed to be ketamine. He orders it online by pretending he's a vet and I am surprised they haven't sussed him out yet because if they checked his transactions history then it would appear that he is only interested in sedating horses.

He began to arrange it into lines with his National Insurance Card.

"Want some K?" he asked.

I shook my head. "No. Sorry mate, I can't. I promised Vanessa."

"Aww man. Come on. Just a little one."

"Kev, I'm not doing any drugs!" I said firmly. "I just came here for my wallet."

"Your wallet?" he asked, raising an eyebrow.

"Yeah, I gave it to you last night to stop me spending money."

It seemed like a wise idea at the time.

"Oh shit man," Kev exclaimed, smacking his hand on his forehead.

"Where did you put my wallet, Kev?"

He rolled up a five pound note, and offered it to me.

"I lost it in a K-hole. You need to help me find it."

I sighed.

"Okay, but just a little one."

I dropped the note on the table, and my head rolled back as I felt waves of turbulence distorting my mind. A few moments later I heard the snuffle of Kev's nostril, as he checked in his ticket to join me in K-land.

I opened my eyes and watched the ceiling above me slipping away, my muscles relaxed, leaving my body still and lifeless, my mind playing helter-skelter. The world turned inside out. My head rested against the cushion.

The line Kev had given me had obviously been far from small, but it didn't matter anymore.

Her face appeared in my mind, and I remembered what brought me here.

I remembered the first time I met her.

Friday night. I finished work, my phone rang, and a voice on the other side gave me directions to where this weekend's rave was being held. After a swift change of clothes I was out of the house and ready.

Free parties are nomadic because if they linger for too long they become stagnant and the authorities send coppers in to snoop around. The location is changed weekly, and this time it was some abandoned warehouse on the other side of town. I soon found myself lost in the derelict quarters of the city, trying to make sense of the somewhat vague directions I had been given. I had been wandering for a while by this point but still not heard any loud music, and I had just swallowed a Rizla filled with MDMA so I was hoping to find it before my mind was blown.

This is a district the council would rather pretend didn't exist and most respectable people avoid. A few years ago some numbskulls decided to build new houses on the other side of town, thinking that it would increase the population – what they didn't realise at the time was that no one actually wants to live here so the same people just moved from one side of town to the other. Streets were abandoned, and neighbourhoods soon became wrecks, filled with street kids, hippies, ravers, drug addicts, all kinds of vagrants and freaks.

And I was just about to meet someone here who would change my life forever.

Years of neglect also mean that blown-out street lamps no longer get changed, but in the darkness ahead I saw movement and squinted my eyes.

A girl on the other side of the street seemed to glimmer as

she ran down the pavement. She was wearing torn up jeans and a black poncho that trailed behind her as she ran. Maybe it was just the drugs beginning to kick in but I found myself strangely mesmerised by her.

"Pikel!" she called.

I stopped in surprise. I had never seen this girl in my life, but somehow she knew my name and was running towards me like I was a long-lost friend.

"Do I know you?" I asked, crossing over the road. I couldn't see how I could have known her; she didn't seem like the sort I usually associated with. She had excessive amounts of purple eye shadow smudged around her eyes, and her hair was a messy brown tangle. She was pretty, but I wasn't sure I liked the effect that the three silver rings dangling from her eyebrow had on her face.

"There's no time!" she gasped. "He's coming for me!"

"What?" I replied. "Who's coming?"

I looked over her shoulder and saw a dark figure running towards us. She was being pursued.

I cursed under my breath, realising that he must be a mugger or something. I fucking hate muggers.

I scanned the ground. It was littered with crap. Stones. Rubble. Fag butts. Beer cans. By the wall was a rusty pipe.

I picked it up.

What the fuck are you doing Pikel? I thought to myself as I faced her pursuer with the pipe in my hand. I couldn't even remember the last time I came to the aid of a stranger. But there was something about this girl: I found myself bound to helping her.

The dark figure carried on charging towards us. He was wearing a large black cloak, and a hood obscured most of his face. The pipe in my hands seemed to be no deterrent – he carried on running.

Now, what to do next? I had a big, fucking ugly pipe in my hand, and he was still coming for me. He was coming in fast and I had no time to think. Instinct took over: I swung the pipe, aiming for his side, hoping to floor the fucker without killing him, but just as it was about to meet the black cape of his cloak, he disappeared and my weapon spiralled through thin air.

He was gone.

I gasped, and turned my head to look up and down the street. Vanished.

My first thoughts were that I must have been tripping, and I abruptly became aware and self-conscious of the fact that there was a girl behind me who had just seen me swing a pipe around at nothing.

"Thanks," she said.

"What?" I blurted, turning to face her. "You saw it too?"

She nodded, and I didn't know whether to feel relieved or even more disturbed.

"What the fuck was that?" I asked, as I tried to think of a reasonable explanation. Maybe that man was one of those hologram things I've seen in the movies, and this was some kind of trick. Or maybe I am actually tripping and she is either just humouring me, or we are having some kind of shared hallucination – I have heard of them.

But when I realised that no matter how hard I tried, none of these "reasonable explanations" I was creating quite added up, I began to feel angry.

"You won't remember me yet," she said. "But I know you, Pikel. We will meet again soon."

Nothing she said was making any sense and I felt like screaming at her. I usually would have but this girl was having a strange effect on me.

I realised that I still had a tight grip on that rusty pipe and dropped it on the pavement.

"So who told you my name?" I asked, deciding I would try and get to the bottom of that little mystery first. Maybe we had a mutual acquaintance and someone had told her about me, or I had met her before and just couldn't remember her.

But I found it hard to believe I would forget someone like her.

"You told me..." she mumbled.

It was a good thing this girl was pretty, because she was damn weird and I would usually be annoyed by now.

"Hey, I tell you what," I said. "I'm on my way to a rave if you want to come?"

She shook her head. "I can't. I must go now."

"No you don't, the night is young," I said, trying to make a charming smile. I wasn't sure how charming it was, I have never tried one before.

Just then I realised that I could see *through* her. The pavement, the walls of the house behind her, all glowing through her clothes and pale skin. I blinked a few times, but the effect was still there. She had a hazy translucence, like a ghost.

"It's happening again," she said, looking down at her glowing hands. She didn't seem surprised at all.

I was speechless. I had taken hallucinogenics before, but as far as I know there was none in that cocktail of drugs I swallowed earlier, and I had never had a trip that was so vivid. She was real. She was a person. Her eyes were like shining sapphires, and her face was set with grim acceptance.

She was fading away.

"Wait!" her eyes suddenly lit up, as if she was remembering something. She reached into her pockets and pulled out a piece of card. "Take this! It's how you find me!"

I grabbed hold of it.

"Don't go!" I blurted, unable to understand this unfamiliar emotion I was feeling. I didn't want her to leave, I wanted to know who she was.

She smiled at me faintly, as her face faded away, into the night. "I'll see you soon, Pikel."

I reached to grab hold of her but my hands passed through the faint outline of her shoulders and she was gone.

I stood there for a few minutes, and stared at the place she had been standing. I wanted to tell myself that I had just been tripping, but deep down I knew there was something more to this. The fact that it made no sense made me angry.

Suddenly my head began to tingle, and I felt waves of heat streaming through my body and my heart pounding against my ribcage. I suddenly remembered the drugs I had taken, and realised I was coming up.

I rested my hand against the wall and concentrated on feeling the cold night air on my face. Slowed down my breathing. Looked up to the sky as my vision blurred, and the euphoria of the MDMA took over.

I opened my eyes and looked at the piece of card in my hands. She had given me this – it looked like some kind of flyer.

"*It's how you find me,*" her voice echoed in my mind.

I held it up to my face and tried to make sense of the lines and shapes on it but the drugs were making them jump around and distort.

I sighed and placed it into my wallet.

"I must be going insane..."

The K-hole was over, and I once again became aware of the walls of Kev's living room around me.

I had been talking the whole time without even realising it.

"I dunno man," Kev muttered beside me. "I've seen some fucked up shit before—"

"But it's the drugs!" I interrupted him. "I know I hadn't come up on them at that point but maybe I have done too many and fucked my head up or something."

Kev shook his head. "Man... You're always like this. I mean, that part where you said you felt angry cause you couldn't explain it. That's you all over!"

"What do you mean?" I asked, sourly.

I must be going insane if I needed K-Hole-Kev of all people in the world to impart wisdom upon me.

"I mean – you, you're so... rational and you like the world to be simple," Kev tried to explain. "And if something weird happens you don't like it cause it, like, breaks your vision of reality. But sometimes weird things happen, dude, and not everything can be explained."

"You're not going to start telling me that ghosts, elves and UFOs and all that shit is real, are you?"

"I've seen some weird shit in my time," Kev replied. "And not all of it when I was on drugs!" he added, scowling when he noticed the expression on my face. "I think a lot of people do, you know, but they deny it because it threatens their... their idea of the world. They try so hard to explain it that they distort their own memories."

I sat there for a few moments and tried to take in what Kev was saying. Yeah, he was a burnt-out drug-user who was a few cans short of a six-pack, but he does sometimes surprise you when he opens his mouth. When you spend most of your life taking narcotics in your living room alone, and your TV is broken, you've got to end up thinking about some things, I guess.

"I mean, remember that time I got you to try those mushrooms?" he asked.

I winced at the memory of that incident.

"Yeah," I muttered. "Hated those things, they just made me think about all this stuff I didn't want to."

"Is that really it, Pikel? Or was it that they were making you *realise* things about the world you didn't want to know? Anyway, the fact that you have come here means that deep down you know it happened."

I didn't really know what to say to that. So I decided to push it into my big hole of 'think about later', which is always a convenient place to sort things that make me feel uneasy. I don't think much.

"Anyway, I have some good news. While we were in the K-hole I found your wallet," he said, throwing it onto my lap.

I felt like a giddy child as I ripped it open. This girl was having an effect on me and I wasn't sure I liked it.

"What does it say man?" Kev asked.

"It's a flyer," I replied. "It's advertising some night in a club called Janus. It's this Friday... but where the fuck is Janus?"

She could've at least given me her number or something.

"I know it," Kev said "Been there a few times. Remember when Dave was seeing that girl who—"

"But you know where it is?" I interrupted him.

"Oh yeah," Kev nodded his head. "I think so..."

Throughout the next week I told myself that I wasn't going to Janus on Friday. That it was a waste of time. She wasn't going to be there because she wasn't real, she was someone my imagination had created when life got a bit boring, and I had picked up that flyer from somewhere to give my fantasies more substance.

That is what I told myself all week, but when I finished work on Friday I realised that I had no intention of going to the rave that night, and a few minutes later I found myself outside K-Hole-Kev's house.

K-Hole-Kev has been to a few free parties and most of his

friends are ravers, but he is not one himself. He doesn't go outside much. The reason for this I believe to be not far from agoraphobia, though leaning more towards plain lazy. K-Hole-Kev would much rather spend Friday night in a K-hole on his couch than get off his arse and venture into the scary world outside. In the early hours of Saturday morning, when the rave is coming to an end, we usually go to his place with the intension of crashing out but, after a quick nap, the weekend's bender is resumed.

But this weekend was going to be different.

True to his name, when K-Hole-Kev does anything it is usually to the extreme. When I entered his house he was waiting for me in the kitchen, prepared for what appeared to be an epic quest. He had wrapped himself in abundant layers of clothes, a big brown coat, beanie hat, and boots.

"Where are you going?" I asked.

"I'm taking you to Janus," he replied.

"But I never said I was going," I said, crossing my arms over my chest, feeling angry that he was being so presumptuous. I had been telling both him and myself all week that I wasn't going to do this.

"I knew you would," Kev said, as he tucked the ends of his trousers into his boots, and zipped up his coat. "Let's find your girl."

My girl? Not only is she not my girl but I am pretty sure she doesn't even exist.

Kev led me to a part of the city not far from where I met her last week. I had no drugs on me that night; I wanted to keep a clear head so that on the off-chance that I saw her again I would know it was real.

We eventually came across a street busy with people, and a girl in a bright orange dress and blue stockings caught my eye. She had a collection of bizarre symbols painted over her face and was walking alongside an extravagant crowd of people who were almost as eye-catching as her. They were heading towards a building which had been discoloured by time and had only a few small windows. The gaps in the roof had been haphazardly covered with planks of wood, and the place gave me the general impression that it could collapse at any moment.

When I realised that Kev was also leading me towards it I came to a terrible realisation.

"Oh no," I said. "Not here!"

Kev smiled. "Yep, here it is. This is Janus."

"But it's full of freaks..."

I took another glance at the mishmash of clothes, hairstyles, piercings and jewellery around me. Some of these people looked very much like their parents had been too busy with their middle class jobs to give them much attention and now they were making sure the rest of the world did.

"Do you want to find your girl or not?" Kev asked as he made his way to the door. I shook my head, realising that I had found a social setting which K-Hole-Kev, the borderline agoraphobe, was more comfortable entering than me.

As soon as I entered the dark, ill-lit room my ears were filled with angry rock music. I cast my gaze about the place to see all kinds of people dressed in distinct fashions sitting around tables together or standing by the walls with drinks in their hands.

"I think the bar's this way," Kev said as he guided our way through the darkness.

We sidestepped around a group of drinkers to a counter where a shabby looking man with a beard was serving drinks. Kev leaned over and asked for two pints of beer while I scanned the crowds of people around us for her face. She was nowhere to be seen.

All the time I was thinking; *what the fuck am I doing here?*

Kev was taking longer than I expected to get drinks so I checked on him to see that he was waving his arms around, engaged in some kind of debate with the barman. I stared, wondering how Kev had managed to turn the purchase of two drinks into such an ordeal. Eventually the barman seemed to back down and Kev handed him some money.

"Why'd you take so long?" I asked as he passed me a drink.

"Ah, he didn't recognise me. He always tries to swindle new people."

"You were *bartering*?"

Kev nodded simply.

I took my first swig of beer and, at the stale taste, hoped Kev didn't pay too much for it.

As I downed the rest of it I realised that in some ways this place wasn't too different from the parties I usually go to. The place was dark, noisy, crowded; the air had that rundown smell of stale smoke and spilled beer, and there didn't seem to be any security guards snooping around.

The people and the music were different, but the essential feel of the place was the same. It had that essence of bedlam – where it feels like almost anything could happen. Raves are places you can party without restriction, and escape from the consumerism of nightclubs. The people in this place seemed to be trying to escape the chains of conventions – of identity, fashion, gender.

In my opinion some of them had taken it a little too far, but the place wasn't too bad.

Just then I caught sight of a familiar face and I almost dropped my drink.

"What's the matter, man?" Kev muttered into my ear.

I could see her at the top of a staircase. The girl from last Friday.

Kev grabbed my shoulder and shook me. "Pike! Man, what's up with you?"

"It's her!" I gasped.

"Where?"

I rushed towards the stairs, but the place was getting busier now and I had to sidestep around a group of punk kids who didn't seem to want to budge. Eventually I got impatient and shoved my way through, leaving a trail of annoyed comments behind me.

I raced up the stairwell two steps at a time and the punters had to cling to the banisters to let me past. When I reached the top, I swung a wooden door open and found myself in a wide corridor filled with people.

"Pike!" Kev called, as he caught up with me. "What's going on?"

"She's not here anymore," I said.

The hallway was big, and had a line of doors on each side. Lingering drinkers were coming and going between the different rooms or talking to each other in the hallway.

"Where did you see her?" Kev asked.

We passed the first room, and I peered inside. It stank of dope, and between the clouds of smoke I could just make out a group of guys sitting in a circle, puffing away at large hookah pipes.

"Whoa, man," Kev's eyes lit up and he paused at the doorway. "You wanna?"

I shook my head. "No! Not tonight! Didn't you hear me? I saw her!"

Kev's shoulders dropped like a child just denied access to Disneyland.

"Where do you think she went, then?" he asked, looking back up the hallway.

"I think she was running away from something," I replied, recalling the look on her face before she fled.

I looked up the corridor and tried to put myself in the shoes of someone running away. There were rooms on each side, but they were all filled with people and I couldn't see an end to the corridor yet, only darkness.

"How far do you reckon this corridor goes, Kev?"

There was no reply.

"Kev?"

I turned around and caught Kev busily leant over a windowsill with a note stuffed up his nostril.

"*Kev!*"

I had only let him out of my sight for a few moments and he was already on the horse tranquilisers.

"Hold on," he muttered. "Was just a little one."

"This isn't the time or the place!"

"There's loads of people on drugs here! *Look* at them!"

"It isn't the *time* then. I said earlier! No drugs!"

"You said it was because if you saw her you, like, wanted to know it wasn't because you were trippin'," he recalled.

"Yes! Now come on!"

"But you've already seen her now, and you were clean. Go on, just a little one!"

Well... He did have a point...

A few seconds later, our nostrils were filled and we were ready for the quest.

The corridor was now much narrower than I remembered, but we compensated for our lack of balance by taking heavy strides. The floor was swaying like a seesaw. Why people make floors in such a way has always been a mystery to me but I always come across them when I have had a bit of K.

I could see all these faces in the corner of my vision leering down at us. They were pissing me off. Why were their faces so big? Why did their mouths keep gaping open like big, black holes? It's the colours. Their clothes were too bright. My eyes didn't like them. My ears weren't keen on their rippling choruses of laughter either.

Why are they all staring at me?

K disassociates your limbs from your body, makes you walk like an insect climbing up a wall. You look like a twat, Pikel. That is why they are staring, a voice in my head reminded me.

I kept my head down and, for a while, became fascinated by the patterns on the floor. Lines, you can always trust lines. Better than those people back there. They were all circley.

I then realised that the chatter of voices had quietened down, the only noises I could hear now were Kev walking beside me, and the faint thumping of the music coming through the walls.

"How far does this tunnel go?" Kev murmured.

I squinted my eyes at the darkness ahead but it seemed to stretch to infinity and I had no idea how long we had been walking for. This place seemed more like some kind of abandoned mansion than a nightclub.

"It's just the K playing tricks with our heads," I replied.

I turned around but there was no one behind us either, the people with big faces and bright clothes had vanished. I shook my head. We must have passed through a door, or turned a corner without realising it.

And then we heard footsteps.

"Someone's coming!" Kev gasped, his eyes widening as paranoia set in. "Quick! Hide!"

Before I could object, he grabbed my shoulder and pulled me into the nearest doorway.

"Kev!" I hissed, as he shut the door behind us. "Do you see two girls and a big, brown, talking dog with us?"

He cast his eyes around us, just to make sure, and then shook his head.

"And you know why that is, don't you?"

He stared at me with a baffled expression.

"Because we are not the fucking Scooby Doo gang, that's why! This isn't a fucking film either. We are not on the run, and no one is out to get us. You're just drugged up and paranoid!"

"Why are you whispering then?"

"I don't know..." I admitted.

"You said that girl was running away from something," Kev reminded me. "I just thought that might mean someone's following her."

"Hold on," I sighed, and peered through a crack in the door, hoping that if I humoured him he would stop acting like such a fruitcake.

The footsteps on other side became louder, and I watched a shadow stretch across the floor. I held my breath, feeling chills going down my spine as I recognised the dark figure in a black cloak.

"What's going on, man?" Kev whispered in my ear, a few moments later. "He's gone, right?"

"I think it was the man from the other night," I whispered back in disbelief. "The one who disappeared."

"The one who was chasing her down the street?" Kev remembered. "Are you sure? Shit, mate, what should we do?"

"Follow him," I replied, as I gently pushed the door back open.

He marched down the corridor, turning his head left and right to peer into the doorways he passed. I could never catch a glimpse of his face, just the outline of his black cloak that covered him from head to boot. There was something menacing about his presence, it was obvious he was looking for something and he was in a hurry.

We followed him from a distance. At one point he drew to a sudden halt so I pulled Kev into the nearest doorway, and we found ourselves in a small cupboard jumbled with furniture and junk. I smothered Kev's mouth with my hand to stifle his breathing, and peered down the corridor. The cloaked stranger was standing in front of one of the doorways. He lifted his arm and a pale, white hand slipped out of the sleeve of his cloak and grasped hold of the handle, pulling it open.

He then walked through and disappeared.

I waited for a few moments and then ventured out, motioning Kev to follow me. We shifted silently down the corridor to find the door he entered still ajar.

It led to a staircase. Kev and I both looked at each other.

"I'm lost, man," Kev said. "This place is huge. Are we supposed to be here? This must be off-limits."

"Go back if you want to," I replied. "It's okay, I can take it from here."

"Nah, man," Kev shook his head. "If you're going up there, I'm coming too."

I reached the top of the stairs and entered a large, open-air balcony; she was there, exactly as I remembered her last week: torn jeans, wild hair, and purple eye shadow smudged across her eyes.

"Leave me alone!" she screamed defiantly, as the cloaked man closed in on her. She was clinging to the railing and had nowhere to escape.

"Only when you stop," a cold voice echoed from the hood of his black cloak. "I have warned you before!"

"I had no choice this time! I had to!"

He took another step towards her, and I knew this had to be the moment for me to step in.

"Get away from her!" I yelled.

The stranger turned around and for the first time I caught a glimpse of the face inside his hood. His skin was pale and blurry – it was all distorted. I tried to focus my eyes on distinguishing his features but they twisted and garbled under the moonlight.

His cold eyes looked through me and somewhere in the pit of my stomach I *knew* he wasn't human.

"Who are you, boy?" he asked.

I clenched my fists, and swallowed my fear. I wasn't going to let this freak of nature get the better of me.

"I am your worst fucking nightmare!" I replied. "Now piss off."

He crossed the gap between us in the blink of an eye and then his hand was around the scruff of my jumper, pulling me off the ground.

"This is none of your business, kid," he breathed into my face, as he held me up in the air.

"Pikel!" Kev yelled, appearing from the shadows. I don't know exactly what he was trying to do but, when he was near enough to us, the man just shoved him aside.

As I watched Kev fall onto the floor something happened, it was like he had flicked a switch in my brain. *How dare you!* I thought, clenching my fists.

I swung for his face. My knuckles connected with his cheek with a crack and he dropped me, placing a hand to his blurry features as I recovered my balance. I clenched my fists again, ready to fight.

But he didn't attack and, for a moment, I thought I saw the distorted line of his lips curve into a smile. The space around him rippled and stretched, like a black hole, and when it cleared he was gone.

"*Again*?" I cursed a few times and then caught my breath, not knowing whether to feel relieved or freaked out. It was just another thing to add to the fucked-up list of events I could not explain.

I turned to the girl as she straightened herself back onto her feet and our eyes met.

"Is your friend okay?" she asked, looking at the ground next to us where K-Hole Kev was lying on his back, waving his arms and legs around frantically.

"Kev!" I called, stepping over to him. "What the fuck are you doing?"

"Pikel, mate, I'm falling! Help!"

"No, you're not, Kev!" I replied, stamping my foot next to him. "See! You're on the ground."

"Is he having a fit or something?" she asked.

"Nah. He's just K'd up," I sighed, grabbing him by the hand and yanking him back onto his feet. He swayed back and forth for a few moments, so I held his shoulders.

"Thanks, man," he said as he steadied. "Man, he pushed

me, and I fell and just kept falling! It was horrible! But you found her, yeah?"

"Yes," I said. I turned to her and was just about to introduce them when I realised I didn't even know her name.

"What is your name, anyway?" I asked.

"Frelia," she said, smiling. "Thanks for the help back there. Who are you?"

I was rendered speechless for a few moments, and then I narrowed my eyes at her angrily. She was just as pretty and enticing as when I first met her but this time it wasn't enough to quell my frustration.

"What the fuck do you mean? We met the other day! You knew my name!"

"Oh shit," she exclaimed, slapping her hand on her forehead, a look of realisation spreading across her face. "I'm sorry... this is *really* hard to explain..."

"I think I deserve a fucking explanation!" I snarled. "I came here for you!"

"Really?" her eyes lit up, and her expression became serious. "I know this must be weird for you but I need you to tell me everything that happened when you saw me."

As she led us back down the staircase I explained everything to her. How last week I met her when she was running from that man. How he disappeared before my eyes, and she handed me a flyer as she faded away.

"It was a flyer like this one!" Kev added as he picked one up from the floor of the corridor. We were now nearing back towards the main part of the club; I could hear the music getting louder.

"Yeah. I think he doesn't like it when other people see him," she casually said over her shoulder. "That's always good to know."

"What do you mean he doesn't like to be seen," I asked, narrowing my eyes. "And how the fuck does he vanish like that?"

"Because... it's what he does," she said. "He travels through time. I think he's supposed to maintain the balance or something. He's probably not supposed to be seen."

I shook my head, trying to make sense of it. A week ago I

would have called her a loony and laughed at her but I had seen him vanish before my own eyes twice now. I didn't know what to believe anymore.

"But that doesn't make sense," Kev butted in from behind us. "If he doesn't want to be seen why is he chasing you?"

Only Kev would be able to actively dissect the details from such an absurd conversation.

"He is trying to stop me travelling through time."

"You travel through time?" I blurted, sceptical. I paused in the corridor and stared at her in disbelief.

She stopped beside me and blue eyes looked into mine and almost made me believe her. She could have told me that the sun was green and I wouldn't have objected much.

"Not exactly," she said. "I can only project an image of myself. My body stays behind... I can carry small things, though. Like that flyer."

"But why?" I blurted. "How do you do it? And why did you bring me here? You forgot my name!"

"Because she hasn't met you yet!" Kev realised.

She nodded. "Yes, he's right. But I know you now, Pikel, and I think I know why I asked you to come."

She reached a hand towards my face, and I found myself closing my eyes in anticipation of feeling her skin against mine. But instead, all I felt was a cold, chilly sensation.

I opened my eyes, and saw that her hand was stroking my cheek but I couldn't actually feel it. She was fading away again.

"I am not really here, this is a projection," she explained. "But you will meet the real me someday. I need your help. Can you help me?"

Without even a moment of consideration, I nodded.

"Something really bad is going to happen in this place," she said, casting her eyes to the walls of the nightclub. "That is where my body is at the moment. I am projecting back to try to change it. I *have* to. Can you be there when it happens?"

Once again I nodded my head without hesitation.

She held her hand out in front of her face; it was becoming fainter by the moment.

"Whoa," Kev muttered under his breath, as he stared at her.

"Shit, man..."

"I haven't got much time left," she said, turning back to me. "You said it was out in town last week that I met you, yes?"

I nodded.

Kev's eyes lit up. "And you gave him a flyer!" he realised, holding up the one he still had in his hand. "Here, this is what you gave him, take it!"

"Okay," she said, slipping it into her pocket. She was fading away quickly, I could now see the wall through her.

"You said something bad is coming!" I remembered. "When?"

She opened her mouth as the last of her faded away. Just before she vanished completely I heard one word.

"Friday."

I still, sometimes, have lingering doubts where I convince myself that Frelia never existed, but they are short-lived musings throughout the week. When Friday comes, I find myself at Janus. I stand in the corner, like a ghost, with a drink in my hand, waiting for something to happen. Sometimes K-Hole-Kev joins me.

I watch the people who drink here and I have even come to know some of them. I think they talk to me because I am a mystery.

I am beginning to understand why they are the way they are. They all seem to be searching for something they feel they have lost. I am too. Every Friday, I stand here, waiting for her.

I know that one day she will be here.

2
The Christmas Puppy

He wasn't my usual type. He was short and lean, with wiry arms and narrow shoulders. A few creases around his wild brown eyes were the only signs that betrayed his age. He wasn't beautiful, he was handsome, and there was something alluring about him. He had something I was drawn to; a quiet charisma.

It was just a typical night out with my friends but on that night it just so happened that he was there. We noticed each other. I saw him looking at me and I looked back.

Like a moth to flame, I crossed the bar to meet him.

Life is full of objects colliding. Some combine and become saturated in each other, others clash and repel, some take away little parts from others and move on. It is basic science.

Most things come into contact with little effect, but every now and then you will find that right combination and the outcome can be explosive. When alkali metals come into contact with water, they create a reaction and sparks fly. Rubidium particles are lonely and strive to fill the emptiness of their electron shell; they rip away the particles of oxygen, leaving hydrogen to dance in red flames across the surface.

Sometimes, when the right two people meet, a reaction occurs and their lives are changed forever. It is notoriously hard to predict which blending of people it will happen to, and some spend years searching for that right complement to themselves with little success for it then to suddenly jump into their life unexpectedly, often at a most inconvenient moment.

But you can't stop it.

The first time his lips met mine my knees went weak. When his tongue entered my mouth it sent waves of electricity rippling through me. When my hands met his body they wanted to tear all his clothes away. I wanted to feel his bare skin against my fingers.

It did not matter that he was a stranger. I did not pause to think about what was to come of it. For that moment, he was mine. We had made a new discovery and were exploring each other.

I wanted to drown myself in him.

The next thing I knew I was in his house and, as we landed onto his bedsheets, ripping each other's clothes away, everything else disappeared. Nothing else mattered. I was lost in the feeling of his bare skin against mine.

"What are your thoughts?"

It was the morning and I was in a bed that wasn't my own. Last night's drinking had left me with a dull headache and just a few hazy memories. I was in the arms of a stranger.

"About what?" I asked.

"About this," he said, running his hand across my stomach. "About us."

I sighed – it was now time for the talk. Last night was something new and exciting, but now it was over. We would probably either exchange fake phone numbers or say things to each other like "I am too busy to have someone in my life at the moment."

Or maybe he'll just be blunt and tell me he is not interested.

"Well..." I said, deciding I would ease the awkwardness of this conversation with some comic relief. "Didn't we agree that this was on a monetary basis?"

He grabbed my shoulders and twisted by body around so that I was face down into the pillow. I struggled against him but he pressed his knee against my back to pin me down and twisted my arm up into the air.

He leaned forward and whispered into my ear. "Want to say that again?"

"Okay," I laughed. "I was joking."

He then let go, and I shuffled back around on the bed to face him.

"From what I remember," he said. "It was *you* who made the first move. I was quite surprised. How old are you anyway?"

"Nineteen," I replied.

There was a silence.

"And you?" I asked.

"Forty-one."

There was a moment of realisation. We had just evoked a barrier between us that we might not get past. Something that needed to be dealt with.

But it had also lit up a devilish light in his eyes and his excitement was intoxicating. We were both suddenly very horny.

He slammed his body against mine and we made love all morning.

"So why an old fart like me?" he asked.

Daylight was starting to peek through the window. A reminder that a new day was beginning, and this moment was coming to an end.

"I consider myself a charity worker," I replied.

"Are the dry replies evasive humour or a defence mechanism to stop people getting close to you?"

"When I get close to people, I get hurt."

"We are close right now," he said, squeezing his arms to pull me in tighter.

I had nothing to say – he was right.

"Is this a one-off or are you doing more voluntary work?" he breathed into my ear.

"The more times you meet, the closer you get."

He nodded.

"The more you get hurt," I finished.

"I don't want to hurt you, I want to get to know you."

"It'll wear off," I dismissed, turning onto my back to stare at the ceiling.

"Wear off?"

"I am the Christmas puppy," I explained. "Men fall in love with me for one night, a few days, maybe even a week if I am lucky. But they all get bored of me in the end."

"I have dogs," he said. "I better let them out before they shit everywhere."

A wave of cold air brushed my skin as he lifted up the

sheets. He stood up, and reached into the pockets of the trousers he was wearing last night.

"Here's my phone," he said, tossing it onto my lap. "Leave your number if you like."

He then swung a dressing gown over his shoulders, tied the thong around his waist, and opened the door. He left the room and I found myself alone on his bed.

I sighed as I heard his feet treading down the stairs. I wanted to leave my number, because I *did* want to see him again. But that in itself terrified me; when I care for others I do so sincerely, but I have learnt though time that not everyone is like that.

Against my better sensibilities, I typed my number onto his phone. And then my name: Tristan.

When he is done with me I will take myself back to the pound.

As I entered the kitchen I was greeted by an excitable brown dog that began to bark and jump around me.

"Chaser!" he yelled from the counter where he was waiting for the kettle to boil. "Leave him!"

"It's okay," I said as I patted his furry head. "I like dogs."

Chaser retreated into the corner where another Labrador was lying broodingly in its nest of blankets and pillows.

"That's Missie," he said, pointing to her. "But watch out, she's a moody git. If she wants pettin' she'll come to you. Otherwise she bites."

I walked over to him as steam began to billow from the kettle. With a click, the light went out – the water was ready.

"I'm afraid I only have normal tea," he said, as he poured it into two cups. "You look like one of those hippy types, so I'm sorry, but I haven't got any of that Himalayan mountain leaf of the yew tree, or any crap like that."

"Normal tea is fine," I said, laughing. "You'd better have sugar though."

"I bet you've forgotten my name, haven't you," he muttered.

"It's Neal," I recalled.

We sat ourselves down in the living room and, as I took my first bite of toast, I worried that while our mouths were busy eating the absence of conversation would feel awkward. To my surprise, it wasn't. After he'd finished eating he relaxed back onto the couch and sipped at his tea.

My eyes wandered his living room, and I found my gaze drawn to a picture of a pretty woman with brown hair and blue eyes in the centre of the mantelpiece.

"Who's she?" I asked.

His eyes darkened.

"My wife."

I sighed. *Great, what have I got myself into this time?*

I looked down at his hand to see a white band on one of his fingers where a wedding ring used to be. Dirty trick that one, I should have noticed before.

"She died."

A silence. Things had just become more complicated.

"How long ago?" I asked, not quite knowing what to say. Sorry would just sound stupid – I never knew her.

"Two years," he said, casting his eyes to the window.

"How long were you together?" I asked.

"Eight years."

Jesus.

"Look," he said, placing a hand on my thigh. "I'm ready to move on now. I just need to take things slowly."

To assess the situation I went back to the place where it all started. It was in this club. We saw each other at the bar. He offered me a drink and I said yes. I fell for those eyes. He was just a simple stranger then. Uncomplicated and alluring.

That was last night. But now I was sober, and it turned out that he wasn't as uncomplicated as I first thought.

It was daytime, but the only difference that makes in this place is the smell of coffee instead of ale. I believe that they built this club on a whim that left most rooms without windows. The walls are dark. The place is an enclosed world outsiders cannot glimpse into and insiders are free from prying eyes.

Janus. The place I met Neal.

"So, he was married..." Namda said from the other side of the table.

Namda is my best friend. She has a round face of pretty

features framed by mulberry locks of wavy hair. She was wearing a baggy patchwork blue dress and a pair of large boots that day, which gave her the appearance of someone much larger than her petit five-foot-three. We are both artists; she likes to sculpt, and I like to paint. She is also my confidant and advisor because she has more perspective than me – sometimes I believe it's because she crafts within three dimensions whereas I am restricted to the canvas.

"Yes," I replied.

"How did she die?"

"Breast cancer."

She shook her head. "Oh Tristan," she said. "You know how to get yourself into these situations, don't you..."

She gazed at the wall for a few moments while her mind calculated the scenario and I waited for her verdict.

"So I am guessing he must be bi..." she mumbled thoughtfully.

"I hope so..."

"Is he nice?" she asked. "That's the most important question."

I took a sip from my coffee, pondering. "I guess so..."

"But I can tell there are doubts..." she finished, knowingly.

I lifted my phone out of my pocket. "Well," I said. "He hasn't text me yet..."

"You gave him your number?" she asked.

I nodded.

She smiled. "Well he won't text you yet – that's against the rules."

"The rules?" I asked. "What rules?

"You're in the honeymoon period," she explained. "You'll never be far from his thoughts but he won't dare to text you until at least ten hours after you left. No matter how much he wants to."

I raised an eyebrow. "Why?"

"Because then he would come off as too eager."

"So let me get this straight," I said, leaning forward and folding my arms across the table. "He wants to text me but he cannot because of some social convention."

"Yes," Namda said, smiling. "And, when he does, you need to wait at least three hours before replying."

"Shall I set a stopwatch?" I asked sarcastically. "Do it by the minute?"

Namda laughed. "Oh Tristan, you're not used to this game, are you?"

"It all sounds a bit retarded to me," I admitted. "Suddenly taking things naturally is needy?"

"I didn't make the rules," Namda said, shrugging her shoulders.

"And two people who want to get to know each other will both wait for the other to text or ring them but not dare do it themselves..."

She nodded.

"It's just as I thought," I concluded. "Humanity is doomed."

I was sitting in my room later that evening when my phone finally buzzed. I picked it up and an unknown number appeared on the screen with a message.

Hey sexy. Hope you had a good day. Let me know if you want to meet again.

I looked at my watch – it was 6:30 pm – and with Namda's advice in mind I made a mental note to make sure to not text him back until after 9:30.

At 7:21 pm I found myself staring at my phone.

If I just texted him back, would there really be anything wrong in it? To set a specific time instead of just doing what you want to do – now *that* seems obsessive to me. What are these mind games that Namda told me about in aid of anyway?

The next thing I knew, my thumbs were pushing away social convention.

Hi, my day was okay. I am free tomorrow night if you like?

I put my phone back onto the desk. It was done now. If he can't deal with the way I roll it isn't meant to be.

To my surprise, a few moments later my phone buzzed and a new message appeared on the screen.

Let me get back to you on that one.

That night I began a new painting. What Namda had told me today about the rules of dating had given me an idea and I began to brush a picture of two people; a man and a woman. They were gazing at each other with desire but at the same time building a wall between them. The man is placing the bricks from his side while the woman is applying the cement from hers. So far the wall is as high as their shoulders, and it will soon block their lusty glances.

I began to flesh out the colours in the man's brown eyes. They gaze at the woman longingly while his hand places another brick between them. I was just adding tones of grey to his irises to signify that he is withholding something, when the sound of my phone ringing suddenly pulled me out of my world of colours and shapes.

I dropped the paintbrush and scrambled for my phone. When I read the screen it said "Namda."

"Hello," I said as I placed the phone to my ear.

"Hey Trissy," she squealed. "How's it going?"

"I'm fine," I replied picking the paintbrush back up. I had just noticed that there was a smudge in the whites of his eyes and I needed to fix it. With most people it would be rude to do such a thing while talking on the phone but Namda knows what I am like and understands. I often get carried away and don't know when to stop, I even go without sleep some nights because something is unfinished and I can't relax until it is done.

"You heard from him?" she asked.

"Yeah—"

"Did you follow my advice?"

"No..." I admitted. "I couldn't be arsed. But don't worry, its fine. He text me back straight away, so I am guessing—"

"That means he won that round," she interrupted. "You're his bitch now. The ball is in his court."

"I am not playing with any fucking balls!" I exclaimed.

"Oh Trissy, don't get pissy," she said, with a chuckle. "I'm just trying to advise you."

"Sorry," I apologised, realising that I had let myself get wound up too easily.

"Anyway Tris, what are you doing tomorrow night?" she asked.

"I'm not sure yet. Maybe meeting up with Neal. Why? What's going on?"

"Sam wants to go out to Janus," she explained. "But don't worry if you have plans with Neal..."

"Well Neal hasn't got back to me yet so I will let you know, okay?"

"Sure, hun. Anyway, give us a ring tomorrow sometime. Bye."

The next day I didn't hear back from Neal, though I wasn't too surprised. I always mentally prepare myself for the insincerity of the men who wind their way into my life – I have had years of practice.

So I had been used again. But, on the bright side, the sex had been good and I hadn't lost anything, so it was time to forget about him and have a good night out with my friends.

I rang up Namda to tell her I would be coming out, and started to get ready.

The thing I have always loved about Janus is that you can dress however you like, and no matter how outrageous it was, no one will bat an eyelid.

I like customising my clothes so that they feel like my own rather than the cheap chain store crap they originally are when I buy them. I went to my wardrobe and selected a pair of yellow corduroy trousers on which I had painted flames rising from the bottom of the legs, and wondered what they would look like with my red shoes.

Only one way to find out.

Dressing yourself can be an art and, just like painting, it is all about colours, shapes, tones, and textures. I carried on the theme of fire and cut tassels into the waist and sleeves of one of my orange shirts, to match the flame shapes on my trousers.

The last thing left was my hair, which is naturally blonde and about three inches long all over. I slapped some gel into my hands and curved it up into the air, like rising flames.

I looked in the mirror and laughed – I looked like a fire demon.

Half an hour later, I was standing outside Janus, casting my eyes up and down the street to see if I could spot Namda or anyone else I knew, when I felt my phone vibrate against my leg.

I held my breath in surprise when I saw the name that was flashing on the screen. It was him.

"Hello?" I said in a bemused voice, when I answered the phone. I somehow felt defensive.

"Are you coming over, then?" he asked.

I looked up and down the road at all the kids filing into the club. I didn't know what to say.

"Err... I don't know," I mumbled. "You said you would get back to me, and... I thought..."

"Well I have, haven't I?" he asked.

"Can I ring you back in a minute?" I asked. I needed time to think.

"Yeah, sure," he replied, with a not-so-convincing air of indifference. "Either way, let me know soon."

With a click he was gone.

"Trissy!" someone yelled.

It was Namda, and I walked across the road to meet her. We quickly embraced but, as soon as I pulled away, she began to quiz me; she has a way of knowing when something is on my mind.

"So what's up?" she asked.

"He rang," I replied. "Just now."

"Are you going to him?"

"I don't know," I said, shaking my head. "He's left it to the last minute... and I've made other plans now..."

"You're going to him," she decided firmly, as she grabbed my arm and pulled me away from the club.

"What about you?" I asked.

"Oh don't worry about me," she dismissed. "I have other friends apart from you, you know. Taxi!" she yelled, raising her hand towards the nearing vehicle.

It stopped beside us and she opened the door.

"Get in!" she ordered.

Namda can be stubborn when she wants to be.

I got into the back of the car and told the driver the name of the small hamlet outside the city where Neal lived.

The driver nodded his head and gripped hold of the wheel. The next thing I knew, I was being carried down the street and I rolled down the window to say goodbye to Namda.

"Have fun!" she called as she waved.

It was beginning to get dark by the time I was walking up the pathway of his country home. My bright red and yellow clothes must have illuminated me from miles away, but the cold night air cast me chilly.

I think he had been waiting by the door for me because as soon as I reached for the knocker it swung open and his arms were around me.

I had prepared a speech about how it was a bit annoying that he had contacted me at such short notice but it was interrupted by his tongue entering my mouth. When he pulled away, his smile made me weak and all was forgotten.

"Sorry for being late getting back to you. Good thing you didn't make any plans, eh?" he said as I took off my shoes.

"Well actually I—"

"You didn't have to go to all that trouble," he interrupted me, as his hand reached over to stroke my gel moulded fire-demon hair.

He looked me up and down and I blushed. My attire wasn't exactly fitting for a visit to someone's rural country home, and he was obviously under the impression that I had dressed up like this for his benefit. I opened my mouth to explain that I had actually made other plans.

But he placed his finger on my lips.

Within moments we were fucking on the floor.

An hour later we were spread out on the couch with our limbs entangled. I turned over to stare at the ceiling but instead my eyes focused on her picture on the wall. It surprisingly didn't bother me too much but I began to wonder if, for him, it was a haunting presence hanging above us, a witness to what we just did on the living room floor.

I could see, in the way he had looked at the picture yesterday morning, that she was the love of his life and nothing could ever replace her, but did that mean he couldn't eventually learn to love others?

"She's beautiful," I said. And I meant it.

He was silent for a few moments.

"Yeah," he eventually said. "She was."

It took me a few moments to build up the courage to continue.

"So you're bisexual?"

He nodded.

"Completely fifty-fifty?" I asked.

He sighed. "I suppose if I had to say one or the other: I am a little bit more attracted to men," he admitted. "But your preference doesn't always choose who you fall for. I mean, I don't often look at nineteen-year-olds but here you are."

In the morning he woke me up with a steaming cup of tea, which I drank down before we took his dogs for a walk.

The dogs chased each other in the distance while we walked side by side through the woodlands and fields. Every now and then he would point to a particular tree or plant and tell me its name, and I soon found myself discovering a whole new world of tall oaks, leafy ferns, canopies of willow branches, bay trees with sweet smelling leaves, the purple petals of foxglove. I had always been a city boy and was now realising that a lot of the world had so far escaped me.

"How do you know all of this?" I asked, realising that I didn't even know what he did for a living. "Are you a horticulturist or something?"

He smiled and shook his head. "No, you just learn these things when you live in the country."

I felt something wet against my fingers, and looked down, surprised, when I realised that Missy was sniffing them. I smiled and stroked the back of her head.

Neal was frowning.

"Are you okay?" I asked.

With a jolt of his neck he came out of his thoughts and his eyes became icy. "Missy hasn't really taken to a stranger since *she...*"

I suddenly felt a barrier between us. It seemed that I had overstepped a mark without even meaning to. The haunted look in his eyes made me want to wrap my arms around him, but somehow I felt it would be inappropriate.

"I wish I had my paints," I breathed, trying to change the subject. "This place is really nice."

"You could bring them next time," he suggested.

"So there is a next time..."

He covered his mouth, as if he had just realised that he had said something he didn't mean to.

"Maybe," he mumbled.

He carried on walking.

We wandered back to his house in silence but once we got there his mood seemed to lighten. He suggested we sit in the garden for a while and disappeared into the house for a moment to return with a selection of cheeses, crackers and wine.

We talked for hours. Not about his wife. About my art, the city, the countryside. We talked about our childhoods, our most memorable experiences, what makes us glad to be alive, and times which made us wish we were never born.

Most of all we laughed. I felt so relaxed around him. I didn't feel reserved. We were very different people, but there was chemistry, and conversation carried out naturally between us without awkward silences or any need to artificially initiate new topics. I could open up to him. I told him my secrets. He told me his.

The sun began to go down and cast the horizon with an eerie glow. The garden dimmed and I realised that a whole day had somehow disappeared.

"I still don't know what you do," I said, taking a sip of wine and watching the sun set.

"Does it matter?" he asked.

"Well sometimes it can be an important part of who you are..."

"We are not all flashy painters," he pointed out.

"I only just scrape by on it," I admitted. "I have very little expenses, I earn enough to pay the rent and the bills, and buy art materials. I have no savings; I don't earn enough to travel or anything like that. I just exist. I'm happy though."

"But you still do what you want to do, in your own time. I am an administrator for a law firm. It pays the bills."

There was no point in denying it – I was lucky.

"What do you *want* to do then?" I asked.

He gulped down the last of his wine, and reached for the bottle to pour himself another. "I have been saving up to open my own bar," he answered.

"A bar? Why?"

"Were you expecting something creative? Nah. Not me," he dismissed. "But... I like to get to know people, and bars are where you see the best and worst in them. That is why I was at Janus that night, I've been going to different places for research."

"Did you find what you were looking for?"

"Only time will tell."

He drank too much wine that day to drive me back home so I stayed another night. It was a sly tactic on his part to get me to stay longer without having to ask, and thus admit that he actually wanted me to stay, but I didn't mind.

In the morning we hopped into his car and he drove me through country lanes back to my home. I wanted to stay longer but I dared not ask. This was complicated for him and we needed to take things at his pace.

In seemingly no time at all, the streets of the city began to appear outside the window and I gave him directions to where I lived. When the car pulled up outside I invited him in to see my flat.

He entered my studio apartment with wide eyes – my home usually has that effect on people. The walls are plastered in blotchy colours and posters, the floor is scattered with discarded paper, paints and brushes, and the furniture is covered with brightly coloured throws that I dyed myself.

As we kissed goodbye his attention was caught by something he could see over my shoulder and he broke away, walking over to the painting I had not yet finished.

"You *are* talented," he muttered.

I shrugged. It was far from one of my best. I had created it to vent my frustration when I was waiting for him to contact me. But he wasn't playing mind games anymore, so now I just wanted to finish it and send it away to the gallery.

He turned around and patted me on the shoulder on his way towards the door.

"When are we meeting again?" I asked.

"Who said we were meeting again?"

His parting words confused me but there was no point in dwelling on them so I went to my studio to finish off that painting I had been working on.

But when I reached the easel, what I saw made me gasp.

The painting had changed.

I shook my head. This was certainly a weird occurrence, though not a new one. This has happened before. Sometimes my paintings seem to have a mind of their own. The characters move, the colours change, new objects appear, others are taken away.

The only person I have ever trusted enough to tell about this phenomenon was Namda, but even my best friend was sceptical. Well this time her theory, that some people sleepwalk, and I sleep-paint, had lost the little credibility it ever had as an explanation. I could clearly remember the painting as I had finished it before I went to Janus that night, and since then I had only slept at Neal's.

The wall between the two people was now leaning towards the woman and looked like it was about to collapse on her. There was no way I had painted it this way. Even her facial expression had changed; she was now staring up at the bricks about to fall on her head.

I angrily grabbed the frame from the easel and dropped it onto a pile of my unfinished and discarded pieces.

After five days of silence I finally accepted that Neal must have got bored of me and moved on. A few hours later he appeared on my doorstep with a bottle of wine in one hand and a Chinese takeaway in the other. He ended up staying for two days.

The cycle began. We would meet almost every weekend. We shopped, we dined, we took his dogs for walks through the countryside, we saw the sights of the city, some nights we would stay up chatting until the sun came up, sometimes we would spend the whole day in bed.

Each time it was over we would part but any mention of future plans were met with ambiguous dismissals. Any comments that acknowledged there was something going on between us would result in him becoming cold and distant.

I kept telling myself that it was because of his wife, but it felt like I was caught in a whirlwind and I was beginning to feel dizzy.

One day, he was dropping me off at my house and I asked him what he was doing next weekend.

"Who said we were meeting again?" he asked.

That devious smile on his face. All this time I had attributed his contrary behaviour to guilty feelings over his deceased wife but, when I saw that look in his eyes that day, I realised that it wasn't all because of her.

He was enjoying this.

"Why can't you just be straight with me?" I asked.

"I don't do straight these days," he said jokingly. "You should know that."

"I don't do mind games."

His expression changed and his eyes narrowed at me grimly.

"Last thing I need is a stalker!" he hissed. "I will call you if I fancy it, ok?"

"Don't bother," I retorted. "I've had enough!"

I slammed the door and stormed across the pavement. I could feel his eyes burning into me as I fumbled for my keys but I didn't turn around.

This is why I don't usually let myself get too attached to people.

It doesn't matter how close people make you feel to them, you can never fully trust anyone. In a society where we no longer have to fight for survival and everything we need is readily available, we have been taught to consume, seek cheap pleasure, and indulge everything in excess. It is all about the packaging. People care little for the product they originally desired.

Media broadcasts images of perfect bodies and weekly fashions tell us how to be; not many people fit the schema and we are caused to feel increasingly isolated from each other. Deflated self-esteem, in a world where the general public have little control over the way they live, has turned us into egotists, searching for ways to make ourselves feel important and special. Sex has turned into something that people give to each other freely, on a whim, and, to many, romance is just a grand scheme to satisfy their shattered egos at the expense of others'. Consume. Consume. Consume. Discard. When people are discarded like a flimsy wrapper their confidence becomes wilted and they lose faith in their self and everyone else.

This is why people play mind games and use each other. Somewhere through this journey we have lost a part of ourselves and we strive to get it back. People would rather sit and stare at their phone, thinking about calling someone, rather than touch the buttons and give away another piece of their self. They have learnt that some will lead them on just to feel special; to know that someone wants them just so they can discard them. They have learnt this because others did it to them first.

They rip away the wrapper, gobble away a few chunks, and discard the rest.

Back to the sweet shop. It is time to fill that hole again.

I performed my usual routine for when I want to forget about someone – removing all traces of their existence. His toothbrush, a t-shirt he had left behind, empty bottles of wine we drank together, notes he had left on the fridge, and I even deleted his number from my phone.

Whenever something bad happens in my life I try to make something good out of it, usually venting it through my art. When I walked into my studio I remembered there was just one piece of him left in my flat.

I went through the stack of canvases on the floor, and found the picture of the two lovers I had painted when I first met him.

It had changed again. The woman was ducking for cover. She was about to be crushed by the weight of the bricks falling on her.

I stared at it, seething with anger, trying to remember it the way I had last seen it.

I then noticed the trowel in her hand was empty, now; there was no cement holding the wall together, and *that* was why it was falling. This was also impossible, as I had clear memories of brushing in those tawny coloured textures in between the red bricks.

I almost burned the painting with the rest of his stuff but I needed the money and it would have been a waste. I finished it off by just adding some finishing touches rather than trying to mend the mysterious changes. If the painting wanted to alter itself so much then I would let it be that way. I just wanted to get it out of my sight.

When I was done I named it 'The Christmas Puppy'. I would take it to the gallery down the road in the morning. They sell my paintings in exchange for a commission. If I had my own shop I could probably make more money but I can never be bothered to deal with the business side of things. This way, I don't make as much money but I get to just concentrate on what I love doing – painting – and the rest of my time I am free to enjoy my life instead of having to worry about the commercial side.

This painting was finished. It was time to begin a new one.

I placed a blank canvas on the easel and stared at it. I didn't have any ideas yet but sometimes, if I just stared at a canvas for long enough, my eyes would project a picture onto it and I could start tracing the lines with a paintbrush. But today nothing was coming.

After a few minutes I glanced back at 'The Christmas Puppy'. It was finished and I had placed it aside, but couldn't shake the feeling that it was somehow incomplete. I knew it would be almost impossible to make any changes to it now as I had already smothered it with varnish, but I felt like it was calling to me. It needed something else to complete its story.

But I couldn't think of what it was.

Fuck it.

I reached for my coat and went to the door.

Sometimes, when I lack inspiration, I go to Janus and drink.

I stepped through the entrance and instinctively walked towards the bar, even though the room was cloudy with smoke and my eyes were still adjusting to the atmosphere. A few kids stared at me but I avoided making eye contact. This place had recently become plagued by clichés in tight black clothes and spiked bracelets – the type of teenagers who like to feel that they are breaking free from the bonds of society and being 'different' but somehow, in the process, all managing to look the same. I try to avoid them.

I bought myself a drink and sat down at a dusty table in the corner. I gulped down rum and coke while my mind stewed over recent events and tried to make sense of the situation. Figure out why I had let this guy get under my skin.

I considered ringing Namda but I knew that if I saw her she would just start asking questions. I didn't want to swallow and regurgitate my issues. I wanted to have a good time and forget about them.

I got up and went back to the bar, realising that the place would start getting busy soon so I should probably get a drink that would last me.

"Can I have a jug?" I asked.

The barman reached into one of the shelves behind him and held one up. It was one of the larger ones – he must have been psychic.

"Can I have vodka?"

He poured a shot.

"More vodka..."

He tilted the bottle towards the jug until I motioned him to stop. After I gave him the signal he placed the vodka back on the shelf and began to walk towards the place where the cola and other mixers were kept.

"Wait," I called, stopping him in mid motion. "Can I have some gin?"

For the next minute or so I guided him with the point of my finger to the different liquors and spirits along the shelf which took my fancy and, after I thought I had enough to get me reasonably wasted, the jug was topped up with some fruit juice and lemonade.

"How much?" I asked.

He had not been taking a precise count of everything that had been poured into it – instead, he held the jug up to his face and narrowed his eyebrows. That was one of the good things about Janus – the tariff was not always fixed or exact.

After a quick exchange of bartering, I got a reasonable price and handed him my money. He offered me a glass with my change, which I turned down.

I lifted the jug to my lips as I made my way up the stairs.

I wandered my way down the corridor and found myself in the room that the potheads had claimed for the night. I am not much of a smoker but I indulged on a few tokes and my large jug was like gold dust to the parched mouths of the stoners. Afterwards, I decided to get some clear air on the balcony but ended up getting into light-hearted small talk with people I vaguely knew in the corridor.

I eventually bumped into Halann, a friend of Namda's, a girl with mousey brown hair and periwinkle gloss painted on her lips.

"Hey Trissy! How are you? It's busy here tonight isn't it? Is Namda out?"

She was speaking very fast. I noticed that the blacks of her eyes were bigger than usual and she was chewing gum. I am no detective, but the signs were telling me she was on amphetamines.

I shook my head, and made a mental note to tell Namda to stop calling me "Trissy" in public – it was starting to catch on.

"Nah," I said. "She's probably sculpting or—"

"Shame you couldn't come out the other night," Halann interrupted me.

"Sorry, I was kind of busy..."

She raised her eyebrow knowingly. "Ah I remember Namda saying... so... you're *preoccupied* at the moment, hey?"

I shook my head. "Not anymore."

"Oh," she replied, sparing me a quick, sympathetic smile. "That's a shame..."

Suddenly her eyes lit up and she grabbed my arm. "I know something that will cheer you up, come with me!"

She spoke to me over her shoulder as she dragged me down the corridor. "I just tried to stick my tongue in this guy's mouth, but he was not so into it. Anyway, it turns out that he is one of your kind. It's a good thing I don't get embarrassed – don't you think!" she exclaimed between giggles.

I laughed with her but inside I was sighing. Why is it that all straight people think that two people are automatically going to be attracted to each other just because they both happen to be gay?

"Anyway," she said as she pushed open a creaky door. "I think he was in here..."

The huge black pupils of her eyes did a scan of the room as she took some large gulps from her glass of water. Eventually she pinpointed our target and grabbed hold of my arm so that we could close in.

He was standing by the window, and at first all I could see was a large black trench coat covering the back of a tall person with broad shoulders.

Halann prodded his shoulder, and he turned around.

"Not going to try any of that again are we?" he asked Halann teasingly.

Halann giggled into her hand. "No. *I* am not going to. But – by the way – here is a friend of mine, Tristan. Tristan, this is Harry."

We shook hands. He was wearing a cowboy hat that cast shadows across his handsomely chiselled face. He had high cheekbones, nice blue eyes, and a defined jaw covered with a manly spread of stubble. I would have guessed his age at somewhere in the middle of his twenties.

"Tristan here is an artist," the ecstasy-induced chatterbox carried on talking as his fingers lingered against my hand and his eyes went down to my feet and back up again. "What do you do again?" she asked.

"I guess I could call myself an entrepreneur," he said, his eyes were set on my face now, and not moving.

"Oh really," Halann squealed. "That's such a coincidence because my cousin, she... oh wait, is that Jarni over there?"

In a split second Halann's legs had carried her to the other side of the room.

Harry and I were alone.

Harry was charming. He was successful. He had a deep, manly voice. He was worldly and well-travelled. He had been to places, seen many things, and had the means to do so again. He had a fine physique and knew how to present himself.

He was also one of the most boring people I had ever met in my life.

So far we had chatted about money, money, trade, economics, money, and more money. He explained to me many of the finer details of how he buys stuff at the right time and then makes profit by selling it at another place later, while I got more and more drunk, taking large gulps from my drink to drown out my urges to yawn.

At one point I thought the conversation was going to get interesting. He asked me about my art, but I somehow got tricked into telling him how much money my art dealer makes whenever she sells one of my works and he – as my new friend – informed me how I could get a much better deal. Within moments he had already planned out how I was going to start my own new business. I tried to tell him that the financial side of it all doesn't bother me and that I was quite happy earning the small amount it takes to keep me alive, but somehow it did not compute.

Eventually he placed his drink on the table.

"So why is a beauty like you single, then?" he asked.

"I... err..." I found myself quite taken aback. I knew I was fairly good looking but I had never really thought of myself as beautiful. If I was, wouldn't I know? I am an artist, after all.

His fingers went to my chin and tilted my head up and we stared at each other.. His hand was warm, and he did have nice eyes. There was definitely an attraction there.

But it just wasn't the same. I wasn't ready for this. I wasn't even sure if I wanted *any* new man in my life. I didn't want anyone to get close to me again.

"I need to go..." I announced. "I have things..."

Harry just smiled. "That's fine, but here, take this."

He handed me his business card. How fitting.

It was time for me to get another drink so I began to make my way downstairs, and spotted a familiar face on the way.

"Tristan!" she called, ushering me over.

It was Frelia – a punky girl who drank with Namda and me sometimes. She was only seventeen, but you would think she was older from her bold confidence and the way she carried herself. I had known her for a couple of years but she was a bit of a mystery and I didn't actually know much about her.

"Hey," I said, as I reached her. She seemed strangely tense and apprehensive.

"I can't stop for long," she said, casting her eyes around us warily. "I just need to tell you something, and I know it will sound weird, but please, Tristan, you've got to trust me."

"What is it?" I asked.

"Something bad is going to happen here one day," she whispered into my ear. "And this place will no longer feel welcome. No matter how bad it gets you must still come. Friday night. When they have taken over be here on Friday night."

I raised an eyebrow.

"I've got to go now!" she said, suddenly taking to her heels and sprinting down the corridor before I could voice any of the many questions going through my mind.

When I reached the main bar downstairs I saw another familiar face. This time, it was Neal – the last person in the world I expected to see.

Even in the dim lighting I could recognise that ruggedly handsome face and that seductive, misleading smile. But it wasn't for me this time. It was for a pretty young woman wearing spiked bracelets he was talking to.

My stomach felt empty as I tried to figure out what this could mean. He *knew* this was the place where I liked to hang out, so I could only guess that turning up here was just another one of his weird games.

I did not want to give him the satisfaction of seeing his presence affecting me so I decided it was time to make a swift and inconspicuous exit.

This plan was unsuccessful. Just as I finished making my way down the staircase I knocked my jug against the banister and it shattered on the floor. At the sound of glass breaking a few faces turned to stare at me but they were quickly distracted by something else. Only one pair of eyes lingered – Neal's. He had noticed me.

Why was he smiling?

Plan A had been a failure of epic proportions. So it was time to initiate plan B: just a simple, hasty exit would have to do now.

He intercepted Plan B by stepping in my path towards the door. Fail.

Plan C.

"What the fuck are you doing here?" I screamed.

Okay, so it wasn't exactly a plan but at least I managed to complete this one.

He held his hands up in the air innocently. "I just came here for a drink..."

"This is my club and you know it!"

"It's a free country."

"You knew I would be here! Why couldn't you go somewhere else? You could have gone *anywhere*! Anywhere but here!"

That wiped the cocky smile from his face but his features twisted into a nasty scowl. His eyes became cruel. I could barely recognise him anymore.

"Get over yourself!" he spat.

I walked past him, swung the door open, stepped outside, and slammed it behind me.

It was late. The street was dark and desolate. I could still hear the burble of people chatting and the door behind me was vibrating with music. I looked at the road but I couldn't see any vehicles and I wondered how hard it would be to find a taxi at this time of the night.

I then realised that I didn't even know what the time was. Just as reached for my phone, the door behind me opened, and Neal appeared in front of me.

"Don't go!" he pleaded.

The cruel ice of his eyes had thawed and they were warm again, it was the eyes of the real Neal, the one who cared about me. The person he was when he wasn't playing weird games. When he wasn't hurting me.

"I'm sorry!" he said, gripping my shoulders. "I just came here... because I wanted to see you!"

He was close. I could smell his intoxicating scent. It enters my nose, warms my chest, melts my insides.

I couldn't understand why he had such an effect on me. He wasn't my usual type. He was twice my age, and shorter than me. I usually go for taller guys; calm and collected guys like

Harry.

There were things I wanted to say to him but his arms were around me and my will to resist wavered. The feeling of his body against mine quelled my will to run. His tongue liquefied the words of protest from my lips.

In the morning I awoke in a bed that was beginning to become not so unfamiliar, with Neal beside me. I sat up and watched him sleeping for a few moments.

I couldn't believe I was there. The amount of times that I believed I would never lie beside him again, but each time I somehow ended up back there. It made each time like a new beginning, and I began to wonder if that was why he kept doing this – was it all in the thrill of the chase for him?

I shook my head. I didn't know. All I knew was that it was becoming tiring.

He was snoring, and I realised that there was no way I would be able to get back to sleep again so I decided to get out of the bed and go downstairs to make us both a cup of tea.

I entered the kitchen with the intention of filling the kettle but both of the dogs started to jump and bark around me. I patted their heads to try and calm them down.

"Down Chaser!" I said. I wondered if all of the fuss was because they were hungry, but then I noticed Missy was scratching the door and understood that they wanted to go outside.

"Okay, okay," I said, reaching for their leads. "I'll take you."

The dogs dragged me through the field as I tried to maintain a tenuous grip on their leads. It was autumn and the air was crisp. I don't often see this time of the day as I usually stay up till late at night painting but walking through the field that morning made me realise why people would choose to live in the countryside. My shoes became wet with morning dew and the clouds had descended from the sky and obscured the hillside in fog.

It felt good to be back here but I also knew that Neal and I needed to talk. Last night we were both drunk and so relieved to be back together that we just enjoyed each other, but now it was morning and I knew that there were still some things I wanted to say, some things that needed to be resolved.

I was going to put it to him straight. If he wanted to get to know me more and spend time with me, that was fine. If he didn't want to I would be a little upset but I would get over it, and that was also fine. I just wanted a bit of honesty. I wanted to know where I stood.

When the dogs dragged me back into the house he was already dressed and waiting for me in the kitchen.

"What are you doing?" he asked.

"I took them for a walk," I replied.

He crossed his arms over his chest and I realised that, somehow, I had angered him.

"I came down because you were still sleeping..." I mumbled. "They kept running to the door... so I thought..."

"You took my dogs out?" he shouted

I hate it when people shout at me. It makes me nervous and I don't know how to respond.

"They wanted—" I began.

"You just thought you would make yourself at home?!" he asked. "You think that by taking my dogs out in the morning you have some kind of hold over me? That you can make this more than it really is?"

I shook my head. "No... it was nice outside... I just wanted to."

His eyes were flaring at me and I didn't know what to do or say.

"You want her shoes don't you!" he carried on. "This is what this is about isn't it! That's why you want me to call you all the time! You think that you can take her place!"

His sudden anger put me in a state of shock and nothing he was saying made any sense. I opened my mouth to speak but his words had tied my tongue in knots.

I didn't know what to say to him anymore.

He carried on shouting but his words lost their meaning and garbled in my ears.

And I realised that I didn't want any of this anymore, so I turned around, stepped out of the door, and covered his pathway with my footsteps.

Ten minutes later I was walking down the road and heard a car pull up behind me. I cursed under my breath – it was one of those narrow country lanes so it probably needed to get past. I sidled up against the hedgerow.

The engine roared for a moment but then the brakes engaged again, and the car halted.

I then realised it was Neal's car. The window rolled down and I saw his face.

"Get in," he mumbled. He still had that cold look in his eyes but there was something else inside them as well now. Something I couldn't read.

I shook my head. "No. Leave me alone!"

"You can't walk all the way back to the city from here!" he exclaimed.

"I'm young, I will make it."

"Well you won't because you're walking in the wrong direction..."

The next thing I knew I was in the car and we sat in silence as he drove me back home.

I still couldn't believe all of the things he had said to me. They repeated in my mind over and over again and I couldn't make sense of them. All I had done was take his dogs for a walk, how had that incurred such a reaction from him?

My tongue was still tied. I couldn't speak. I had nothing to say to him. Was this all to do with him having commitment issues after the death of his wife, or did he just enjoy fucking with my head because it made him feel good about himself? I just didn't know anymore.

I just sat there beside him and thought about what I would say to him if I could.

I never wanted her shoes, Neal. I wanted to stand in my own shoes. But you never gave me any. I was barefoot, and you asked me to walk across hot coals.

And I did it for you.

But not anymore.

The scent of your sweat still lingers on my skin. I can still feel your lips on mine, but my ears remember, and keep repeating your poison. I still have red marks in the shape of your teeth on my nipples. It is all I have left, and they will fade away.

They say that once you have kissed someone their saliva stays in your mouth for six weeks. Yours will be in mine for another five weeks, six days and seventeen hours. When you make love with someone how long do they stay within you?

You unravelled my skin, twisted your fingers through all the muscles and sinews, you caressed my cheek while you snapped my bones and sucked the blood out my arteries to nourish your soul.

Before you went away you took something. My insides are twisting in knots.

I wish I had never met you.

When I got home I undressed so that I could get into the shower to wash him away. When I took off my jeans I emptied the pockets to find Harry's business card.

I stared at the number for a few moments but I knew that I was not ready for that yet.

I tossed it onto the table in case it appealed to me another day.

3
Bruises

He lived for order. For procedure.

Each day he'd wake to his digital alarm clock. He'd shower and then shave with his electric razor. He'd brush his teeth and then dress in a suit and tie.

Downstairs, Weetabix with skimmed milk and a spoonful of sugar. Then he'd get into his BMW (which he filled with petrol every Tuesday).

Life was routine. His job was something to do with numbers. When he got home he would open his freezer and choose which of his selection of microwave meals he would eat that night. They all had numbers on them too; listed daily nutrients. He'd take one out of its box; place it in the microwave; ping; eat; throw the plastic in the bin.

Every three days the dishwasher was filled, then, with the press of a button; clean plates. He took Prozac to keep his mood in check, and Codeine for his back.

When I moved in I disturbed this order.

I cooked meals. The first sight of me chopping vegetables, dirtying his knives and spilling scraps of food over the kitchen counter freaked him out, but he eventually acclimatised to it and my meals were integrated into his system. With his sense of order it was only fair that he also started cooking meals for me every now and then. He tossed a pre-sliced stir-fry pack, cubed chicken breast and some ready-to-wok noodles in the pan, and, a couple of minutes later, came to the dinner table with two steaming plates, looking very proud of himself.

In the first few months when we made love he experimented, but eventually he had me deciphered like a puzzle at work. He knew the points where I was most sensitive and the exact order to roll his tongue over them.

I was part of his routine.

One day, when he was at work, I broke the routine. I broke

the brush off his broomstick and tore a section out of our bed sheets. I piled up some of my possessions – in no particular order – onto the sheet, tied it in a bundle onto the end of the stick, and slung it over my shoulder.

On my way out the door I kicked his suitcase down the stairs.

My feet were light on the pavement; my body was on autopilot. My mind was racing, but I could think of nothing at all. My legs led me to the only place I could think of.

Janus.

I opened the door to the dingy interior. It had been a long time since I'd been there but this place had always felt like home: the same rock music was blasting out of the speakers, angry kids were sitting in the corners, the air stagnant with nicotine.

I bought myself a drink at the bar.

"Hey!"

There was no mistaking that voice. I turned around to see Pag wobbling his way towards me with a wide grin that was split by a missing tooth. I was there when he lost that tooth; I never found out how he'd got into that fight with those kids – he couldn't even remember himself – but I'd helped him out all the same.

He greeted me with, "Dude!" as he landed on the stool next to me. It must be easy being Pag: to him it didn't matter whether you were male, female, old or infant, tramp or royalty, everyone had the same name – dude.

"Not been 'ere for a while. Where the fuck have you been?" he asked.

"I tried the settling down thing. Didn't work," I replied, hoping he wouldn't ask more questions.

He looked at my bundled possessions tied to the end of the stick. It was balanced against the bar counter. "Wow, dude. You okay?"

I nodded.

"Well, it's good to see you," he said.

I smiled, and I was about to take another gulp from my drink but he jumped from his seat and snatched it from my hand.

"Nah. Fuck drowning your sorrows," he said as he slammed my glass back down on the counter. He grabbed hold of my sack of possessions and handed them to the barman, who accepted them silently. I was just about to protest – that was now all I had in the world – but Pag grabbed my arm and pulled me out of the room.

"Where are we going?" I asked as Pag led me up the stairs.

"Mr M. He has all the things you need."

We were now in a quieter part of the club. This place could be a maze sometimes: different rooms were cut off and opened each week. It seemed like it was always in a peculiar state between development and repair.

We passed through a grimy corridor on the third floor and reached a small room. Pag opened the door and there was a man wearing sunglasses, sitting at a table, with two men standing before him like bodyguards.

Pag walked up to them. "We want to see Mr M."

"Why do you request the presence of Mr M?" one of the bodyguards asked monotonously.

"Why you think man? *Drugs*," he said in a hushed voice.

Pag stepped past them but, just as I was about to follow, one of them blocked my way with a firm hand on my shoulder. "One at a time."

I scowled but sat myself down on the nearest chair to look at Pag and try to guess what he was saying by reading his expressive hand movements.

Eventually he came back. "Your turn," he said, winking.

I walked past the two men and nervously sat down with Mr M. For a while he just stared at me while he stroked his chin. I found him unnerving. I hate sunglasses. You can never tell if someone is looking at you or not. The club is a dingy enough place as it is so I'm not quite sure what benefit he could possibly be gaining from wearing them.

Pag's friends are always a bit fucking weird.

"You seem tense," he eventually said, in the manner a doctor asserts just as they are approaching diagnosis. "Upset. Let me offer you a choice."

He opened up both his hands and there was a pill in each one.

"If you take the one in my right hand it will numb your

mind, ease all those little thoughts that trouble it. The one in my left hand will help you gain insight, and see through the boundaries."

What's this garbage he's waffling on about? I wondered, beginning to suspect that this dealer had been sampling a little too much of his own wares.

"Can't you just give me a tab?" I groaned. "Or an E or something? What did Pag have?"

He shook his head. "You're at a crossroads. Two possible doors now lay before you. You must choose one."

I clenched my fist under the table, keeping a tenuous grip on my frustration. Did I really have to listen to this inane drivel just to get my hands on some drugs?

I looked back at his hands: two options before me. One pill to make me numb, and another that sounds like it could, potentially, turn me into an overanalysing, hysterical wreck. The former option seemed tempting just after leaving someone I thought was the love of my life. I could escape it all. Have a night of ignorant bliss…

Only to wake up in the morning where I started? No. I needed to evolve. I needed to take the left pill.

I grabbed it and placed it in my mouth.

Is this really the right choice? I looked at the remaining pill resting on his other palm. *Who says I can only open one door, anyway?*

Fuck it.

I snatched it from his hand.

"Don't!" Mr M shifted forward in a vain attempt to stop me.

It's too late now, Mr M, I thought, feeling rather pleased with myself as the duo rolled down my throat.

"You… shouldn't have done that," he said.

I walked back to Pag.

"Sorted?" he asked.

I nodded.

He put his arm around me and led me back down the stairs. "We're in for a fucked up night, dude!"

Next thing I knew, Pag and I were back downstairs in the main bar. A group of kids waved at him from one of the tables so he grabbed my hand and guided me over to them. He started to greet them with hearty handshakes while I stood there, awkwardly, not recognising any of them. Where was Halann? She and Pag used to be inseparable. The three of us used to be inseparable, but then I stopped coming here. How long had I been away from this place?

Pag sat himself down in the middle of the gang, and the only space left for me was at a small table to the side. I looked over at him but I couldn't make out what he and his friends were saying to each other, let alone join in the conversation.

I shrugged and turned to the girl sitting on the other side of my table. A petite goth girl with a slender frame and a cigarette balanced between her tiny fingers. She took a toke but wasn't really inhaling – it was just an accessory.

"That's Jenka, by the way," Pag yelled at me.

She looked up from a piece of paper she was writing on and smiled.

Thanks Pag, I thought. *You just chat to your friends and leave me with this crackpot.*

"So… what is that?" I asked. It was a weak attempt at conversation but her eyes lit up as if she'd been waiting for someone to ask.

"I am writing."

"Cool," I replied, suppressing a yawn. When were the pills going to kick in? "What are you writing?"

"It's about bruises," she said.

I raised an eyebrow.

She held up the paper and began to recite.

Bruises

*Love is like a bruise. The first time is
agony. It penetrates you. Gets beneath
your skin. There is nothing you can do to
soothe it.*

Have you ever heard of Savlon?

*After that first time, every now and then
you meet someone.*

I meet people everyday...

They want to nurse that bruise.

Yes, I think you need a nurse. Great idea.

*They lull you into security.
They caress the bruise softly with their
fingers.*

What is this? Porn?

*But only so they can jab their finger in,
to swell it again.
Bruises build up over time.
Bruises make you less desirable.*

Well, don't shove them in my face.

*After retaining a certain number of
bruises you become desperate for
someone to nurse them.
You can pull clothes over your bruises,
but everyone will find out one day.
Once they undress you.*

It's not their fault you're a slut.

*I once met a man, he had a thing for
bruises.*

Perv.

*He undressed me with his words, his
sweet caresses.
And then he battered me.*

With what, a stick?

> It gave him pleasure to see all the patches
> on my body.
> He liked to think they were all his, but
> they were not.

I don't know... sounds like you have issues with him...

> No.

Really?

> They were not his.

You sure?

"So, what do you think?" she asked, placing the paper back on the table.

"I think it's good."

I think it's the most pretentious, sentimental piece of crap I have ever heard in my entire life.

Everything around me began to distort. She made a reply but her voice swirled around me in vibrations and I was unable to distinguish the words.

I turned around and tried to get Pag's attention but he was too busy talking to his friends.

"Pag?"

He looked at me.

"Which pill did you take?"

He looked confused.

"Don't worry," I sighed. *Great! Fuck knows what I've just got myself into.*

I started to feel claustrophobic. Everyone's faces surrounded me and the lights flickered. The room started to sway as I walked away to catch my breath. Colours were manifesting in the shadows and the shadows were manifesting in the sounds. I staggered, falling to the floor. Out of the corner of my eye something else was falling and it took a few moments for me to work out that it was my own reflection.

But was it my reflection? It seemed to move independently and it was drawing me closer. I crawled forwards and gazed into the mirror. My features were twisting and distorting. My eyes were darting about like flies around a light bulb.

I reached forward to touch the surface but it cracked and a shard shot outwards and embedded itself in my hand.

I gasped and tried to prise the shard from the wound, but my veins sucked in the pieces of glass like a vacuum. Blood was oozing out of my palm. But instead of trickling down my skin, it was spreading along all directions of the surface. Within moments my whole arm was red.

Then it spread to my shoulder. I was hyperventilating. I could feel the blood spreading up my neck, to my face.

I looked around for Pag but I couldn't find him. I was enveloped in darkness. All that was before me was the mirror, and the cracks were growing. Just as I felt the blood spread past my jaw, up my face and to my eyes, the mirror exploded in a burst of shiny particles.

I was back in the bar. It was the height of the night and I could feel vibrations against my feet as music boomed from the speakers. I was still looking for Pag but I couldn't recognise anyone. The air was full of smoke – I couldn't even see the walls, and everyone seemed to be dancing alone in a grey abyss.

One woman in particular caught my attention and, as our eyes met, time started to slow down. Her skin was oily and her dress was so drenched with sweat it clung to her. She was looking at me seductively and I felt something stirring within me.

"Come closer." Her fingers ushered me towards her. Like I was a cat.

I crept forward.

"Closer," she whispered.

She was now a foot away from me.

"Closer still."

Our chests were touching. I could feel her breath on my neck.

"Closer," she whispered in my ear.

Our bodies were entwined.

"Don't ever get that close to me again!" she howled. Her palms slammed into my shoulders and sent me reeling back to the floor.

She was gone and I felt a numbing pain in my shoulder. I pulled back the neck of my t-shirt, and there was a purple hand shape underneath my skin.

A bruise.

I sat on the floor for a while, rubbing my bruise, but it just seemed to make it ache more. I must have looked like a complete invalid but I didn't have the will to get up.

"Help!" I cried, over and over again, until, eventually, someone came over. She looked a bit like that Jenka girl and she leaned down to examine my shoulder, her dark eyelashes stretching apart as her eyes widened.

"Oh no! You're bruised," she gasped. She grabbed my

wrist with icy fingers and pulled me to my feet. "You need to see the Artist," she said and started skipping across the room, almost wrenching my shoulder out of its socket.

"The Artist?" I asked.

But she was oblivious and just giggled to herself as she dragged me towards a door.

Where's Pag? He's left me alone on this, the fucker! We were supposed to be in this together.

She pulled open the door and in the frame was a vortex, swirling like a purple whirlpool. "She'll help your bruise," she said, excitedly. She pushed me in.

I felt an odd sensation in my stomach, but I wasn't falling. I didn't feel my feet land on the ground, but when I opened my eyes I found myself in a chasm of spiralling colours with plasmas of red swirling around me.

There was a woman in a purple dress. Her bony face was deathly pale and streaks of blackened tears were running down her cheeks. She had a razor blade in her hand. She was playing her wrist like a violin.

"What are you doing?" I asked.

"I am an artist," she said. "My wrist is the canvas, the razor, my paintbrush. My blood is the paint and the scars are the final piece."

"But where is the feeling in it?"

She paused. "There is none… it's about taking the feelings away."

"But isn't that what art is about? Everything's got to have a meaning."

"No. You're wrong," she said. "Art is a release; art is an expression of your innermost demons."

I followed suit and joined in her exquisite dance. We drew the blades across our wrists and each time I felt myself becoming more grounded. We grabbed hold of white cloths to soak up the blood and sat together in silence.

It was interesting. My anguish died a little with each cut and now when I thought about him all I felt was numbed sorrow.

But when I looked down at my bloody wrist I began to feel a bit ashamed. There is never a right way to deal with your anguish: some people let it build up until it consumes them, some take it out on others, this was a way of taking it out on yourself.

I didn't know what the true answer to the problem was, but it wasn't this.

The Artist smiled at me encouragingly – as if me smiling back would reassure her that what we'd just done was acceptable – but I didn't feel like smiling. She took my arm and traced her fingers across the red lines while her tongue explored her lips.

"Where are we?" I asked, pulling my arm away and getting to my feet. This place was making me feel dizzy and this woman was beginning to freak me out.

"Do you want to go back now?"

I nodded, but I couldn't for the life of me see a way out. All I could see around us was swirling, purple mist.

She rose to her feet and ambled towards me. I felt nervous as she drew close but she smiled reassuringly and placed her hands across my eyes.

My stomach lurched and then my feet once again touched solid ground. Her hands left my face.

We were back in the club. It was dark, the air was stuffy, smoke was clogging the room and people were dancing all around us. I scanned their faces but I still couldn't recognise any of them. There was still no sign of Pag.

The Artist was pulling back the sleeve of my shirt.

"What are you doing?" I gasped, pulling my arm away.

"What is the point of making art if you don't want to show it to anyone?" she asked as she turned to the crowd, raising her scarred arms for them all to see.

"I don't want to show this to anyone."

The crowd drew closer, surrounding us. Some of them were weeping with sympathy, others were cheering encouragement. They all looked up at her like she was a goddess, and then turned to me expectantly.

When I didn't respond they grabbed me. Dozens of hands held me still while they forced my sleeve back to admire the cuts lined across my wrist. I struggled and struggled but they only laughed. I felt my blood boiling and then I lost it, clenching my fists and knocking them away, kicking and lunging.

They drew back and stared at me, aghast.

"What the fuck is this?" I screamed. "Why are you all here?"

They scowled.

"Since when did pain become a statement?" I asked, turning to the Artist. "You don't know pain. You just want people to notice you."

"Leave her alone," one of the kids in the background yelled. I tried to work out who it was, but they all had the same faces, the same hair. "She's just being herself."

I laughed mirthlessly. "None of you have any idea what you are, do you?"

"I'm different," one of them shouted. I couldn't make him out from the others either.

"You're an insult," I said.

I turned back to the Artist and slapped her across the face. White powder exploded from her cheek and a red handprint began to form under it.

"The people you copied that from didn't do it because they wanted to make a show of themselves," I said. "They did it because they wanted to punish themselves. They felt like the world was trying to control them and it was something that was truly theirs. That no one had control over."

I grabbed the Artist's black hair and pulled it off – her head was shiny and bald underneath it. "You're not an artist. You're a fake."

I was expecting to be assailed by a horde of long nails and spiked bracelets but instead the crowd all turned their attention to the Artist.

"Fake! Fake! Fake! Fake!" they chanted, glaring at her with mania in their eyes. Within moments I had dethroned her; her subjects were malleable little things.

"Haven't you got better things to do?" I yelled. They went silent and stared at me devotedly. They were my subjects now.

But I didn't want them. I began to walk away but they followed me, so I quickened my pace. They grabbed for my arms and I elbowed them off. I tried to run but one of them was clinging to my ankle.

"Stop," he begged, with tears in his eyes. "Tell me what I should do."

"Go home, sit on your couch and let the TV guide you," I suggested as I kicked him aside. "At least then you'll be honest with yourself."

I ran out of the room but could still hear the stampede of footsteps as I slammed the door shut and bolted it behind me. The door rattled and shook on its hinges, so I reached for a chair and tilted it against the door handle, hoping it would hold them off for a while.

I turned around to make my escape down the winding corridor, and saw Pag in front of me.

"Dude!" he said, smiling like a long-lost friend and placing his hands on my shoulders. I could tell he was wired: his pupils were dilated.

"Where the fuck have you been?" I said, pushing him back.

"Dude, I turned round and you were gone."

I shook my head. "You left me on my own with that weird girl."

"Jenka? She's okay. She's just—"

"She's one of them," I said.

I turned back to the door. It had stopped shaking. The kids were either trying to find a way around, or had found another distraction.

"One of who?" Pag asked, raising one of his eyebrows.

I shook my head. Pag had a good nature but he could be incredibly simple sometimes. It was one of the things I'd always loved and hated about him.

"What the fuck has happened to his place?" I whispered. I gazed at the walls; they were covered in posters. Men with long black hair trailing down their shoulders and shiny leather trousers stretched tightly around their skinny legs. Angry women with short hair and baggy t-shirts that had logos like *blak shreik* stitched onto the front. They all had uncountable bits and pieces of metal sticking through their ears, mouths, nipples, and cheeks; wrapped around their fingers and necks.

Pag hung his head low and turned his eyes to the floor. "Things have changed—"

Just then I noticed that he had a spiked bracelet wrapped around his wrist, his t-shirt had a white logo saying *spookify* above the breast, and his hair – I'd seen other people with hair like that tonight.

I took a step back.

"What the fuck have they done to you, Pag?"

I met his guilty eyes. Pag had always had the clearest blue eyes I'd ever known. Truthful eyes. But now they were misted over by something else.

"I tried—" he began.

"You tried?" I punched the wall. The weak plaster crumbled against my knuckles and showered down to the floor. "Don't you remember? It was you, me and Halann! We fought for years to be free from all this shit! We made our dreams real! We were free! And you surrendered freedom for some spiked bracelets and a shitty haircut?"

"Don't you ever get tired of fighting?" he said. "I've been fighting my whole life."

"You gave up!"

"You left me here!" he said, pointing at me. "So don't go acting all high and mighty. Those kids were the only ones left!"

"Those kids are the exact kids that we came here to escape from. And you gave in? How could you be so weak?"

I turned and ran. It was time to get out of this shithole.

"Yeah, that's it… run away! Go back to your rich boyfriend's cushy little pad!" Pag shouted as I ran down the stairs. "Some of us don't have that luxury. Some of us have to help ourselves—"

I opened the door and felt the cold night air against my face. It was dark outside but the night was clear. I walked out into the street and took a look at Janus. It used to have crumbling walls and disjointed windows but had recently been repainted and had a shiny sign crowning its roof. I preferred its more decrepit look. It had more character.

I stood there for a while, staring at a place that had once felt like home but was now a place I no longer felt welcome. I felt someone poking my shoulder. I turned my head and gasped in surprise, feeling a surge of elation when I saw Halann beside me. She still had the same mousy blonde hair and purple lipstick glossed over her lips – it was good to see at least one of my old friends hadn't changed.

We hugged, holding each other tightly.

"You don't know how glad I am to see you," I whispered into her ear as I rested my chin on her shoulder.

Eventually she let me go and I stepped away.

"But how did you find me? I just mentioned you—"

"Pag texted me," Halann replied, holding up her phone.

I resisted the urge to scowl at the mention of his name. I tried to remind myself that whatever Pag was wearing now he was still a nice person. Deep down he was still Pag, though now he was pretending to be something else because it was easier.

"Why aren't you going inside to see him?" I asked.

"We don't talk much anymore," she said softly, turning her eyes to the club.

"What happened?"

She shrugged. "There was always the odd wannabe turning up there for the wrong reasons and the numbers just grew and grew. Then it became the new fad and—"

"Where do you hang out now?"

"Nowhere." She shook her head.

"What do you do then?"

She smiled at me impishly. Pag had always been the simple, fun-loving one; I was the dry, cynical one; and Halann was the mischievous and creative one.

She curled her finger, and I followed her through the backstreets. It was dark and I stumbled along on clumsy feet between the roads. Eventually she stopped, bent down to pick up a rock, and passed it to me.

I held it in my hand quizzically. She picked another, clenched it in her fist and suddenly launched it at the window of a house nearby.

The glass smashed and she turned to giggle at me for a quick moment before we fled the scene of the crime. We wound our way through alleyways, laughing to each other between panted breaths.

We became creatures of the night and journeyed through the town in shadows. We were a storm of chaos, ravaging our way through the streets. She was the wind that guided our way and I was the lightning blasts of destruction.

We had never wanted to be part of society and that was why we went to Janus.

Well now we didn't have Janus, and we were angry. If they were going to fuck up our world, it was time we fucked up theirs.

We trashed the town in vandalising bliss and I felt giddy on my feet. We set car alarms off, spray-painted anti-capitalist slogans onto the walls of banks, broke into the butcher's to steal animal carcasses to leave outside the vet's, and blocked up supermarket car parks with trolleys.

We stopped to rest outside a house. As I caught my breath I looked at Halann. She was drawing an anarchy symbol on the wall with red lipstick.

"What are you doing?" I asked.

"They took away the only place we could be free," she spat angrily as she circled the 'A'.

I shook my head. "Rebelling isn't being free," I realised. "Purposefully going against the grain is still letting them affect you."

"But it's the only thing I have left—"

I looked at the sign she'd made on the wall with lipstick. Was this really the only future we had left?

"I have to go," I said, walking away. "I'm sorry but this just isn't for me."

The distraught expression on her face was one I had to turn my back on because it pained me. Halann had, also, always been the emotional one.

I wandered through the town aimlessly, looking for any signs of chaos. But everything had been structured into roads and buildings and cars and pathways. You couldn't just walk in the direction you wanted to go anymore; you had to skirt your way around the lines and sectors society had created. Even the countryside was sectioned off into fields, farmlands, forests and fences. It was then that I realised that even Janus must have been organised for it to exist in the first place. It had never been pure chaos, it was just a piece of chaos we trapped in a box, but still, it was *our* chaos, and one day it imploded.

My phone was ringing. I picked it out of my pocket and looked at the screen. I had thirty-six missed calls. All from him.

I flipped it open and held it to my ear.

"Are you there?" His voice brought butterflies to my stomach.

"Hi," I mumbled.

"Where are you?" He sounded worried.

"Fuck knows," I replied. I scanned my surroundings for some landmarks but they were all blurred and distorted.

"Why did you rip the bed sheets? Are you leaving me?"

How could I explain? How could I put it into words for somebody like him?

"Things are too organised. I went to Janus, but they've stolen it—"

"That weird club you used to go to? How can someone steal a club?"

"You don't understand."

"Are you okay?"

"No. Society keeps organising things and it's really pissing me off."

"Okay… so it's not something I've done then?"

"It's you as well. It's your house."

"You don't like my house? You always liked it before. You have your own room. I helped you decorate it."

"Everything there… everything you do… is so… organised. It's the dishwasher… you put plates in and press a—"

"You want me to get rid of the dishwasher?"

"It's not the dishwasher!"

"You just said it was."

"No. Look, forget the dishwasher. The dishwasher is just a metaphor. I've had a really fucked up night. Some weirdo offered me these two pills, and I couldn't decide so I—"

"You've been taking pills again? You know how I feel about them."

"They aren't normal pills. They're—"

My knees suddenly buckled and I fell to the ground.

I woke to the feeling of soft sheets against my body and

bright sunlight from the window blinding my eyes. I covered my face with my hands as my eyes adjusted and I noticed that my arm had been bandaged up.

I could feel his eyes on me. He was sitting by the side of the bed. Had he been watching me sleep all this time?

He looked at me nervously, as if he was afraid to say anything.

"How did you find me?" I asked, sitting up with my back against the headboard.

"Your mobile. I had to break a few rules at work but I managed to locate you."

I shook my head. So now they could locate us by our mobile phones? What was next?

He passed me a glass of water and I drank it all in one go.

"I got rid of the dishwasher," he said. "So you don't have to worry about it anymore."

He still didn't get it, but he'd found me, brought me home, bandaged my arm, and watched me. No one had ever done so much for me before and it made me nervous.

Home. This was my home.

"I'm sorry," I said between trembling lips as surges of guilt wracked my mind.

He rose from his seat and made his way to the window to look outside. Then he turned back and his eyes were drawn to my bandaged arm.

"I think you need counselling," he said, turning back to the window. "I know a great one, he—"

"Oh yeah. I bet he would love to organise me," I said. "Tick some boxes. Then place me in a box. Give me some lovely tablets, and then ask me to pay for them. I'm okay, thanks."

"You're not well."

"I'm fine." I met his eyes as he turned back to me. Couldn't he see in my eyes that I was still me? Still sane? A bit peculiar, maybe, but that would never change.

"And I won't do that again," I said, indicating my arm. "I promise. That was just an experiment—"

"You did that as an experiment?" he asked, raising another puzzled eyebrow.

"Look, I know a lot of the things I do and say are weird

sometimes. But you have to trust me. I'm fine."

"Are you leaving me?"

"No—" I sighed. "But things have to change."

He sat down and wrapped his arms around me. I placed my head against his shoulder and remembered what was so good about us. I always want to see deeper into things; I float so high to get a view I sometimes get my head stuck in the clouds. And society has buried him so deep into the ground that he's lost his vision. We need each other: I'm the vision and he's my anchor.

"Oh… and get the dishwasher back," I muttered into his ear. "It's useful."

4
Red Rivers

Our lips parted for a moment. Just long enough for him to pull away, place his hands on my neck, and look into my face.

"Where you from?" he asked, while I tried to remember how I ended up here. It was all a blur, a distorted sequence of events. The last memory I had was of dancing in the darkness with flashing lights around me, feeling the wet, sweaty skin of other people brushing against me as we bumped into each other in a drunken Friday night haze.

I became aware of a pair of blue eyes staring at me between the shoulders of people. He was handsome. I checked behind me to make sure he wasn't looking at anyone else but there was no one. He was really looking at *me*.

I edged myself away from the guy who was grinding against me at the time. Eventually his hands left my hips and I danced my way through the crowd. As I got closer to him a perfect set of white teeth flashed a smile at me. We danced for a while. Face to face. He pulled me in closer and our lips met.

The next thing I knew I was here. Sitting on his lap by a table in a dingy corner of the club.

"That far away?" he asked. "Wow. What's your name?"

"Elaine," I replied, as I flicked a grey cloud of dust from the end of my fag into the ashtray. When I turned back around I caught his eyes engrossed on my breasts.

"Nigel," he introduced himself.

A brief silence as we smiled at each other. I reached into my handbag, drew out my tin, and began to roll another cigarette.

"You're on pills, aren't you," he said, knowingly.

I blushed. "How'd you know?"

"I probably have about ten years on you," he said. "You think I can't tell? How old are you, anyway?"

I knew my game was up when I paused to think, but he was smiling mischievously and, for some reason, I found myself trusting him so I leaned over and whispered into his ear.

"Seventeen."

He grinned and shook his head in mock disapproval.

"Tell me, Elaine," he said, his expression suddenly turning serious. "What are you doing seventy miles away from home, on pills, at seventeen?"

That did get me thinking.

He had a point – but what could I say to him? That 'home' to me is a dank, threadbare hovel where my mum splays herself on the couch, drinking herself to death and shouting abuse at me because I look too much like my sister, who died four years ago. Or should I tell him that I am out with two friends of mine who I got into a weird three-way sex affair with a while ago – until they decided they wanted to cut out the third party, cast me aside, and we are now trying the 'friends' thing. I took an E so that I could face this night with a smile.

No – I didn't want to tell him any of that. So instead I pushed the bad feelings away, giggled, leaned forward and kissed him. This diversion seemed to successfully distract him, and his lips felt nice.

Then I pulled away and lit up my fag.

"Want one?" I asked as I took a drag.

"No," he shook his head. "I don't smoke."

I sat myself on his lap and he placed a warm hand on the flat of my stomach.

"So," he said, looking back up at my face. "Tell me about yourself. What do you do?"

"College," I replied.

"Doing what?" he said, as his hand began to slowly move down lower.

"Art," I mumbled, pausing for a moment to remember. "Philosophy, and history."

"Intelligent then..." he commented.

"Ha ha," I giggled. "Not really."

His eyes suddenly cleared. "I am serious. There is something about you..."

"What do you mean?" I asked, raising an eyebrow.

"None of these other people," he said, casting his head around the eclectic range of people in the room. "Drew my attention. But you did. You have something which they don't."

I could have melted in his eyes, as he turned back to me, but his words made me feel uncomfortable. I don't like compliments. They embarrass me.

"I need the loo," I said, as I got up from his lap. "I'll be back in a minute."

I walked through the busy dance floor and a few dark corridors filled with people, towards the nearest bathroom. This club was some kind of hangout for clichés of teenagers dressed in black. There were a few hippy types and other eccentrics scattered around, but wannabe-goths seemed to have the run of the place. The only person who really stood out was a young man who was dressed plainly, in jeans and a grey hoodie that covered most of his face. He was just standing by a doorway – an observer watching the events around him without any inclination to involve himself, almost as if he was waiting for something.

"Do you know a girl called Frelia?" he asked me.

I shook my head and swiftly walked away.

I reached the bathroom and, after I had finished doing my business, I got out of the cubicle to wash my hands. There was a girl with strawberry-blonde hair at the sink; she was wearing a tight blue dress that attracted my wandering eyes to the curves of her body. I then swiftly realised that she could see me in the mirror and turned my gaze back to the sink.

"I know you," she said. "You're Elaine."

"Yes..." I replied. The fact she knew my name made me feel defensive; it made me wonder what she had heard about me. "Sorry, but I don't know who you are."

"Oh, me?" she shrugged. "I'm Fran... sorry... just, I've heard of you."

"Oh, and what did you hear?" I asked, forcing myself to smile.

"Nothing really," she said, as she moved to the hand dryer. "I just know people who know you, that's all."

The sound of the hand dryer saved me from a few moments

of more awkward conversation as I finished washing my hands. When I turned around again she was gone.

There were too many amphetamines pumping through my veins for me to have the patience to hold my hands under the dryer so I just rubbed my dripping hands on my jeans. I gazed into the mirror in front of me for a moment and sighed as I saw only the same familiar features. The E was giving me a temporary glow of happiness but the only thing it had changed was making my eyelids swell and my pupils huge. I shook my head. Once a boy called David used to tell me I was beautiful, but I am not. I am not even plain. Plain can be good; it is like a blank canvas you can make of what you want.

But I am not plain. My face is crudely sculpted. My cheekbones are high and swollen and I always have dark shadows beneath my eyes.

I suddenly remembered myself and realised that this was not the time for such thoughts – I was in a club for goodness sake! I practiced a smile in front of the mirror but it faltered. I hate my smile.

I noticed a movement out of the corner of my eye and looked in the mirror to see Charlene walking into the bathroom.

"Are you okay?" she asked. She looked a bit concerned. "I've been looking for you."

"Did you see a girl when you came in?" I asked.

She turned around. "What girl?"

"Ginger hair," I said. "Bit taller than me."

"Don't think so," she shook her head. "Why, what's wrong?"

"She was just weird," I shrugged. "That's all."

Charlene was the girl I came here with. Our friendship has become tenuous recently because we got into a three-way relationship with a guy called Greg, which lasted a few weeks. She and Greg cut me out.

She stood herself at the mirror and began to coat her lips with red lipstick. "We were a bit worried. You disappeared with some guy...."

I looked at her reflection. She is pretty. I don't blame Greg for choosing her over me. I should have known that the three of us sleeping together wouldn't last. I don't think Charlene is even bisexual, I think she just did it because Greg was into it.

"He's called Nigel," I replied. "Don't worry, he's nice."

She gave me a warm smile that was missing the layer of ice that had grown between us recently. I knew why: now that I had a guy interested in me I posed less of a threat to her having Greg to herself.

"Can I bring him back tonight?" I asked.

"I'll check with Greg, but I don't see why not," Charlene shrugged as she placed the lipstick back in her handbag.

When I was walking back into the main bar there was a girl in a blue dress talking to Nigel. It was too dark for me to know for sure but she looked a bit like that weird girl I met in the toilets. I quickened my pace towards the table but missed her by a few moments and she walked away, soon disappearing into the dancing crowd.

He smiled at me and placed an arm around my shoulder.

"You okay?" he asked.

I opened my mouth to ask him what that girl wanted with him when I suddenly felt really hot. Heat rose in my chest – it felt like my insides burning up, melting, yet the air around my skin went incredibly cold.

"Elaine!" he yelled, grabbing me by the shoulders and shaking me. I tried to hold my head up, but the waves of intense sensations coursing through my body were too much and my neck rolled back.

"Sorry..." I mumbled. "It's just hot... and I..."

"Wait there," he said, rushing over to the bar. "I'll get you some water. I'll be right back!"

I placed my back against the wall and tried to catch my breath. I could feel the thudding of my heartbeat hammering against my chest and my shirt was coated in sweat. Eventually a hand guided a cold glass of water to my lips and I gulped it down. It tasted like heaven.

"Feeling better now?" he asked, when I opened my eyes. I sat myself back up, feeling alert and awake again.

I nodded. "Thanks... sorry about that."

He shook his head and placed a hand on my shoulder. "It's okay. Just make sure you drink water. Ecstasy dehydrates you."

I rested my head against his shoulder. I had only known this guy for a short amount of time but I already felt so comfortable around him, and just then he had shown me that he cared. He was gorgeous as well. God knows what he saw in me.

"Why did you do this?" he asked as his fingers lingered on the pattern of white lines on my wrist. With time the lacerations had faded from their fleshy pink to a faint white, but they were still visible. I usually wear something with sleeves to cover them up but it was too hot in this place.

"They're my Puberty Marks," I replied.

"Puberty Marks?" he repeated, quizzically.

"Yes: they are like birthmarks, but people tend to get these ones during puberty," I said. I had never really done anything of real value in my life but I was proud of the fact that I had given up that habit. "It's rude to ask a girl about her Puberty Marks, you know."

"I can see a lot of pain in you," he said, clasping my hand between his own. "And I want to help. I can't explain it, Elaine, but I feel really drawn to you... I'm sorry if I am being a bit heavy. I've only just met you but I want you to be my girlfriend."

He turned away, like he had said too much.

"It's okay," I said. "I feel the same."

Greg and Charlene joined our table and the rest of the night was a blur of drinks, listening to music, chatting, and resting back in Nigel's arms. Later on, though, there was some kind of fight on the other side of the club and the atmosphere soured. We didn't stay long enough to find out what had happened and decided to make a hasty exit. We caught a taxi back to Greg's place and he and Charlene soon went to bed, leaving Nigel and me in the living room.

We rested on the couch for a while in silence and I closed my eyes, feeling the pills wearing off. I was coming down.

Eventually I opened them again and realised that Nigel was playing with his phone. It looked like he was texting someone.

"What are you doing?" I asked.

He quickly put his phone away and smiled at me. "Oh, nothing. You look tired. Do you want to go to bed?"

I nodded my head, yawning. "Hold on a moment."

I got up and made my way up the stairs towards the bathroom. I felt clammy and sweaty from the night out so I stripped off and hopped into the shower, quickly cleaning myself. I didn't want to leave my new boyfriend waiting for too long but I didn't want to get into bed with him all sweaty and smelly.

I dried myself off, went to the sink, and brushed away the stale taste of a night out of my mouth with a line of toothpaste.

Just as I was rinsing my mouth out I heard the doorbell go.

Who could that be? I wondered. Greg and Charlene were both asleep and I certainly couldn't remember them inviting anyone else over.

I quickly made my way down the stairs and saw a silhouette of a girl with strawberry-blonde hair through the glass of the door. I opened it – it was the weird girl I met in the club. I stood there for a moment with my mouth gaping open. What the hell was she doing here?

"Hi, it's me," she said. "From earlier, at Janus. Fran. You remember?"

"Yeah..." I mumbled, unable to hide my surprise. I was just opening my mouth to ask her what the hell she was doing here when she interrupted me.

"Sorry," she said. "I'm a friend of Nigel's – he texted me your address. I need to see him."

"Oh..." I muttered, suddenly realising that I was standing in front of a complete stranger wearing nothing but a towel. "I guess you better come in then... he's in there," I said, pointing towards the living room. "I need to get dressed..."

I sped up the stairs as she walked into the living room. This was all getting very weird, and I felt an urgency to get back downstairs so they weren't alone. I hurriedly dressed myself and walked back down.

Should I knock? I thought as I hesitated outside the door. They could be having a private conversation.

After debating with myself I stepped inside, but they weren't there. I cast my eyes around the room and quickly realised that the door to the spare room was open. I walked up to it and heard a gentle sigh on the other side.

When I saw them squirming against each other on the bed, with their hands exploring and their lips joined, I could only stare in horror. Nigel looked at me and smiled. It was a knowing smile, it was conniving, and told me he knew exactly what he was doing.

He had planned all of this. All those words he had said to me, and all the kindness, was part of a plan which led to this moment.

I slammed the door shut, and sat myself down on the couch. Nigel groaned loudly, making sure I could hear that he was having sex with a stranger in my friend's house. Enjoying the humiliation it caused me.

They carried on throughout the night as I sat there on the couch. Inside I was screaming. I didn't make a sound. I wanted to disappear.

Eventually it stopped. There was silence. I sat there. I didn't move. Nigel might hear me. I didn't want him to have the satisfaction of knowing I was still there.

I saw something in the corner of my eye.

At first I ignored it. *It must be the pills*, I thought. *Maybe I am just dreaming. Please can this be a nightmare?*

It stayed there, no matter what I thought. I stared straight at it. It was a girl. Standing by the window. Her outline was translucent and glowing faint blue. She had a haunted look in her eyes.

"Who are you?" I whispered.

"I am like you," she said, softly.

"Like me?" I muttered. I shook my head violently to try to dispel the illusion, but she was still there.

"We are all like you..." a second voice whispered.

I jumped at the sound. There was another girl beside me, on the couch. She was skinny and her bones clung to her skin. I couldn't see her face because she was leant forward. She was beset with the same ghostly hue as the other girl.

"We know *him*."

A third voice. Another girl huddled in the shadows in the corner of the room. She was petite – couldn't be older then sixteen – and clad in black. I could barely see her cadaverous eyes between the lank strands of her ebony hair.

"What's going on?" I gasped. I was trembling with fear but too scared to move.

"We are the shadows which follow him," said the one standing by the window. "And we all have our stories."

Stacy's Story

I once had a happy life. We lived on a nice estate on the suburbs, and my father was in the Navy. One day he sailed away and never came back. My mother said he had docked his ship into a more desirable harbour.

She changed after that day. Slowly, but surely. Her voice became a haughty rasp of bitterness, and sometimes she would go into a helpless rage and beat me. The first few times she did it she woke me up the next day with a bar of chocolate and a teary, regretful apology. Over time this became less frequent. The beatings increased.

At school I was the girl who ate my lunches in the toilet and spent my breaks in the library. I was humiliated daily, and when my mother noticed bruises on my body which were not hers, she beat me for refusing to tell her where they came from.

I met a man on the internet. He was older, but kind and gentle. He made me feel special. Wanted. I poured my heart and soul out to him. In a life of despair he brought a glimmer of hope. Nobody could hurt me anymore because I would just close my eyes and think of him. He told me we would meet in the flesh and run away together. That he would do anything for me. And I believed him.

One day I came home, and it was one of those rare occasions my mother was in a good mood. She was actually smiling. With a glimmer of light in her eyes, she told me about someone special in her life she wanted me to meet.

The moment he walked into the room, there was no mistaking that it was *him*; I looked at pictures of that face every day. I even had a print out of one of them in my purse. I stood there in shock, not believing my eyes. I wanted to scream.

My mother placed an arm around his shoulders and scorned me for being rude to her new boyfriend. I was forced to compose myself, and shake his hand. He smiled.

From that day he was always in the house. At night I used to have to bite my pillow to stop myself from screaming when I heard them making love in the room next door.

Once, when my mother was away, I heard my door creak open in the middle of the night. I looked up to see him in my doorway with a mischievous look in his eyes, and a smile on his face which I hadn't seen for weeks. The smile I used to believe belonged only to me.

He said he was sorry.

That he loved me.

I knew deep down that it was a load of crap, but when you have nothing to live for you will settle for a fleeting moment of happiness – even if it is false.

I slept that night in his arms and for the first time in weeks I was smiling. But when I woke in the morning there was a space next to me which was cold and empty. I never saw him again after that, but one day my mother received a letter in the post. After reading it she screamed and dropped it to the floor.

She ran at me with a knife.

Steph's Story

I ran away from home when I was sixteen because my stepfather abused me. To survive I became a whore, a beggar. Anything that meant I would never have to go back to that place.

One day a man offered me a warm bed for the night and a meal. It was winter and I was freezing – how could I turn that down?

The first time we had sex I thought it was just part of the deal: I was used to letting men utilise my body in exchange for creature comforts. But there was something different about this. It wasn't the usual mechanical thrusts from a glassy-eyed man staring guiltily at the sky that I was used to experiencing. He was kissing me. Looking at me, rather than through me. Making love to me.

After staying there for a few days he said that he loved me and wanted to help me.

My life had meaning again. I stayed in his flat and, a few weeks later, I got myself a job. It was only temporary, in a supermarket to help with the holiday season, but it was the first time I felt like I was worth something and I was so happy. I raced back to the flat to tell him, only to find he wasn't there and everything was gone: the TV and furniture, his clothes, his possessions. I was baffled, confused. God spare me: I was even worried about him.

At first I was in denial to the truth that was all around me. He had not left me. He loved me. He would be back soon. There would be a perfectly good explanation for all this.

I stayed there for two days and eventually a man burst in through the door, claiming to be the landlord. He accused me of squatting and threw me out onto the streets.

"Nigel Harris doesn't live here anymore!" he screamed. "He left weeks ago!"

I am not quite sure what happened to me after that. I just wandered the streets, unaware of where I was going. Not caring. I wanted to die.

Jenka's Story

I didn't grow up in a troubled family. I don't have a story of abuse which compares to those two girls. I was just the weird girl in school that no one liked. People confused me. I felt alien. Depressed. Insecure. Lonely. Outcast. Lost.

I used to slice open my skin to reach into that place where I felt hollow, and every time I would wish I had the guts to push down harder. Make my wrists run red rivers and gush the light out of me.

I met him at Janus, and he filled that void inside me. He told me that the mere sight of me brought butterflies to his stomach. When he saw my scars it didn't scare him away – he said he wanted to help me.

I gave my virginity to him. He devoured my body and cast me aside. He would ignore me for days at a time, but always come back for more eventually. He would say anything to get me back: that he was sorry, that he got scared, that it was only because he liked me so much and he didn't know how to handle it. But it was only so he could hurt me again.

And each time, I believed him. Each time, he would take another piece of my soul and then pretend I didn't exist, until he wanted more.

Until he vanished completely.

That night, I cut down harder.

"This is the beginning of your story," Stacy said. "Can't you see, Elaine? He wants to hurt us. He enjoys it. All those nice things he did and said to you tonight were just leading towards *that*," she turned her eyes to the door of the room where he had sex with that girl.

"But why?" I whispered. "Why would someone want to do this? You're all dead! How could he do that?"

Jenka shook her head. "There's no reason for it, Elaine. Some people are just sick. Sick in the mind and soul, and sometimes there is no cure for them. It is just the way they are."

"It is time to end this," Stacy said, as she lifted herself from the floor and floated towards the doorway. Jenka and Steph followed her. "Come, Elaine," she implored, turning around to face me. "You need to be here."

I silently got up and followed them towards the bedroom. They opened the door and I saw him lying there on the bed next to Fran. I narrowed my eyes. Could it really be that he did all those things to these girls? That all of the things he did to us where just schemes to cause us pain?

He was sleeping so soundly. He looked satisfied and at peace.

"Wake up, Nigel," Stacey said.

"Nigel!" Steph cooed.

He stirred from sleep and slowly opened his eyes. For a moment he just looked around the room in a dream-like haze. But when his eyes cleared and his mind began to gain clarity, his face twisted in horror.

"What!" he gasped, shifting, turning his head to stare at each of us in turn. "What's going on?"

"We are really here, Nigel," Jenka whispered, leaning over the bed and smiling at him menacingly.

"We never really left you," Stacy whispered.

"No!" his hands went to his face and he rubbed his eyes. He looked up again. They were still there. "This isn't—"

"It's really happening," Steph interrupted him, floating to his side and placing a hand on his shoulder.

The other two girls closed in on him – he was surrounded. He tried to get out of the bed and run but their glowing hands pushed him down.

Suddenly, the figure next to him floated out from the bed sheets and I gasped when I realised it was Fran. She was translucent and ghostly, now. Just like the other girls.

"I am Francesca," she said, looking at me. "And I am his girlfriend."

I turned my eyes to the floor. There was me thinking that I was the victim of all of this but it turns out that *I* was the woman on the side.

He had played us so well.

"My story is not important," she spat, shaking her head. "We are all one story. His story."

He opened his mouth to say something.

"Shut up!" she snarled. "This is ending right here, Nigel! Right now!"

"It will!" he groaned, with desperation in his eyes. His gaze fluttered between the ghostly apparitions around him.

"Your crimes must be dealt with," Jenka said flatly. "We cannot let you do this anymore."

"It is time to end this," Steph concluded, nodding her head.

"It will!" Nigel whimpered.

"Death is not enough punishment for him," Stacy said, turning to the other girls.

"He needs to suffer."

"We need your help, Elaine," Steph finished.

The four of them turned to me expectantly.

"Me?" I gasped.

"We need your permission," they said in unison.

"Why?"

"It's just how it works," Fran said, simply, shrugging her shoulders. "We can't do this unless you say yes."

This must be a dream... I thought to myself.

But I knew by now it wasn't.

I looked at Nigel. He was now cowering in fear. He looked so pathetic now I almost felt sorry for him. Almost.

But then I looked back at the other girls and remembered their stories and all the things he had done to them. The calculated and perverse pleasure he got out of their suffering. Did such a person really deserve to live?

"I am Elaine," I said, my voice shaking in cold anger. He looked me in the eyes. Imploring me.

"I am the last girl you ever fucked with."

A look of joy crossed the girl's faces and they smiled. They all turned back to him while Fran reached into a bag on the floor and retrieved a shining blade.

"We will be together forever, Nigel," Jenka whispered as she and the other girls straddled him. He tried to push them away but his hands just slid through their transparent figures. The girls began to giggle.

"And forever together."

I closed my eyes. I did not want to watch this.

"It hurts, but only for a moment. Then *all* the pain is gone."

"It will be over soon, Nigel."

"You will be with us forever."

A scream. His scream. The scream of a man. I did not know a grown man could scream like that.

The four of them started giggling again.

"Just like you always said to us."

Another scream.

"Come with us, Nigel."

The screaming softened to a passive wail.

"We will be together now."

The girlish laughter reached a heavy climax.

"Together forever."

"Just like you always said to us."

The laughter suddenly died out and all I could hear was silence. Eventually I dared myself to open my eyes and his bloody remains were spread across the bed. A knife was protruding from his chest. The girls had vanished.

Charlene was racing down the stairs.

5
Shadow Sisters

This tale begins with a dream.

I lay back with my limbs stretched out on a bed of grass. A gust of wind blew the reeds and they swayed before my eyes and tickled my face.

I sat up and saw there was an endless landscape of green hills around me, and the sky was a welkin of bleary, merging colours.

"Where is the sun?" I whispered, realising I could not see the source of light which lit up this world. A dim haze seemed to exist everywhere. I did not know where I was or how I had got to this place

There was a girl beside me. She was a slight figure with black hair and a bird-like face of small features, a pointed nose, and azure blue shimmering eyes. "You are searching for the source?" she asked, looking at the heavens. "If you want to find the source, you must first find their place."

She circled a finger around us. There were animals grazing. Plump sheep with woolly coats and cattle with their heads buried in the grass as they devoured the vegetation. Some of them were more outlandish species that I could not distinguish and their forms flickered like candlelight in the wind as I tried to decipher what they were.

"Discover their purpose," she challenged.

"That is no problem," I said. I reached into the fold of my dress and pulled out a flute. It was carved from wood and of simple design. When I held it to my lips and began to play, aureoles of blue and orange rippled around me as my song filled the sky. The heads of animals perked up and they fixed their eyes on me as I skipped along the hillside, twirling a spiral dance around the meadow.

"I have rounded them up," I said, appearing before the girl with a trail of animals behind me. "Where do you want them?"

She shook her head.

"The task wasn't to lead them," she said. "It was to guide them to their purpose."

"What's their purpose?"

"That's not for you to know," she said. Her eyes became angry and she snatched the flute from my hands and dangled it in front of my face. "You should be more worried about your own instrument."

"My instrument?"

She smiled, brought the flute to her lips, and blew a breath into the wooden tube. A piercing shrill swept across the air and tingling sensations crept through my body, making me quiver. I looked down, realising that her song was causing a burning desire between my legs.

I gasped. She blew harder, and my hands went to my crotch as I became horribly self-conscious of the strange effect her song was having on me. I looked up at her, begging her for mercy.

She smiled and carried on playing.

I woke up that morning with a sharp intake of breath and wetness between my legs. My eyes opened wide at the revelation that it was all a dream.

Funny how you only ever realise how bizarre dreams are *after* you wake up.

With a heavy sigh I pulled my hand out of my knickers and rested my head back on the pillow.

Like most fifteen-year-old girls on a Saturday, I slept the rest of the morning. Dreamlessly. Unlike most fifteen-year-olds, I was woken up by the sound of my mother practicing yoga in the living room. She was under the instruction of one of those guidance videos and we live in a bungalow with very thin walls.

"Stretch and hold. Breathe deeply. Feel the mercurial energies of water flowing through your chakras."

I sighed and tried to ignore the sound of the woman's infuriatingly placid voice as I made my way to the shower. A few minutes later I was clean and dressed. To get to the kitchen I had to walk through the living room where my mother was standing on her head, stretching her legs up high in the air.

"Morning mum," I said as I tiptoed past her.

"All that black doesn't suit you, you know," she said, although I wasn't sure how valid her opinion was, viewing me upside-down. "It's your eyes, Faye. Your eyes are too light."

I didn't reply. She said the same thing to me a few weeks ago when she took me shopping for clothes, but she still bought them for me. Such passive guidance was typical of my mother: she is one of those New Age types who believe the young should be free to blossom without being smothered with oppressive confinements. This didn't stop her enrolling me at the local school.

"What are you doing today?" she asked as I doused my cereal with milk. She was now curved up in the Bow Pose, rocking back and forth. "I have meditation class this afternoon but I am free tonight if you want to spend some time together? We'll get a—"

"I'm going to a party with Amy and Harriet," I said apologetically. "I think we're staying at Amy's. Is that okay?"

I could tell she was disappointed but she nodded her head. "Just make sure you take your phone with you. Does Amy's mother know where you're going?"

"I think so," I said casually. I then turned away so she couldn't see my face. I have never been a good liar. If her mother really knew where we were going that night Amy would be grounded for weeks. "They're coming later to pick me up. Can they hang out for a while?"

"I guess so," she said as she straightened her legs and rolled back onto her side. "Just behave yourselves."

After my mother left the house, I picked up my bass guitar and began to practice. The speakers of my computer blasted out music from a playlist of my favourites while I plucked away at the strings. It is only when my mother is out that I get to practice this loudly because she says that the music I have been getting into recently is bad for the soul. She thinks that everything is bad for the soul. TV. Radio. Fizzy Drinks. Computer games. Artificial preservatives and flavourings.

It's not that I don't like my mother. I mean, as far as mothers go, she is pretty cool. I know this. She believes me sensible enough to not get into trouble, so I can leave the house without her asking too many questions. I know I could talk to her about almost anything and she is such a beatnik there is not much that would shock or surprise her.

It's just that when you're growing up sometimes you just want to be normal, and it is a continual effort to fit in when your mum sends you to school with a lunchbox filled with bean salad and picks you up at the end of the day dressed in tweed.

I was in a zone of sounds and rhythms for most of the afternoon until my fingers began to feel sore and I looked at the clock and realised that Amy and Harriet would be here soon. I had not put any makeup on yet so I rushed over to the mirror and hastily applied thick measures of black eyeliner around my eyes, followed by a smothering of dark lipstick.

After covering my face in powder and smearing cerulean shadows above my cheeks Amy and Harriet burst into the room. Amy was wearing a netted top, miniskirt and tights, all in black; and her hair was tied up, apart from a few rebellious strands she had carefully gelled across her face. Harriet, her ever-present shadow, was in a black dress and leather boots. They both had spiked bracelets strapped around their wrists.

With a bottle of vodka in one hand and a lit cigarette in the other, Amy looked me up and down. "Faye, what the hell have you done to your eyes?" she asked, turning to Harriet. They both cackled at me.

"Here," she said, passing her cigarette over to Harriet, who began to suck away at it without inhaling. "Let me fix that up for you."

I wanted to tell them to stop smoking – my mother had smelt it last time they came over and told me off – but before I could get a word in Amy was sitting beside me, rummaging through her makeup.

"Take this," Harriet said, passing me a bottle. I took a swig and restrained a shudder as the vodka trickled down my throat.

"Close your eyes a sec, Faye," Amy requested as she dipped a brush in some dark purple powder. After applying, she blew a warm, smoky breath of air over my face. "That's much better," Amy marvelled as she admired her handiwork before turning back to Harriet. "Don't you think?"

Harriet agreed immediately. I looked at my reflection in the mirror; the mauve under my eyes made me look like I had not slept for a week but I shrugged. At least they weren't laughing at me anymore.

"You didn't tell your Mum where we're going tonight, did you?" Amy asked, narrowing her eyes at me.

I shook my head. "I said we were going to a party."

"Mine thinks we're having a sleepover," Harriet added.

"Good," Amy smiled. "I think we're covered then."

"Where *are* we going, again?" I asked.

"*Janus*," Amy replied, rolling her eyes, as if by not knowing the name I had just committed blasphemy. "Where else would we go in this shit town?"

"Is Paul still coming?" Harriet asked, a sudden light appearing in her eyes. Paul was a boy at school she had a crush on.

"Paul?" I asked. "But you said this club was a place for... well, you know... people like us?"

Amy shook her head, smiling. "Paul has seen the darkness now. Didn't you notice all those badges he's been sticking on his bag recently? I sit next to him in maths. He's learning to play guitar."

"Oh," I muttered. This news actually annoyed me though. Paul was one of those popular kids. The sort of guy Harriet would not have stood a chance with a year ago. Amy, Harriet and I had always been outsiders, the sort who just didn't fit in. I was never really bothered by it but I could tell that Amy wanted more.

A while ago Amy changed. She started to listen to heavy music with distorted guitars and screaming vocals, and she adopted the styles of some of these musicians and dyed her hair black. She introduced Harriet and me to it all and the three of us – the outsiders – found something we had never had before: an identity. People began to see us in a different way.

The moment that really turned it all around, though, was when some of the bands we liked aired on the radio and other people began to like it. Kids at school started dressing like us and Amy turned into a guru who lent them CDs and gave them advice on where to buy the darkest and most outrageous clothes. Suddenly we found ourselves with not just an identity, but also something we never even dreamed we would have: status.

But Paul becoming one of us vexed me. We were in the same tutor group at school and he had been teasing me for years over the way my mother dressed; the fact that I lived in a bungalow; my wild, wavy, auburn hair which refused to be tamed until the day I discovered black hair dye and hair-straighteners. Paul, who had always tried to make my like hell for being a bit different, was now assimilating himself with me.

"Oh, and Faye," Amy said, bursting the bubble of my thoughts. "I think Steve is coming as well, and guess what!"

"What?" I asked, shrugging. Steve was a boy I had a couple of classes with. He had never been nasty to me or anything, but he was quiet and I had always thought him a bit boring.

"You can't tell I told you this," Amy whispered, even though it was just the three of us there. "But a little crow told me he likes you!"

"Oh," I said, surprised. It wasn't often boys fancied me. Not that I knew of anyway.

"He's cute Faye!" Harriet slapped my shoulder. She then turned to Amy. "Is Josh coming?"

"Yes. I rang him earlier," Amy replied. Josh was her boyfriend; they had been dating each other for a few weeks. He dressed like a skater but his only real hobby was smoking weed. He was nice enough, if a little dull in the head. "Looks like it's a triple date!"

I sighed. Neither of them even asked me if I fancied Steve.

After a few shots I was feeling much more relaxed. The afternoon drained away while we sat on my bed, chatting, drinking, smoking, and teasing each other. Eventually my eyes were drawn to the clock on the wall and I realised my mother was due back soon so I began to motivate them to get up and make a swift exit.

"Hold on, missy," Amy answered. She had a stick of mascara in her hand and was applying a few more garish touches to Harriet's face.

I stubbed my cigarette out on a plate and sighed. They always did this. Even when we arrived there they would be taking regular trips to the bathroom to paint their faces in front of the mirror. I have never understood how they could be so vain.

I heard a duo of cackling behind me and turned to catch the sight of Amy and Harriet falling on the floor together. They tumbled around in a drunken black bundle of limbs and laughing.

I cursed and grabbed Harriet by the arm, hauling her back onto her feet. Amy was still rolling around in fits of laughter.

"How much's she drunk?" I asked. Harriet shrugged.

"Get up, Amy!" I yelled, but she wasn't listening. Her attention was drawn to something under my desk and she stretched her arm out.

"What the hell is this?" she exclaimed, pulling out my flute. "Jesus, Faye! What are you, the Pied Piper or something? You *still* have this?"

Harriet began to mime playing, (quite badly, she wasn't even holding the imaginary flute the right way round) and skipped around the room like a Morris dancer.

"Stop it!" I yelled, pulling Amy back up and dragging her out of the room. "We need to go! *Now!*"

Harriet grabbed their bags and they both carried on laughing as we left the house. Just as I reached the front door, it opened itself, and my mother was there, standing in the frame. She looked at me, and I could tell by her expression she knew something was up. But, being my mother, she didn't yell, she just gave me *that* look. The disappointed look.

Amy and Harriet abruptly went quiet and breezed past her, making a swift exit down the street.

"Faye," she said, softly. "You've been smoking! I can smell it!"

"Sorry, Mum," I said as I reached for my coat.

Janus was everything Amy promised: dark and dingy, full of people wearing black clothes and spiked bracelets, angry rock music blasting out of the speakers, tonnes of underage kids drinking.

And I found myself unexplainably uncomfortable and disappointed.

We bought drinks and then Amy made us stand by the crowds of people gathered near the speakers. It was too loud for us to have much conversation and I started to feel bored.

So bored I was actually glad to make a visit to the bathroom. Amy led us up a rickety staircase and then down a winding passage cluttered with people drinking and talking. The thumping music from downstairs quietened and the chatter from the crowds of drinkers filled my ears. This part of the club was markedly different; the light bulbs were dim, the walls were faded and the drinkers were more diverse. The hall downstairs was a world of black clothes, dark hair and spiked jewellery, but this world up here was full of variations, styles and colours. Men in torn jeans and straggly hair drinking cider, a boy in a green elf hat sat against the wall smoking a pipe and rocking his head back and forth, I even looked through the doorway of a room we passed to see a group of girls playing hopscotch on some lines they had chalked on the floor, one of them was wearing a large frilly dress, like she was out of some kind of pre-Raphaelite painting.

I then saw a familiar face at the end of the hallway that made me gasp. I stopped and stared, blinked a few times, to make sure I was really seeing what I thought, but there she remained.

It was the girl from my dream. My vision of her was distorted by the smoke of cigarettes and the shoulders of people standing between us, but I knew that face. I was about to walk over to her but Amy grabbed my arm and pulled me into the girls' toilets.

She and Harriet began to paint their faces in the mirror again. I opened my mouth to say something but quickly realised that I couldn't really say anything that wouldn't sound ridiculous. I had just seen a girl I had never met before, apart from when she made me orgasm with a flute in a dream I had.

Now I wasn't going to tell them about that, was I? So I went into a cubicle and relieved myself.

When we left the toilets I turned my head to look up the hallway where I had seen her, but she was gone. I tried to convince Amy and Harriet that this place seemed interesting and we should explore more but Amy pulled out her phone.

"Josh just text me," she said. "The boys'll be here soon."

"Amy," I said as we made our way back downstairs to the bar. "How's the guitar going?"

"So-so," she replied, shrugging. "It's so cool we're in a band though! I can't wait!"

How can we be in a band when we've never played together? I thought to myself.

"Okay..." I said. "How are you doing with it all? What can you play?"

"I dunno..." Amy said, shrugging again. "Paul said he is going to teach me the power chord. Apparently that's all you need. What can you play?"

I began to list the ones I could remember from the top of my head, and with each addition Amy's eyes widened more. Eventually I realised I was losing her, so I stopped.

"How did you learn so quickly?" she gasped.

I practiced...

"I mean. Did you manage to find tabs for all those songs?" she asked. "I was looking at some of them the other day on the internet, and they just confused me!"

"I don't use tabs," I said. "I can read music... and you can figure most of them out by listening anyway..."

"You *what*?" Amy exclaimed, staring at me as if I had just told her I was one of the X-Men and I had laser beam tits.

"Harriet," I said, turning to her. She was leaning over the bar counter trying to get the attention of the barman. "How's the drums?"

"I tried to get some but Mum said she doesn't want the noise..." she replied. "I'll bug her again at Christmas."

"So let me get this straight," I said, looking at both of them. "Neither of you can actually play yet?"

"Chill out," Amy said, passing me a glass of whiskey and lemonade. "It's a work in progress. We'll get there..." She pointed to the other side of the room. "Look! The boys are here!"

I counted to ten to calm myself down. I probably wouldn't have even taken up playing bass guitar if it wasn't for them, and I also felt kind of guilty when I asked my Mum to buy me one because she doesn't earn much money. It was almost six months ago that we decided we would learn how to play so we could start a band. We were going to call ourselves 'Shadow Sisters'.

By the time we joined the boys, I had managed to mask my anger. The three of them were waiting for us near the entrance. Josh was in a pair of baggy jeans, a red t-shirt, and his hair was spiked. Paul had evidently gone through a dramatic transformation from trendy to goth in a matter of days. Steve lay somewhere in between, wearing baggy black garb.

"Wow, Amy," Josh said, in his droning, lazy voice. "This place is so... cool..."

Amy wrapped her arms around him and started kissing him. The rest of us all looked at each other awkwardly for a few moments.

"We should go sit somewhere," I said, looking around for a free table. I pointed one out. "Let's go there."

"Where's the bar?" Paul asked.

"I'll show you!" Harriet exclaimed. She grabbed his arm and led him through the crowd.

"Get me a beer," Josh called, tearing his face away from Amy for a moment.

"And a rum and coke for me!" Amy yelled.

While they were gone the rest of us wandered over to the table. Amy and Josh continued to make out. Occasionally, she pulled away from him to exclaim how much a song that was playing "rocked", and sway her head for a few moments, but their main activity generally endured.

This left Steve and me sitting next to each other in silence. I felt awkard so I just looked at the people dancing in the middle of the room; but I could feel his eyes on me. Every time I looked at him he turned away.

Eventually he spoke.

"Josh told me you guys are in a band," he said.

I narrowed my eyes at the back of Amy's head. Is that what

she had been telling everyone, when she couldn't even play yet?

"We're just learning to play first," I replied.

"That's cool," he said. "I've been trying to start one but I can't find anyone else to play. Paul said he's going to learn but I don't think he realises it takes time and work. What do you play?"

"I've been learning bass," I said. He had my attention now. "What about you?"

"Guitar," he replied. "A bit of drums. I used to play cello... but don't tell the others."

I looked at him, realising that I didn't know him at all and it was wrong to think him boring just because he didn't talk much. Amy talks a lot but not much of it has value.

"How long have you been playing for?"

"I don't know…" he said, shrugging. "Cello since I was little. I'm grade seven. I started playing guitar when I was twelve – but mostly acoustic. Drums; not very long."

"Nice," I said, realising that I had found someone who actually knew a bit about music. "I'll tell you a little secret as well; I can play the flute."

"Really?" he said. His eyes widened and he looked around self-consciously to make sure that the others couldn't hear us. Amy and the other kids in school tended to look down on anything musical that didn't have a place in heavy rock. "What grade are you?"

"I don't know," I said, shrugging. "My Mum's been teaching me since I was little."

Harriet and Paul came back with drinks, so we both had to shuffle along the bench to let them in. Harriet soon began to ply him with puppy eyes and lots of questions, which was good because it meant Steve and me were free to carry on chatting about music. Amy and Josh disappeared at one point and returned with another round of drinks, and I reached the stage of drunk where everything starts to sway and blur.

At some point in the conversation Steve's attention was stolen by something over my shoulder and I turned around to see that Harriet had finally made her move: she and Paul were kissing.

Steve then looked at me and I could tell what he was

thinking; his two friends had both made a successful move on their prospective dates – therefore, he was lagging behind. He hesitantly began to lean towards me, as if he was unsure. He was giving me plenty of time to pull away. I looked at him. He had proved himself interesting; that had been probably the longest conversation I ever had with a boy.

Our lips touched and held in place for a moment. Neither of us seemed to know what to do. He started pouting his lips like a goldfish. This was doing nothing for me.

His hands were on my shoulders. This was doing nothing for me.

The tip of his tongue entered my mouth. I pulled away.

"Err..." I said, turning away and covering my mouth. "Sorry... I need to go... to the loo."

I made a swift exit before he had a chance to reply and disappeared into the crowd. They were all dancing wildly, shaking their black hair around and raising their arms up to the ceiling. An angry song reached a heavy bridge and I found myself in the middle of a mishmash of shaking limbs and heavy bodies colliding with each other. They knocked me to the floor and I screamed, but no one heard me. A foot came down on my leg and I yelped again, quickly shuffling away.

By the time I crawled back onto my feet I was angry. I shoved my way past them, searching for a way out. It was hard work because they were all too busy making a big show of how violently they could dance to notice me. I fought my way out and went up the stairs. When I reached the toilet, I stood in front of the mirror and thought about the kiss. Why was it that Amy and Harriet enjoyed it so much?

My hair was a mess, my skirt was torn, my makeup was smudged, and I found myself wishing I was like Amy and had a backup supply with me so I could reapply my face. I stumbled up to the mirror, planning to fix myself up a bit, realising just how drunk I was.

Fuck it, I thought, and gave up trying to straighten my vest top. I walked out of the toilet with the intension of going back downstairs to see if Steve and I could pretend that whole thing never happened, when I realised I was back in that weird corridor again and I remembered the girl I'd seen earlier.

I searched the rooms. Some of them were empty but a few were filled with people partying. I scanned their faces but none of them were hers. As I made my way further down the corridor the place became quieter. In one room there were two people sitting opposite each other in the lotus position; one of them opened their eyes and gave me a knowing look that sent shivers crawling down my spine. I moved on.

I turned a corner and opened a door. A series of faces turned to look at me and stared. Several eyebrows knotted together.

"What are you doing here?" a boy demanded. He had dreadlocks and was wearing a denim jacket.

I was dumbstruck. I had no idea why, but I could feel hostility and it wasn't just my imagination: many of them *were* scowling at me. One of the girls got up and walked over to me. She wore a more sympathetic expression than the others but I could still see some kind of disapproval in her eyes.

"Come," she said, putting a hand on my shoulder "You must be lost. I'll take you back downstairs."

"Wait," a voice called out. Everyone turned to a small figure sitting in an armchair at the back of the room.

It was the girl from my dream. She was staring at me.

"You want to speak to her?" the girl with her hand on my shoulder asked.

She nodded.

I was led across the room to her. I was nervous and I didn't know what to say; if I told her I knew her from a dream she would think I was a freak.

"Be careful what you say," the girl guiding me whispered into my ear. "Be careful what you *think*. She sees..."

I was too nervous to fully take in what she was saying. We were now nearing up to her and she looked exactly as I remembered, with her pointed chin, but otherwise small and delicate features. Her hair was a thin layer of black, shiny velvet running down to her jaw.

The one who was guiding me then left, and I was alone with her. Most people look you up and down the first time they meet you but this girl just studied me with her ghostly blue eyes and there was something about them that made me feel exposed.

"You've seen my face before, haven't you..." she eventually said. Her voice was a little different to how I remembered it in the dream, more of a whisper. A gentle sound, but it had a tone of authority.

I didn't know what to say so I just nodded.

"What did she say to you?" she asked.

Her eyes were still on mine, and I somehow knew it would be impossible to lie to her. "It was a dream," I said.

She nodded her head, unsurprised. "What happened?"

I told her about how I herded the animals around the meadow by playing my flute. I left out the bit at the end, of course, but I think she caught me blushing when I thought about it.

"You play the flute?" she asked when I finished.

I nodded.

"Patrick!" she called out, turning to a table a few feet away. A boy wearing a checked shirt and scruffy jeans lifted his head. He had a mousy face framed with locks of wavy brown hair. "She plays the flute."

He narrowed his eyes at me. He was one of the boys who scowled when I first entered the room, and his expression had not changed much.

"Play then," he eventually said.

"I don't have it with me," I answered.

He shook his head and turned back to the girl from my dream. "A true flautist would always carry it with them."

"Do *you* play the flute?" I exclaimed, suddenly feeling angry.

"No," he shook his head. "I play the violin."

"We need a flute player for our band," the girl cut in.

"Not her!" Patrick objected. "She's—"

"We'll just give her a trial," she said, turning back to me. "Is Tuesday evening good for you?"

I was about to ask her what sort of music they played (as well as some of the other numerous questions going through my mind, such as what the fuck was she doing in my dreams) but there was something about Patrick's arrogance that vexed me. "Tuesday's fine," I said, through gritted teeth. "What's your name anyway?"

"Ellen," she replied. "I'll call at your place."

"Fine!" I agreed, as I turned around and stormed out of the room. "And I'll show *you* what a real flute player is!" I yelled at Patrick as I passed him.

It was only after I slammed the door behind me that I realised I never told Ellen where I lived.

When I returned back to the table in the main bar Amy and other others questioned me on where I had been. I told them I got lost – which wasn't far from the truth. I had a feeling I shouldn't tell them about the people I just met.

After that, the rest of the night was pretty boring. Amy carried on making face with Josh, Harriet gave Paul a sickening amount of attentiveness, and Steve was being distant with me, so conversation was stilted. I was glad when Amy finally decided it was time to call it a night and the three of us went back to her place.

On Tuesday I had an English lesson with Steve, so I sat next to him. Things were a little awkward at first but I got him talking about music again and it soon dissipated. I made a conscious effort to make sure I didn't say anything to lead him on so he wouldn't get the wrong idea. That kiss had been wrong for me but I hoped we could be friends.

I arrived home to my mother stirring a pot of lentil soup on the hob and we ate at the table together. I think she was beginning to forgive me for letting my friends smoke in the house at the weekend. She's not the sort of mother who grounds me or anything when I do wrong, but she always makes it clear when she is disappointed. After we finished eating I offered to do the washing up.

I was just running the water when I heard a rapping at the door, followed by the sound of my mother's voice talking to someone in the hallway. It wasn't often we had visitors so curiosity got the better of me and I quickly dried my hands and walked over to see who was there.

I stopped in surprise when I saw Ellen standing in the doorway.

"Hi Faye," she said.

"Hi," I replied, suddenly feeling nervous and flustered. "I'm just—"

"I'll finish the dishes," my mother interrupted me as she ushered Ellen into the house. "Would you like a cup of tea, Ellen?"

Ellen shook her head, and looked at me. "No thanks, I would like to talk to Faye."

"Sorry about Patrick the other night," she said, before I had a chance to ask her how she found out where I lived. She sat herself on the end of my bed. She was wearing a purple dress that had been tassel-cut from her knees to ankles that day. "He's a bit cautious around people these days."

"He doesn't even know me!" I said, placing a hand on my hip.

"I know it seems unfair," Ellen said. "But there have been a lot of people who dress like you coming to Janus recently. It has taken away a lot of what Janus used to be... it's hard to explain..."

I looked in the mirror; at my black trousers, corset, and spiked bracelets, as if seeing it all for the first time. I started dressing like this originally because Amy and I were experimenting, and it gave me a sense of identity which I had never felt before.

When I recalled the main bar of Janus, that night, it was filled with people dressed just like us. Everyone who was a bit different seemed to be hiding out in all those other rooms and corridors up the stairs.

I opened my mouth to say something but she silenced me by raising her hand.

"You don't need to justify yourself to me," she said. "I never judge a book by its cover and I know that you are not the same as the rest of those people... even if you don't yet. That's what my sister was trying to tell you."

"Your sister?" I gawped.

"Yes," she nodded her head, simply. "In your dream. That wasn't me."

"But she looked just like you!" I gasped. "And it was a *dream*... this doesn't make any sense."

"I was a twin," Ellen said, leaning forward and placing her

hands on her knees. Her face became serious. "At least I was supposed to be... she died when we were born. And now... well, she follows me. How do you think I found my way here? It was her."

I stared at her, dumbstruck. I didn't really know what to believe anymore – there were too many coincidences surrounding this sequence of peculiar events to deny that there was something mysterious going on and dismiss what she was saying. This wasn't much stranger than some of the stories friends of my mother had told me about, but experiencing it yourself is much more overwhelming.

"But anyway," she said, resting her head against the wall. "She sent you to me because I asked her to find a flute player for our band. Where is your instrument?"

I picked it up off the floor. It was strewn with a pile of mess, still where Amy dropped it the other day.

"Play," Ellen said.

I held it to my lips, and placed my fingers against the notches. It had been so long, but the weight of it was familiar and comforting.

After I finished playing Ellen took me to Janus to meet the rest of the band. I wanted to ask her questions about the music they played but I was too much in awe of this girl to say anything. The things she told me about her twin sister and the dream I had were streaming through my mind and even though none of it was logical, with everything that had happened, I couldn't deny it.

When we reached Janus she led me upstairs and through a series of winding corridors, followed by another set of staircases. She opened another door and we stepped into a large, dimly lit hall. Patrick was sitting in the middle of the room with his arms dangled over the backrest of his chair, and another boy I didn't know was next to him.

"This is Jack," Ellen said, pointing to the stranger who was tuning an acoustic guitar. He had long golden hair, and reminded me of a younger version of one of my mum's friends. He smiled at me, and I took an instant liking to him.

"And I believe you've already met Patrick..." Ellen said, dryly, as she walked over to a pile of sheets scattered over the floor. I stood before the two boys nervously as she began to leaf through them. There was an unoccupied drum set a few feet away.

"Faye," Ellen said as she returned with a selection of papers in her hands. "Can you play any of these?"

I scanned them. Some of them were folk songs my mother taught me when I was younger but most of them I didn't recognise. There was also an electric guitar propped up against the wall, so I guessed this band must be a fusion of styles.

"Any of these are fine," I eventually said. "This one looks interesting. Can we try it?"

The corner of Ellen's mouth curved – she seemed impressed. Patrick however, narrowed his eyes at me sceptically.

"We'll see how you do, *Jezebel*," he muttered.

I guessed that nickname was a dig at the way I dressed but I decided to take it as a compliment: Jezebel was originally a powerful and beautiful princess in the ancient Hebrew texts; it was the later influence of Christianity which demonised her into a fallen symbol of dark and destructive femininity.

You're not as clever as you think, I thought, smiling at him sweetly.

Just then we were interrupted by the thwack of the door bursting open with such force that it rebounded from the wall. A tall girl with long arms, torn clothes and messy hair marched into the room in giant strides.

"That's Amelia," Ellen whispered to me as she strode right past us and sat herself in the middle of the drums. "She doesn't mean to be rude... but she's just... abrupt, about things..."

It was only after Amelia positioned the drums sticks in her hands that she finally looked up and acknowledged that there were other people in the room. "We ready or not?" she asked, staring at us expectantly.

"This is Faye," Ellen said, gesturing at me. "She's... auditioning for flute."

"Hi," Amelia muttered, barely glancing at me before turning back to Ellen. "What are we playing?"

"I might give Faye a chance to practice first," Ellen said,

passing me the notes for one of the songs. "Just so she can—"

"Let's just do it," I said. "It looks pretty easy."

"You sure?" Ellen asked.

"Let's just get this over with!" Patrick muttered as he held his violin up to his chest and pressed his jaw against the chinrest.

"Fine," Ellen said, placing a reassuring hand on my arm before stepping over to the microphone stand. "Patrick, you start, and Faye, you come in on the fourth bar, okay?"

"You *do* know what a bar is, don't you?" Patrick muttered behind me. I chose to ignore him, and readied the notes for the song on the stand.

Patrick raised his bow to the strings and began to play. A soft winding note filled the room, and he drew the bow back, weaving the strings into a melody. Asshole or not, he was a good fiddler – there was no denying it.

But I wasn't going to let myself get distracted. When he reached the end of the second bar I raised the flute to my lips and prepared myself for the cue. My hands were almost shaking with nerves but I kept a steady pitch as I blew the first note. I was determined not to give Patrick the chance to be smug.

I was concentrating so hard on the note that I almost forgot about the others – but then an acoustic guitar began to drone behind me, echoing across the room, followed by the tapping of Amelia on the drums.

The song built up speed and I felt a wave of elation when I realised that we actually sounded quite good. Amelia was in her element; her eyes were distant as her arms flailed around, smacking the sticks into different parts of the drum set. Jack gave me a quick nod of approval as he strummed his guitar, and even Patrick was smiling.

But none of this prepared me for the moment Ellen reached for the microphone and pulled it closer to her lips. An eerie soprano filled the room that was both haunting and beautiful. Her words were an indecipherable glossolalia, but the feelings they stirred within me were ominous and poignant. I stared at her, mesmerised, as our melodies entwined. It was at that moment that I realised just how in awe of her I was.

I was back in the meadow with Ellen lying beside me.

"I am glad you are getting more acquainted with your instrument," she said, smiling at me devilishly as she placed a hand on my thigh.

I sat upright at the sudden revelation that this was a dream, again, and took a look around me. The meadow was a little brighter than last time, as if spring was underway and merging into summer. The grass was long and green and dotted with wild flowers. Sheep were grazing, but they had been crudely painted black and had fake pointy ears strapped around their heads. One of them tilted its head up into the air as if it was a wolf preparing to howl, but the noise it produced was an unpleasant amalgam.

I shook my head; this was just getting weirder and weirder.

"Okay, so I know I am in a dream now... isn't this usually the part where I wake up?" I said.

"Usually, yes," Ellen replied. "But this isn't a normal dream, is it."

"Why are the sheep trying to be wolves?" I asked.

Ellen looked at them and shook her head. "They are scared. They think it will stop the predators from singling them out..."

"What do you want me to do this time? Play a song that'll stop them being stupid?"

Ellen laughed. "Of course not, I am more interested in *you*..." she said, swiftly flashing a hand towards my head and snatching something from my crown.

It was a pair of wolf ears, attached by string.

"What?!" I muttered, putting my hand on my head self-consciously. "I never put them on!"

"Of course you didn't. This is all metaphorical!" she said, waving her arm across the scene around us, tossing the fake ears to the hills. "Don't you get that yet?"

A bright ray hit my eyes and I covered them. It was the sun. I tried to peer at it from under the shadow of my palm but it disappeared behind the clouds again.

"I saw the sun!" I yelled triumphantly. "I found it!"

"You're getting there, but you've got a little further to go yet," Ellen replied as she gently pushed me down so I lay on my back. "The clouds are still clearing."

"What are you doing?" I asked as she positioned herself between my legs.

"I'm going to help you get better acquainted with your instrument."

"But I don't have my flute."

Ellen laughed, shaking her head. "I don't need a damn flute. This is *metaphorical*, how many times do I have to spell it out?" She lifted up one of my legs, and positioned her fingers as if my thighs were the notches of a flute. "Let's see if this is subtle enough for you."

She leaned down and placed her lips on the mouthpiece.

The next day Ellen called at my house and when I answered the door I blushed and could barely look her in the eyes. I invited her in and she sat in the living room while I went to make us both a cup of tea.

I returned, sat down next to her, and we were silent for a few moments.

"Why are you nervous?" Ellen asked.

I looked at her and remembered the dream. The memories were exciting and the fact that they were exciting made me nervous. I was caught between elation and shame, liberation and denial.

I didn't know what to say. I felt my cheeks flush and I turned to the window.

"I think I know, Faye," Ellen said, looking down at the steaming cup in her hands.

"I'm not ashamed anymore!" I whispered, looking at her. "I know what I am... and I know what I—"

I still couldn't find the words to say it out loud. I just couldn't. I looked at her but she was staring at her tea.

I put my hand on her leg.

"But I know—"

"Stop," Ellen said. She spoke softly but it was still distinctively commanding. I drew my hand away. It was shaking.

"It was Jessica," she said, finally looking at me. "She's been—"

"Jessica?" I repeated. "Who's Jessica?"

"My twin," Ellen replied. "In the dreams; that's not me,

Faye. It's Jessica. It's all her."

My jaw dropped, and a terrible embarrassment crawled into my stomach. "So you're not..."

Ellen shook her head.

I looked at her and knew it to be true. The girl in the dream had the same face, the same figure, same hair, but the eyes were different. The way she held herself was different. *She* was different. She was not Jessica. Tears welled into my eyes. "But," I said, trembling. "But... I haven't ever. This is the first time I have..."

I cried and cried and cried. And Ellen held me as I wept into her shoulder.

After the tears were over I felt surprisingly lightheaded. It was like all my life I had been carrying this huge weight around with me which was now gone.

"So you like boys," I said, as wiped my eyes.

Ellen shook her head. "I don't like... anything... in that way, anyway."

I stared at her. "What?"

"I am asexual," Ellen said, shrugging. "I'm not sexually attracted to men or women."

"Is that possible?" I asked, in disbelief.

Ellen nodded. "It's probably more common than you think. I tried having sex when I was younger, with boys, even with a couple of girls Jessica drew to me... but I never really got it, or enjoyed it much. I just kind of did it because it was what people did. It took me a while to realise why."

I looked up at the ceiling; truly realising just how different Ellen was to Jessica. There was something wild and vivacious about the mysterious girl who visited my dreams, whereas Ellen was notably recondite and collected. I looked at Ellen as if I was seeing her for the first time. Both of the twins were beautiful and enigmatic in their own way but I knew now that it wasn't even Ellen I had a crush on. It was Jessica.

"So... you're a lesbian," Ellen said. Hearing the word spoken out loud felt strange to me and I wasn't sure I was completely comfortable with it.

I nodded. "I guess I am... but please don't tell anyone... I'm not ready for that yet."

Ellen nodded. She didn't seem to be phased about it at all, which was a surprising relief. "That's okay. So, what do you want to do before band practice? I have some notes with me. We can—"

I shook my head. "No," I said. "Can we... go shopping?"

There was something else I was ready to admit to myself now: I had been feeling increasingly uncomfortable with the clothes I was wearing, and it was time for a change. My experience with Ellen that morning was exactly the push I needed to do something about it.

When I told Ellen that I didn't have much money she recommended we try the charity shops, and I was surprised to find a lot of things there I liked. I scanned the dresses, trousers, skirts and tops hanging up along the isles thinking about what *I* wanted to wear, rather than what Amy would like. I liked black, but I was tired of wearing it all the time.

I hated to admit it but my mother was right.

Shopping with Ellen was a strange experience. I was used to Amy advising me on what to wear and my mother trying to tell me what to *not* wear. I bought purple dresses, red netted-vests, denim skirts and purple tights. When I got home later I combined them with my old clothes in new and exciting ways. I discovered a new passion for trying out different outfits in front of the mirror and feeling waves of elation when I found combinations that worked. I was experimenting, and enjoying it.

When we arrived at band practice later I received a couple of surprised looks. Jack pretended not to notice but he did give me a second glance, whereas Patrick looked me up and down with one of his eyebrows raised.

"What's with the change?" he asked.

"None of your business," I replied, coolly, as I opened the carrier case for my flute.

His face softened. "Well, for what it's worth, you do look a lot better."

"That's brilliant," I replied, dryly. "I have always craved your approval."

"I don't know what the hell you two are talking about," Amelia cut in from behind her drum set. "But can you flirt later?"

"I thought I was being nice..." Patrick muttered, shaking his head. "What are we playing tonight then, Ellen?"

I know it must seem like we all hated each other but, despite Amelia's cut-off attitude and the occasional verbal battle between Patrick and me, as soon as we picked up our instruments and starting playing it all went away and a profound chemistry surfaced through our music. I had only been in the band for a couple of weeks but it felt like a lot longer and we were becoming stronger with every session.

At the end of practice that day, Amelia dropped her drumsticks and left the room without saying a word, while the rest of us lingered for a while. Patrick and Ellen chatted while Jack sat in the corner with his guitar, experimenting with different riffs and tunes. I decided to leaf through the catalogue of notes they had compiled of their songs for me.

"How come we never play these ones?" I asked, holding up some of the later pages. I had spent the last few days practicing them in my room and I was quite intrigued by them. Most of the songs I had played with them so far were an amalgamation of folk and progressive rock with an ethereal-wave edge, but these particular ones seemed like they would sound much more haunting and solemn than the rest of their stuff.

Ellen and Patrick hesitated for a moment and looked at each other.

"We..." Patrick began, and then hesitated. I could tell from his expression that he wasn't even quite sure of the answer himself. "Don't play those often."

"Why?" I asked.

"I don't usually have the vocal range for them," Ellen explained. "I guess they are special songs... they can only be played at the right time and place... it's hard to explain..."

"You should learn them though," Patrick said. "We usually only play them live. It's all up to Ellen really," he said, turning to her. "When the time is right you'll need to know them... especially with that gig coming up."

"What gig?" I asked.

"We are thinking about playing in the battle of the bands next week," Ellen said.

"Next week?" I blurted. "Isn't that a bit soon? I've only just joined!"

"I think you're almost ready," Ellen said, turning to Patrick for confirmation.

"You're a natural," he admitted grudgingly. "I was surprised when you said you haven't been in a band before. You took to playing music with us very fast."

I shrugged. "My mother and I go around festivals in the summer selling strawberries. Sometimes in the evenings her friends join us around the fire and we play music together... I guess I'm just used to playing as a group."

Patrick's eyes widened. "You do that every summer? Your mum sounds cool."

Ellen grinned. "You're full of surprises, Faye."

I smiled. I wasn't used to having friends who thought my mother was cool. Amy used to say it was 'lame' that I was taken away each summer, and I was always trying to talk my mum into letting me stay behind so I could spend the holiday with my friends. One thing I have never admitted to her, though, was that I always have a great time and am glad she made me go by the end of August.

"So are you cool with playing next week?" Patrick asked.

"Where is it?"

"Here, at Janus," Ellen replied. "At the main bar on Friday."

I usually spent the weekends with Amy and Harriet, so I knew I would have to come up with an excuse, again – I still had not told them about joining the band, or anything, really. Truth was: I had been avoiding them as much as possible, but I knew that time was running out and they would figure out something was up soon.

"I'll do it."

When I got home from school on the day of the battle of the bands Amy rang me. I don't really like lying and I am not very good at it so I withheld some of the truth. This is how the conversation went:

Amy: Hey Pixy, how's you?"

("Pixy" is the name she started calling me when she noticed the change in the way I dress. I don't really get why everyone is making such a big deal about it anymore; most of the clothes I am wearing are the same, I am just applying them in different ways with my new ones. Amy tried to bully me out of it until some of the kids in school said that I actually looked quite good. Now she just calls me "Pixy" and pretends it doesn't bother her.)

Me: "I'm fine." *Apart from being fucking nervous about my first live performance tonight.*

Amy: "That's good. I didn't see you at lunch break? Where were you today?"

Me: "I was—" *Hiding from you.* "—in the library."

Amy: "Oh you little geek you." (Fake laugh) "We're going out tonight. Want to come with us?"

Me: "I'm not sure if I can..."

Amy: "Oh, come on Faye, you're turning into a real bore recently. We're going to Janus! There's a battle of the bands on!"

Me: *I know. My secret band I haven't told you about are playing.* "Okay, yeah. That's cool. I think I'll be there."

Amy: (Another squeally, fake-sounding laugh) "Awesome, Faye. And Steve is coming too." (Suggestive tone)

Me: "That's good... I like Steve." *But not in **that** way. Did I forget to mention that I am a lesbian now?*

Amy: "Harriet stole some gin from her parents. Shall we come over and drink it?"

Me: "No, sorry I can't." *I think my mother hates you, so I don't want you here.* "Shall I just meet you at Janus? You two live on the other side of town anyway."

Amy: (Another fake sounding laugh) "Okay Faye. Have it your way. We'll be there by seven."

Me: "See you there." *I'm arriving at 6:30, so I can stash my flute somewhere and have a meeting with the band before the gig starts.*

I put down the phone, feeling quite guilty. Not just because I was not being truthful to Amy, but also because, by extension, I was lying to myself. I had come so far in breaking out of my shell and discovering who I really was, but there was something about Amy which still had a hold on me. It was probably because I had known her for so long and she had always been there to guide me.

I knew she was going to find out by the end of the night but I just didn't have the guts to tell her yet.

When the pre-gig meeting with the band was over I excused myself from their company and ventured downstairs to the main bar to meet Amy and Harriet. Janus was busier than I had ever seen it that night and most of the tables and chairs had been pushed to the back of the hall. Several groups of youngsters dressed from head to toe in black were waiting avidly by the stage as the first band – a group of teenage boys – readied their instruments and equipment for their set.

Our band was last up to play but that didn't do much to help my nerves. The thought that in just a couple of hours I would be up on that stage felt surreal.

I was interrupted from my thoughts when I heard a familiar duo of girly laughter and I turned around to see Amy and Harriet walking towards the main bar, drunk and giggling.

"There you are!" Amy cried out, grabbing me. "You stranger, you! Josh and the boys are saving us a table!"

We bought some drinks and joined the boys. Amy and Harriet went straight to Josh and Pauls' laps like a pair of kittens. With the implication that we were the third pair in a triple date, there was a bit of awkwardness as I sat myself down next to Steve. Luckily, we were saved by the first band beginning their set.

I watched the spectacle with thinly-veiled horror. They were called 'Deathyard Dolls', and they maxed out distortion effects on their amps to hide the fact they couldn't play very well. The vocalist screamed into a microphone while strumming a riff that consisted of three chords on his guitar; the whole effect was a sub-quality attempt at imitating bands currently successful in their genre.

"These guys are awesome!" Amy exclaimed as she raised

her drink to the ceiling and shook her hair. Harriet soon followed suit.

I looked at Steve and I could tell by the expression on his face that he was, also, far from impressed. Neither of us bothered to say anything though; I have realised recently that trying to discuss the finer qualities of music with Amy is like trying to hack down a brick wall with a stick.

The next few bands were not much better; two were marginal improvements on the first, but only because the musicians seemed a bit more experienced. The most depressing thing about it all was that the massive hoard of wannabes gathered around the stage waving their black hair and pale arms around were enthralled by them. It seemed that all a band needed to do to be liked by this crowd was make as much noise as possible. Some of the bands these people were trying to rip-off were quite talented, but these amateurs had neither the talent to pull it off, nor anything original to add to the genre.

The fifth band was interesting. They consisted of two guitarists, a bassist, a keyboard player, drummer, and two vocalists. Their songs shifted subtly between soft tunes and winding, heavier riffs, and the addition of a keyboard added texture to their sound.

"These guys suck!" Amy proclaimed between gulps of whatever it was she was drinking – I am not even sure *she* knew by this point.

"Yeah," Josh agreed.

"I think they're the best so far," I said.

Amy glared at me for daring to question her judgement. "It's just boring."

"The guitarist is *really* good."

Steve surprised me by backing me up and nodding his head. "I agree with Faye. They've composed their music really well. Most of the other bands were just pointless noise."

"Whatever!" Amy retorted. She pointed at the throng of people by the front of the stage who were notably less animated then they were for the rest of the bands. "I think the crowd speaks for itself!"

The sixth set were a punk band. The boys were dressed in

torn jeans and white wife-beater t-shirts. They yelled out "Fuck authority!" at the end of their last song, and received a marginal applause. I found the whole thing extremely cliché.

While they were packing away their equipment I saw Ellen and the others making their way towards the stage, and realised I was up next.

"I need to go now," I announced, as assembling nerves crept into my stomach.

"Where are you going?" Amy asked.

"I'm playing next," I said as I got up from my chair. "In a band."

"You're in a band?" Steve turned to me in surprise.

"A band?" Harriet asked. "But *we're* in a band."

I ignored her. "I joined this one a couple of weeks ago... I've got to go."

Amy's mouth gaped open. She was notably angry and shocked, but rendered speechless by surprise, so I left the table before that shifted.

"Good luck Faye!" Steve called as I walked away. I swiftly crossed the hall and negotiated my way towards the stage. When I got there Jack was just testing the equipment and Ellen was clipping her microphone to the stand.

"There you are!" Patrick said. "I was thinking you'd backed out on us."

"Sorry to disappoint you," I muttered as Ellen passed me my flute case and I opened it.

"That girl's got a flute!" one of the audience members yelled out. I looked for the speaker but swiftly remembered that it would be hard to spot him out because most of them looked the same anyway.

So far this evening the crowd had shown a marked preference for sub-standard heavy metal and I suddenly became conscious of the fact we were about to play a fusion of softer styles they had probably never listened to before. I had a terrible feeling that this was going to go horribly wrong and feared a bad reaction from the crowd. It almost made me want to turn and run but then I looked at the band-members who were relying on me and realised that they were the people I truly respected, and I didn't want to let them down.

Why should I care what these strangers thought of me? I

knew that we were good, and it was time to show them that.

"Are you ready?" Ellen whispered.

I nodded.

Ellen turned her microphone on and brought it to her mouth. "We are Sunset Haze."

Amelia let out a yell and smacked her sticks together a few times before pounding them into a rhythm on her drum set, Jack soon joined her with the opening tune on his guitar, and I readied myself for my cue.

We wisely began with one of our rockier songs, and, in my opinion, we had never sounded better, but it was also clear that the garish crowd in front of us were mostly unimpressed. Some of them lightly nodded their heads in time with our music, so I could tell that on some level they were enjoying it, but it was like they were afraid to let themselves go while others around them didn't. At the end of the first song there was a brief silence. I heard a few distasteful mutters from the crowd and I looked over to where my friends were sitting to catch Amy looking at us with a stony expression as she whispered something into Harriet's ear.

Jack replaced his electric guitar for an acoustic and we began the next song.

The crowd were even less impressed by one of our more folk-inspired tracks, but the song itself was uplifting so I concentrated on playing it well. Patrick swayed back and forth as he played the violin, like he usually did, enjoying being a part of the music even though it was being underappreciated. I admired him for his carefree spirit.

Something odd happened during the third song. The crowd got bigger. The area by the front of the stage was still filled with a mostly disinterested nest of teenagers coated in black but around the fringes of the main bar, an assortment of people filtered into the room. I turned my eyes to the stairs to see that they were all coming out from their hiding places in the upper rooms. The edges of the crowd were suddenly filled with people dressed in clothes of all colours and styles. A girl wearing a purple blouse and red skirt began to dance, twirling around to our song with a smile on her face of pure, uncomplicated joy.

Many gave her scathing looks but she carried on, without

caring, and was soon joined by others. My spirits were lifted, and by the end of the fourth song we had generated a fairly good buzz of people.

Then, after the fifth song drew to an end, something extraordinary happened.

Ellen started dancing around the stage in a state of catatonia. Twirling her body around as her arms jerked and twisted like a pair of angered snakes. There were several gasps from the audience and I stared at her in concern. Everything about the movements she was making was unnatural and completely different to the calm, collected, and graceful girl I knew. By the end of the song she was shaking so violently I thought she was having a seizure. She fell to the floor.

I dropped my flute and ran to her side, grabbing her shoulders.

"Ellen!" I said, shaking her. "What's the matter?"

Her eyes shot open and a wild grin spread across her face. Her features were the same but it was like she was possessed. I looked her in the eyes and then realised I recognised the essence behind them from somewhere else, but not anywhere in the waking world.

The girl I was holding wasn't Ellen anymore. It was Jessica.

"This is it," Patrick whispered, appearing at our side. "It's time to play those songs we told you about. Yes, Jessica?"

Jessica nodded excitedly.

"You learned them, right, Faye?"

"She knows them well enough," Jessica answered, winking at me devilishly as she pushed herself back onto her feet. "Let's get this show on the road."

At first I was too shocked to even move. I just stared at her as she readied the microphone. I then remembered that there was a whole audience watching me and composed myself. I picked up my flute, trying to hide my entwined state of shock, excitement, and confusion.

Jack plugged his electric guitar back in and pushed one of the buttons on the switch-amplifier. He began to flick the chords and a distorted haze of sound filled the room. I held the flute to my lips and readied myself. I had never played this song with the others before but Jessica's presence was electrifying and filled me with confidence. I was determined to do it right.

I blew my first note, and the rest of the band members joined in with their instruments. The noise we created together was ominous and hauntingly beautiful. The startled crowd before us (even the ones who didn't like us) were immediately drawn to the sudden change in our sound and fixed their eyes on the stage, silently hypnotised by our music.

Ellen – or rather, Jessica, I should say – then let out a wail just as the song reached the first verse. She sang an indecipherable mouth-music, just as indistinguishable as her twin's, but even more enticing and moving. I found myself dancing around on the spot as we played, feeling elated despite the arcane and dark tones of the sound we were generating. I didn't even understand why the music was so mesmerising but that didn't even matter. It was as if Jessica had brought a piece of the otherworld with her and was channelling it into our music.

I played and played, losing myself, and it was only when the last song was over that I became aware again.

Jessica finished the performance with a graceful bow and the rest of us followed suit. We failed to capture the hearts of many of the original audience, but the newcomers who ventured from upstairs were all cheering and that was good enough for me. I scanned my eyes across the crowd to see that Amy was now near the front with her arms crossed over her chest.

"What the fuck was *that*?" Amy yelled, when I went to talk to her.

"I'm sorry. I know I should have told you—" I began but I was interrupted.

"*We're* supposed to be in a band. A *good* band. Not that bullshit I just saw! What the fuck is wrong with you?!"

"Nothing is wrong with me!" I exclaimed. "And we'll never be a band because you can't be arsed to learn!"

"Faye!" Harriet suddenly cut-in, appearing beside Amy. "You betrayed us! I can't believe it! I'm never speaking to you *ever* again!"

"Oh will you just *grow up*!" I yelled.

"Is that why you've been dressing like *that*?" Amy yelled, flouncing a discarding wave at my outfit. "They made you dress like that, didn't they? You're such a loser!"

"No one made my dress like this!" I screamed. "In fact, for the first time I am dressing how *I* want to dress, not how you make me."

"I never made you—"

"Yes you did!" I interrupted. "You always do. You pressure people! You want them to be like you because you think it makes you cool and fashionable. Can't you see that you are *all* just a bunch of fucking wannabes?" I exclaimed, waving an arm at the crowd of disgruntled, fake goths gathered around the stage, waiting for the results for the battle of the bands to be announced.

I knew that what I said must have rang something deep within her, because Amy's eyes widened and she gasped, covering a hand over her mouth.

"Faye!" Harriet squealed, with tears in her eyes. "It's okay. I know you don't mean it... just come back with us. We'll talk..."

I shook my head, which just caused more tears to pour from Harriet's eyes. It made me feel guilty, but I knew this was something I had to do.

Because I had just realised that I had spent my whole life until now being pulled by strings. I think most people are. Strings that your friends, parents, school, television, and other facets of society wrap around you, each of them pulling and grinding, wearing away at your essence as they play you to whatever tune suits their purpose.

Once you become aware of these strings you realise that they have always been there. You didn't even notice them before, but you suddenly see them all around you. You see that most people are tangled, and the worst thing is that most of them *like* it that way because it makes them feel secure.

But *I* wasn't happy. I only really began to find happiness recently when I starting stretching my limbs. I was miserable before then, and I didn't even know it.

It was time to pull myself free.

It was time to cut the cords.

"What's going on here?" Ellen called as she shuffled her way through the crowd towards us. I turned to her and realised by her eyes and movements of her body that she was still possessed by Jessica. For some reason I assumed she would leave once the performance was over.

She fought her way through until she was beside me, and put an arm around my shoulder. "Is there a problem here?" she said, looking at Amy and Harriet. They both seemed to be unnerved by her and neither of them said anything.

The next thing I knew Jessica's hand was on my neck, and she pulled me into her lips. We began kissing and it was heaven. I kissed her back, finally understanding what it was all about. Amy and Harriet were watching me kiss a girl, and I didn't even care.

By the time we pulled away from each other we had an audience of boys cheering at us. I blushed.

"I don't need your bullshit anymore," I said. "This is the real me, Amy, and if you don't like it you can screw yourself!"

Amy was too overcome with shock to do anything at first. She just stared at Jessica and me with wide eyes. I didn't even look to Harriet to see what her reaction was – because it didn't concern me. Not anymore.

Then Amy's eyes suddenly went red with rage and she dived at me. I tried to jump away but I wasn't quick enough and my cheek was stung with the impact of her hand slapping my face. I covered my head in my hands and backed away.

"Get away from my friends!" someone screamed, stepping between us.

I looked up and saw that it was Amelia, and she now had Amy held up in the air by her neck. I stared. Of all people, *Amelia* had stepped in to my defence.

She turned to me for a quick moment to smile and give me a playful wink, before lowering a terrified looking Amy back to the floor, grabbing her by the shoulders and dragging her out of the club.

This time, I knew it was a dream from the moment I opened my eyes. I was in the meadow again. The sky was blue, the sun was shining, the animals were grazing, and Jessica lay beside me.

"Oh... I'm back here again," I said, smiling at her. "What is it this time?"

"Nothing," Jessica said, positioning herself behind me and placing her hands on my back. "This is purely a pleasure visit."

"Oh," I said, blushing. "Well... that's nice. Thank you."

"Well... actually, there was one other thing," she said, as her fingers traced my spine. "Patrick has been bugging my sister to get a cellist for the band... and I hate to admit it but he is right... and I also think you know the right person."

"Steve," I realised. "Really? You want him?"

"Why not?" Jessica said. "He stuck up for you when you were playing that night, you know. Amy and Harriet were bitching, but he defended you and said the music was great. I saw it just before I took Ellen's body. I think he's had enough of Amy's crap as well."

"So you're going to start messing around with his dreams?" I asked.

She shook her head. "No... part of all that was for my pleasure, you know. Steve can be *your* little project. He's already on the right course."

"Good," I said, smiling. "I hate to think of you playing with his 'instrument'... makes me a little jealous."

Jessica laughed. "I only use that method with certain... special people," she said, circling around me until we were face to face. "Steve already knows which way he swings."

She placed a hand on my breast. "I hope you don't mind if I still make the occasional visit?"

"Not at all."

"Good... so anyway," she said, looking down. "How is your instrument? I believe it needs a little tuning..."

"Oh for goodness sake!" I retorted. "Are the metaphors *still* necessary?"

6
Going Back

I woke up that morning with only two things on my agenda; turn up to college for a lecture and then go visit my mother in the afternoon. It all sounds like a pretty lucrative and uneventful schedule. You really wouldn't expect someone to complicate a day like that, would you?

You obviously don't know me yet.

I arrived at college in the morning with great punctuality and sat myself near the back of the classroom. It was for my A Level in Religious Studies, and the topic that day was the Ontological Argument. I swiftly became extremely bored.

It's not that I don't like philosophy – I mean, why the hell would I have enrolled myself in this class in the first place if I didn't?

I like talking about shit, and the beginning of the year was interesting enough. We explored the Cosmological Argument – a theory which follows a logical process: that everything in the cosmos is governed by a chain of cause and effect. Throw a brick at a window and the glass will break. A man and a woman having sex, can lead to a child being conceived. In a void of nothingness, before even time existed, a singularity appeared and created everything which exists in a massive explosion of elementary particles.

But what caused this miraculous event to happen? The Universe must have a cause outside of itself, and for St Thomas Aquinas, it was God. It is a fairly interesting (if debatable) point. Even an agnosto-atheist like myself (the 'agnosto' bit is the scientist in me; I don't believe in God but I will not completely discard the idea until it has been thoroughly disproven) left the room that day asking myself some questions.

But today:

"The Ontological Argument works on the premise that if

we, as intelligent human beings, have conceived of the greatest possible being, then it must in fact exist," the teacher began.

What?

I tried to listen for a while as the teacher droned on about the theory in more detail. There really wasn't any more detail. I allocated ten more minutes of time for this 'philosophical theory' to materialise into something rational, but it failed to elevate itself from "God exists, because we say he does".

I would have stuck it out for the sake of the exam at the end of the year, but I am a girl of principle and I signed up to this course for philosophy.

But it was okay; I am always prepared for such a situation. I kept my gaze turned towards the front of the room, pretending to be riveted by the lesson, while slipping my hand into my bag. When my fingers had successfully located the tub of Tiger Balm in there I pulled it out and unscrewed the cap.

After a quick glance to make sure no one was looking, I dipped my finger in it and smothered it under my eyes.

It usually takes about ten seconds to work, which gives me just enough time to hide the evidence. Once my secret contrivance was safely concealed, the tears began to flow. I didn't even need to pretend to rub my eyes because they were stinging like crazy, but I did let out a few dramatic sobs to achieve the whole neurotic-teenage-girl effect which has never failed to get me out of a lesson.

And then the eyes of the classroom were focussed on me. I looked down at my desk, feigning embarrassment. It was all a charade – I don't do embarrassed.

"Something wrong, Frelia?" Mr Harrison asked.

I tore my hands away from my face to look up at him so he could see my red, wet, welted eyes.

"I'm sorry Sir..." I sobbed. "It's just... just..."

His eyes widened, and I could tell he was starting to panic. If you try to tell a teacher that you must leave because of an emergency or appointment they scrutinise you with all kinds of questions, but as soon as you cry it's like you are infected with a contagious disease and must leave before anyone else catches it. Sixth-form college is a centre of development for the adolescent, and is therefore no place for teenage angst or emotions.

"It's... o-ok if you want to leave, Frelia," he stammered.

"No, Sir," I said, shaking my head and spilling tears on the desk. "It's okay. I'm sorry! It's just that I—"

"Just go!" he said, pointing towards the door.

Well, if you insist.

I didn't even need to proceed to phase two and make allusions to my menstrual cycle. Nothing freaks out a male teacher better than that one.

I rubbed the remaining balm from my eyes as I left the buildings of the college and made my way towards town. I still had some time to burn before I could go see my mother so I wandered around the park, smoked a few fags, watched the ducks, and even convinced myself at one point that, maybe, there was some saving grace to the lesson I just walked out on. A quick read of the textbook reaffirmed my conviction that there wasn't.

I looked at my watch to judge if I had burned enough time and then made my way alongside the lake. There was a guy standing behind a table, trying to advertise something. I made a point of not making eye contact as I went past but he caught me with the words:

"Free samples!"

Did he just say free? I thought, realising that I was actually quite hungry. I walked over to him. He was a skinny man with a bald head, dressed in robes. Oh, wait – scratch that – *orange* robes. He was a monk.

A monk with very nice blue eyes and a cute smile, I might add.

"Hey," I said, looking down hungrily at the selection of cakes and pastries.

"Hi!" he replied excitedly. "Do you want to try some of these? They are from the new Buddhist cafe down the road. They are vegetarian."

I'm not a vegetarian, but I was *very* hungry.

"I don't have to be Enlightened or anything, do I?" I asked, raising an eyebrow.

He laughed and shook his head. "No, of course not. You don't have to be a Buddhist to come to our cafe, either."

"I thought monks weren't supposed to make money?"

"It's a charity," he explained. "All the profits go to the International Temple Foundation."

"Okay," I said, shrugging. I ate it. It tasted a bit like cheese wrapped in cardboard but, hey, it was *free*. I picked up a piece of carrot cake for desert.

"I like those rings in your eyebrow," he said. "And your jeans. Did they come like that?"

"Nah," I said, shaking my head. I thought of returning some kind of similar compliment but swiftly realised that he was a monk and had no stylistic features. I could have told him he had a nice smile, but that would have been bit... well, you know. "I tore them up. Thanks for the food."

"What's your name?" he asked.

"Frelia," I replied. "Yourself?"

"I'm Stephan," he said. His arm twitched as if he was making to shake my hand but then thought better of it.

"So how long have you been a monk, then?" I asked. He looked quite young and probably only had a few years on me.

"Oh, just a few weeks," he said. "So, do you want to come to the cafe sometime? I work there three hours a day in the afternoon. Everything is ethically traded!"

He looked me in the eyes and, to my great surprise, it was in *that* way – he was flirting with me.

"Maybe..." I replied. "But I often have college around that time."

"Or we could just meet up this evening? You seem interesting – I would like to talk to you!"

I stared at him for a few moments. "You're asking me out on a date?" I blurted. "I'm pretty sure you're not supposed to be doing that – you're a *monk*. Isn't it a vow you have to take?"

"One of all 376 of them," he replied.

"Wow. Must have taken them a while to come up with that list," I said dryly.

He laughed. "I like you. You're blunt... anyway it doesn't have to be a date," he said, although his eyes were saying something completely different. "Just two... friends, meeting up. How about it?"

Did I mention he was cute?

You are probably beginning to notice that I am a bit weird. I have inventive ways to get out of boring lessons, I feel no embarrassment at crying in front of a classroom of fellow students, I am an atheist doing a course in religious studies, I arrange to go out on dates with random Buddhist monks that I meet at the park, I have a few facial piercings, too, and I dress a bit funky.

Well, I guess this relates to what I mentioned earlier about everything in the universe having cause and effect:

No idea who my father was. Switched between three children's homes, followed by seven foster families. Short time in juvenile detention. Arrested for the first time when I was 12. Virginity taken at 13. Blah, blah, blah. I am sure you get the idea; in some ways it's all quite cliché.

So yes, I am a bit weird, but please be assured that if you could see my face right now it would bear an expression of deep, engrossed, profound, and heartfelt concern.

And, anyway, if you think I'm fucked up, just wait until you meet my mother.

Okay, so, the first thing you need to know is that to meet my mother you need to go through some procedures.

"Can you place the bag on the belt please?" the security guard asks.

"Okay, sir," I reply as I pull it off my shoulder.

His eyes are drawn to my torn jeans and then travel up to my black t-shirt and poncho.

"Are you carrying anything sharp with you today?"

No, I decided to leave my machete and knuckle dusters at home for this special occasion.

I shake my head.

"Any electrical equipment in your bag?"

Just a bomb, kind Sir.

There I go again. Stop it, Frelia, there is a time and a place for that.

"No."

"Nothing in your pockets?" he asks me suspiciously.

"You can frisk me if you want to," I say, winking at him.

Oops... there are only so many opportunities for a gag I can resist.

He seems embarrassed for a moment, but then recovers and ushers me to step through the barrier.

"Visiting time finishes in one hour," he warns.

"Oh, don't worry. I won't be *that* long."

And there she was, sitting at a table, in a bare, white, insipid room. Dressed in a robe. Her hair was thin and although she's pretty, her face is let down by dark patches under her eyes. It is like something from a movie. The only thing missing is the white sock-things over her hands – they came off about three years ago so I guess that's progress.

"Frelia!" she exclaimed as I opened the door. She got up from her seat and raised her arms as if to embrace me but then seemed to reconsider and sat back down.

"Happy Birthday, Mum," I said as I sat on a chair opposite her.

We sat in silence for a few moments.

"So how are... Harold and Jean? Was that their names?" she asked.

I shook my head. "I don't live with them anymore."

"Oh," she said, her expression becoming sad. "Why not?"

"Well, they got themselves what they really wanted; a nice baby, warm and fresh from the womb, and still soft and malleable – so why would they keep a mouthy teenager in the house."

"They kicked you out?!" she asked.

"No," I said shrugging. "Just, you know. I was cramping their style. It was a mutual agreement. I still meet up with Jean for coffee sometimes."

"So where are you living now?" she asked.

"A special home stay for sixteen to eighteen year olds. It's run by a couple. They're nice enough. I get to live there and go to college, and they get money from the state for putting a roof over my head and nice, bubbly feelings of positive karma. It's a good arrangement."

She put her cold hands around mine, tightly.

"But you're happy?" she asked, with an anxious look in her

eyes.

"Yes," I said. "I mean, I'm not ecstatic or anything. Just, you know, normal. Content and all that stuff. How are you?"

"I'm okay..." she said, shrugging. She was lying – I could see a deep sadness and restlessness in her eyes. "As much as you can be in this place."

"How's the treatment?" I asked.

"They still think I'm crazy..." she replied.

I shook my head. "I hope you get better soon, mother..."

Her eyes became shiny, as if she was holding back tears. "I wish I could see you more, Frelia," she said.

I looked down at the table, feeling guilty. "I think about you a lot... but it's... hard, Mum."

Her hands pulled away from mine and then went back to her lap. She looked down at the table.

"I didn't ask to be put here, Frelia."

No, I thought. *You just wrote "Unknown Mystical Being" as my father on my birth certificate... I can't imagine why the social services were concerned by that little stunt.*

"Tell me who my Dad is," I said. "I need to know, Mum."

She looked at me with teary eyes, and I fleetingly thought that this was going to be the moment I had been waiting for my whole life. I was finally going to know.

"He was... well he appeared from nowhere... he could do that... I think he was a time lord," my mother said. I turned away, crossed my arms, and looked at the barred window. "But one day—"

"*Time Lord*? Come on Mum, this isn't an episode of Dr Who!" I exclaimed as I stood up and reached for my bag. "This is my *life*!"

The terrible thing about it all was that I knew she actually *believed* it. Sometimes I wished my mother was just a liar rather than crazy.

"I'm... sorry," I said, looking down at the floor. "I should go now... I have college things..."

"I love you Frelia," she said as I left.

So that's my mother. Don't know what exactly I inherited from her apart from my looks and a stupid name. I guess I must take after my father, whoever he was.

Time Lord indeed!

If *I* was crazy, I would like to think that I would at least be more original.

So the two objectives of attending college and wishing my mother a happy birthday didn't go exactly to plan, but it wasn't a complete waste of a day; I still had my (non)date with a Buddhist monk to look forward to.

I went to meet him at the park, at the same place as earlier. He was waiting for me on a bench, and greeted me with a wave as I walked over.

"Hi!" He seemed, for some reason I couldn't fathom, *really* excited to see me. "You're here! How was your day?"

I guess some people would find this a bit creepy, but I actually found his enthusiasm for everything quite charming. I smiled. "It was... okay I guess," I replied. "Did you give away any more cakes?"

He nodded. "Yeah, and then we prayed to Amitabha and... oh sorry! I don't want to bore you. Here!" he said, ushering me towards him. "Come, sit."

"Thanks," I said, parking myself next to him. "Are you allowed to be alone with me? I thought you had to have a third party around when near a member of the opposite sex?"

"Not all monastic orders are the same," he replied. "The one in this town is Tibetan. We are trusted to spend time with whomever we want, but any breaking of vows is still a cause to leave. So anyway, Frelia is an unusual name; your mum must be interesting."

"Oh yeah," I replied. "She's a fucking treat."

We sat on the bench for an hour or so and chatted. When he found out I was studying religion we had much to talk about, because he was versed in all kinds of philosophies and beliefs from around the world. We had quite a lot in common; we both wanted to travel and had an appreciation for the simpler things in life. He didn't really tell me much about his life before he was a monk but it was obvious that he was quite educated. I didn't really tell him much about mine either; not because I am ashamed of my history, but more that talking about it all opens an exhausting can of worms.

The way he always seemed so cheerful and excited about

everything was quite cute. He had a childlike innocence in that way, though he was also quite worldly and knowledgeable.

Eventually, he told me that he was due back at the monastery for three hours of silent meditation but he had just enough time to be a gentleman and walk me home. The time had passed so quickly.

"This is where I live," I said as we reached it. "Thanks for walkin' me. I've had a really good time on this... well, whatever it was."

He smiled. "Me too! We should meet again!"

I laughed, shaking my head. "Okay. I'll come to the cafe some time."

"Or tomorrow?" he asked, looking at me hopefully.

He was giving me the puppy eyes.

"Alright. I'll come meet you after college. 6 o'clock?"

He nodded.

We stood in silence for a few moments and he looked at me

"Well if you weren't a monk, and this was a date, this would be the part where you kiss me," I joked, trying to ripple out the tension of an awkward moment.

And then he kissed me.

The next day we met up at the bench again but he insisted we went for a walk along the lake. We strolled around in silence for a while but, once we were hidden between a cluster of trees, he made to put his arm around me.

"Sorry," I said as I shuffled away. "But I think we should just be friends."

"Good friends," he said, smiling.

"No," I shook my head. "I mean that... I don't want to mess things up for you. They will kick you out if they find out you kissed me."

"That was just a slip up—"

"That's the thing, I don't want to be some guy's 'slip up'," I said.

"I didn't mean it that way... I really like you!" he exclaimed. "I was thinking about you a lot today."

"This is so weird! I like you too, which is why I just want to be friends. There's no future for us. Don't you see? You live in a monastery, I'm at college."

"I'm not going to be a monk forever!" he said. "You know, in East Asian countries most of the population become a monk for just a year of their lives, and then they just—"

"But you are *now*. Listen," I said, placing a hand on his shoulder. "Let's just be friends for now. I have enough weirdness in my life without all this."

He sighed.

"So," he said. "What's weird in your life?"

I ended up telling him everything. Well, not everything, but most things, and he listened. He wasn't put off by it at all, in fact, he was very understanding. I thought that all of the things about my past would draw him away from me but for some reason it seemed to make me even more intriguing to him. When I tell people about my childhood it is usually interrupted by expressions of concern and apologies – I hate it when people do that; my past isn't their fault and it doesn't bother me anymore so why should it bother them? He actually *liked* the fact that I was complicated.

I wasn't used to that.

By the end of the conversation he was due back at the monastery again so he walked me home. He didn't kiss me that night but I walked into my house feeling like we had truly connected. I had not opened myself up to someone like that for a long time.

We met every afternoon after college for the rest of the week, usually to sit somewhere in the park and chat, but we also went for walks around places and he even helped me with my homework. Each evening he would walk me home at the end; and on the sixth night we had another 'slip up' and kissed again.

We kissed for a prolonged amount of time, and I am pretty sure that his wandering hands were approaching second base by the time I pulled away.

We had a repeat of the 'friends' conversation the next day, and everything was restored back to order.

Three days later we had sex.

If you ever have sex with a monk at the park, you'll find the robe is handy: it's easy to slip off, so there is no awkward fumbling around with buttons, zippers, and sleeves to get them naked...

It also doubles up as a very comfortable blanket.

The next day, I meant to go and meet him but instead I found myself accidentally walking straight past the park, into a shop to buy a bottle of whiskey, and then through the derelict quarters of the city and into a favourite haunt of mine, Janus.

I don't go to Janus very often anymore, partly because I've been busy with college and seeing Stephan, but also because it has been invaded by a particularly annoying bunch of teenagers who have taken over the main bar downstairs while the rest of us are under siege in the upper rooms. Luckily for me, I have been going to this place for several years and know all the nooks and crannies; there is a secret entrance at the back which leads to the hallway upstairs, so I can reach the hidden rooms where the more authentic characters hang out without having to encounter any of the wannabes.

I made my way down the hall and peered into some of the rooms my friends usually hang out in. It was a Thursday so the place was fairly quiet but I did open one of the doors to see a group of my arty friends lounging on beanbags around a coffee table. Namda was there.

"Frelia!" she called as she saw me. She patted the beanbag next to her. "Where've you been? I haven't seen you for *ages*!"

"Oh, don't even go there," I said, rolling my eyes as I drew out my bottle of whiskey and took a swig. "I think I have got myself into... a bit of a situation."

"Oh, really?" Namda asked, her eyes lighting up. "It's a guy, isn't it?"

"How did you know?" I asked.

"You kind of have this glow about you," Namda replied, winking. "Little gleam in your eye."

That's what I like about Namda: talk to her about a problem and you don't end up crying on her shoulder, you come out of it laughing and seeing the funnier side of it all.

"So," she said, nudging me with her elbow. "Tell me! What's he like?"

"He's nice," I said. "Sweet, understanding. Clever as well."

"So... what exactly is wrong?"

"He's a monk."

"A what?" she said, leaning closer.

"A friggin *monk*!" I exclaimed. "Robes and everything."

"Is that a problem?"

"How's your knowledge of Buddhism?" I asked.

"Not great," she admitted, shrugging. "I heard they like to... meditate, yeah?"

I laughed. "Yeah. Monks make vows of sobriety... and celibacy."

"So he won't have sex with you?"

"No," I said, shaking my head and taking another swig of whiskey. "That's the thing. We *have*!"

She covered her mouth to stop me seeing that she was laughing, but it was a futile gesture and we both exploded into a fit of giggles.

"Well, *anyway*," Namda said, holding her chest as we managed to gain control of ourselves again. "Seriously, Frelia. Can't you see? If he betrayed his Lama – or whatever it is – for you, he must really like you."

"I like him too," I admitted.

"Well, what the hell you doing here then?" Namda exclaimed.

By the time I had drunk enough 'courage' whiskey and made my way back to the park, I was an hour late to meet him (well technically we never actually agreed to meet, but it was the time we had met up every day for over two weeks now) so I wasn't expecting him to be there.

I was in for a big surprise: not only for the fact that he was there but also for the state I found him in: leant over of the arm rest of the bench with an empty bottle of liquor tilting from his limp hand.

"Stephan!" I yelled as I ran over, grabbing him by the collar of his robe. He stirred and his head swam around in a drunken haze as he came around. His unfocussed eyes circled around me for a moment before settling on my face.

"What the hell!" I exclaimed. "You're drunk! Oh shit! Stephan, it's almost seven o'clock. You're due back at the monastery soon!"

He smiled and shook his head dizzily. "You came..."

"*You* need to *go*!" I yelled, running my hands through my hair as I realised that he was due for his daily three hours of silent meditation and I couldn't see that going very well, with the swaying and everything. What could I do?

"No," he blurted, flapping his arm. "Not go back!"

"What?"

He looked me in the eyes. "I left. Gone! Monk no longer."

"You left?" I gasped.

He nodded.

"But why?" I asked, as guilt crept into my stomach.

I knew why – because of me.

"I think... I love you, Frelia," he whispered.

I couldn't get much sense out of Stephan in the state he was in but two things were clear to me: he could not come back to my place (because my homestay had rules about having members of the opposite sex over); and, secondly, Stephan moved here from a different town to join the monastery, so he didn't have any friends of his own to crash with.

Which left me with only one option: to see if one of my friends could put him up for the night. There was a certain friend of mine who owed me a favour... but it was kind of awkward.

In my early teens I lived with a family who fostered several kids under one roof and one of them was a girl called Pandy. She was a little older than me, and had had a pretty cushy upbringing until her parents died in a car accident. We were like candy and peas, but being girls of a similar age we became friends over time.

Anyway, one night we snuck out to a rave together and there was a big bust up by the police. We were both in possession of various class As but at the last moment I had a flash of conscience and got her to give me hers so I could take the rap for it. (I already had a criminal record by then and there was no sense in both of us going down).

To cut it short: I was arrested, she was escorted home by the police, and the social services stepped in and decided it was best we were separated. *But* because I took the rap for the drugs she escaped from it all with a clean record, so she owes me a *big* favour.

After the whole affair was over she went through a sudden transformation and became a born again Christian, and quite an obstinate one at that. Our friendship has been a bit stilted since then.

I rang the doorbell. A light came on and then a shadow appeared at the window. The door opened.

"Frelia?" she said, making no effort to hide the surprise in her voice.

The door opened a little bit more. She was no longer the girl I grew up with, but a creature I did not recognise. Tied back hair, white blouse, plain black trousers – all loose fitting to stop any male eyes being drawn to her figure – and no makeup.

"Hey Pandy," I said.

"It's Pandora," she said indignantly.

"What?"

"*Pandora*," she repeated. "That's what people call me now." Her eyes drifted to the figure slumped over my shoulder and widened.

"Ok, *Pandora*," I said. "Look, I know this is a bit random, but I *really* need a favour."

"Who is *that*?" she exclaimed.

"He's a monk," I said, giving him a little jolt to wake him up. He lifted his head, looked up at her and smiled.

"He's drunk!" Pandora said.

"Yeah... he's a drunk monk. Anyway, I—"

"Just come in! Quickly!" she said, her gaze turning to the neighbourhood self-consciously. She ushered us both inside.

"Look, I'm sorry," I said once we were inside and she shut the door. "But this is an emergency. He left the monastery and he has nowhere to go. I can't—"

"Just put him upstairs," Pandora said, sighing. "In the spare room. Second door on the right."

Once I had put Stephan to bed – safely lying on his side – I went back downstairs, and found Pandora in the living room.

"Thanks, Pandy," I said. "Sorry! I mean Pandora."

"It's okay," she sighed grudgingly. "I still remember what you did for me, Frelia."

"I'll find something for him tomorrow," I promised.

She shook her head. "Don't worry, I won't send him off into the streets! As long as he behaves himself, mind."

"Thanks," I muttered. I looked around the living room and considered sitting down somewhere, but the chairs, carpet, walls and everything were all so clean and white. It was like she had built this pristine world of purity around her; a world I wasn't welcome in.

"So..." she said. "Who is he?"

"Well... I met him at the park a couple of weeks ago. He's—"

She raised an eyebrow. "Are you having relations with him?"

"Relations?" I repeated, not quite knowing what she meant at first. When I did, my face must have given me away because she gave me a look of grave disapproval.

"Oh don't look at me like that," she said, fingering the crucifix at her throat. "Is it difficult for you to accept that I might feel concern for you? I know your lifestyle is your way of dealing with... all that stuff that happened to you, but I just hope that you can overcome it all and stop being a victim of your circumstances."

"Spare me the amateur psychoanalysis," I said, folding my arms across my chest. "I'm a bit more complicated than some leaflet you've read."

"Sorry," she said, turning away. "I love you Frelia... I just find it hard to respect the way you live your life. I turned mine around and, trust me, it gets—"

You think you would've got your lovely job at the bank if I hadn't taken the rap for you! I thought, biting my tongue. I just couldn't get how she could be so high and mighty about it all when I could remember her when she was a fifteen year old girl dancing around wildly in a short skirt which barely reached her thighs at illegal parties, making out with older guys, chewing her gums because she had taken way too much Ecstasy – I was actually the sensible one who had to tell her to calm down a lot of the time.

"You weren't always so perfect," I said, flatly.

"I sinned," Pandora admitted, solemnly. "But I am a better person now. If only you could see—"

"Look," I interrupted her. "Can we not do this? I don't want to fall out with you, Pandy. I'm sorry, but this is me. I'm pretty aware of myself and I'm not going to change. Hell, I actually *like* myself now, and it took me a while to get there, so just be happy for me."

She studied me for a few moments and then nodded her head resignedly and patted the space beside her on the sofa. "Come," she said. "Sit down."

We talked for a while. She told me about her job, her church friends, the voluntary work she does to help disadvantaged children in the community, and a few other things. I admired her for all the time she devoted to various charities but I got a general impression that she wasn't letting herself have a social life anymore and she was turning into a very lonely and repressed woman. In the last two years she had dated only one guy, and he was from her church and ran for the hills when he found out she wasn't a virgin (I guess when women become 'born again' their hymen is left behind, but far from forgotten).

I told her about college, the new home-stay I was living in, and my plans to travel the world after it was all done. Every now and then we would both laugh about something, and for a fleeting moment I caught a flash of the Pandy I used to know when we were young girls sharing a dorm together. It was a bit of a relief because this Pandora person felt like an alien sometimes.

A lot of the people I know who have siblings complain about them all the time, and it often seems to me they don't actually like each other very much but are woven together by a habitual bond in their childhood. I guess in many ways this complexity would make Pandora the closest thing I have to a sister.

I called in at Pandora's the next day after college and found Stephan comfortably making himself at home in the living room, dressed all smartly in a white shirt and black trousers. He looked up at me from a newspaper he was reading and smiled.

"What's with the new look?" I asked, suddenly realising that I didn't even know what his 'look' was – I had only ever seen him in robes.

"She took me shopping," he said. "I've got to look respectable if I'm going to get a job."

"You're getting a job?"

"We're going to need money if we're travelling the world."

"Really?" I exclaimed, with an unexpected surge of elation. "You want to travel with me?"

He nodded. "You said you wanted to and so do I! Who better to do it with than you?"

I jumped onto his lap and we touched noses for a few moments. Then he kissed me hungrily.

I then heard a throaty "Ahem" from nearby, and tore my lips away from Stephan's to see Pandora standing in the doorway with her hands on her hips.

"I know I can't stop you doing that sort of thing altogether," she said, her eyebrows joined together into one hard line. "But I would appreciate none of that business under *my* roof."

"Sorry, Pandora," Stephan said as I pulled away from him.

"Aren't you supposed to be looking for jobs?" she said, turning her eyes to the newspaper he had dropped on the coffee table.

"Yeah!" he said, smiling at her politely. "I'll get right back to it!"

"Would you like a cup of tea, Frelia?" she said. "The kettle's boiled."

"Yes please," I said.

"So... I can't kiss you here?" Stephan whispered when she left.

"Not unless you marry me," I replied dryly.

He then looked at me and, for a moment, it looked like he was actually considering it.

"Don't you dare!" I exclaimed. "Anyway... I'm going to help her make tea."

I got up and walked over to the kitchen where Pandora was pouring steaming water into three cups.

"You've got him well trained," I joked.

Pandora shook her head but there was a strange expression on her face, like she wanted to smile but was desperately trying not to. "Well the quicker he gets a job, the sooner he can get his own place."

"Thanks for doing this for me, "I said.

"It's no problem," Pandora shook her head. "*Deal thy bread to the hungry, and that thou bring the poor that are cast out to thy house. When thou seest the naked, that thou cover him; and that thou hide not thyself from thine own flesh'*. He can stay here until he lands back on his feet. This is what Christians do, Frelia. Can you help me carry these over please?" she requested, indicating to two of the cups on the counter.

"Plus," Pandora whispered just before we reached the doorway. "After spending the day with him I have to say; he's not too bad. He's clever and thoughtful, and he can't stop talking about you. It's quite annoying, really," she smiled. "I think he's a keeper, Frelia. He'll be good for you."

The following weeks fell into a steady routine. I had college, and Stephan spent most of the days searching for jobs and attending interviews. We usually met up in the afternoons and evenings.

Now that the whole monk issue was over we seemed to be making up for lost time and our sex-life went on a turn for the better. We mostly made love in the evenings at the park, and other secluded areas around the town, which added an element of danger that I actually found exciting. I sometimes went to see him at Pandora's place, but not as often because the strict no-more-than-a-foot-of-proximity-under-my-roof rule kind of stuck and we were still in the honeymoon period, and finding it hard to stay away from each other.

Pandora mothered him. Cooking meals and giving him advice on interviews and job applications were tasks she performed with a heavy sigh of exasperation and an air of condescension, but I think she secretly enjoyed it. She would never admit it but I think she was actually quite lonely, and Stephan's presence *was* having a positive effect on her: she steadily became more relaxed in her demeanour, a sense of humour occasionally surfaced and, even though she knew that we were most likely having premarital sex, she stopped trying to chastise me for it because she saw Stephan as a good influence on me.

One day I went over to see them and Stephan opened the door with a gleeful smile. He pulled me straight into the living room where Pandora was in the process of opening a bottle of wine.

"You're drinking?" I asked, staring at her.

She smiled. "Oh, I do have a little bit of fun sometimes you know. Just not in excess. Anyway, this is a special occasion!"

"I got a job!" Stephan exclaimed, no longer able to hold back the news. In a moment of elation he put his arms around me. Pandora narrowed her eyes, but said nothing about the slight transgression.

"Well done!" I said, pulling away from him. "Where?"

"With Pandora!" he said, beaming at her. "She got me one at her place. It's only as a clerk," he said. "But it's a start!"

"I was only a clerk a few years ago," Pandora said as she passed me a glass of wine.

We all clinked our glasses together and drank.

Don't ask me how it happened, but after a few more glasses I managed to convince both Stephan and Pandora that they should come out to Janus with me for a couple of drinks. Pandora seemed far from impressed when we got there and I led them through the derelict corridor but she relaxed a little by the time I got her settled into one of the rooms around a table with my friends.

It was a Tuesday, so it wasn't very busy but Namda was there with a load of her gang from art college. I knew her friend Tristan quite well but didn't really recognise any of the others. I soon gathered that the handsome guy with his arm around Tristan was his new boyfriend whom I had heard about.

I was a little worried at first how Pandora would react to having a gay couple in her midst, as I was not quite sure how strong her new convictions where when it came to homosexuals. Luckily though, Harry turned out to be some sort of businessman involved in trade and investment, so he and Pandora soon found common ground and were chatting about stock markets and many other things that generally made me want to yawn. Stephan – with a great amount of enthusiasm for his new job – listened to their conversation intently.

"So this is the new man," Tristan said, as he drank from a cocktail he had just purchased from the bar. "He seems nice."

I smiled. "He is."

"Does he still have his robes?" Namda asked, winking at me suggestively.

"I think so... unless Pandora burned them," I replied, shrugging. I looked over to see that she and Tristan's new boyfriend were still droning on about conversion rates. Something about that guy and Tristan being together didn't quite ring with me: Tristan, with his wavy blonde hair, faded jeans, tie-dyed t-shirt and denim jacket, barely scraped by on the sale of his paintings and had very little interest in money – he was the very essence of bohemia.

"Who is that girl, Frelia?" Tristan asked, I could tell that their conversation was boring him to death as well. "You've never mentioned her before."

"It's... complicated."

"You know... I was a bit surprised when I found out that Harry and Tristan were... well, you know, that way... but I quite like them," Pandora said.

She had spent most of the walk back from Janus in a thoughtful and contemplative silence, and it was only when we reached the edge of her neighbourhood that she finally spilled out what was on her mind.

"Your friends are really cool, Frelia," Stephan said, siding up next to me. "And I like Janus."

I smiled. "We'll go again sometime if you like."

He nodded eagerly.

We were now outside Pandora's house and she walked up the pathway to open the front door. As she was unlocking it I pulled Stephan close to me. "You're not in the house yet," I whispered mischievously before kissing him.

When we parted Pandora was staring at us.

"I'll get my own place soon," Stephan promised, just as he followed her to the front door. "I'll meet you at the park tomorrow. After work."

"If you ask me," Liam said. "The Design Argument is proof

that God exists. One only needs to look outside to see that God made the world for us. The trees, plants, animals. They were given to us by God."

It was our last Religious Studies lesson of the year, and Mr Harrison had just sparked off a debate around the Design Argument – a philosophy focused on the premise that the complexity of our world points towards intelligent crafting.

Liam was one of those pompous zealots who'd been getting on my tits all year (not literally, he is far too perfect and precious to debase himself with a carnal sin; plus there is the fact I would rather eat my own face). Our debates had mostly been formal and polite up till now, but there has always been an air of arrogance about him that vexed me. I could tell from his mannerisms and the way he *looked* at other people that he considered non-believers lesser people.

"The Design Argument doesn't *prove* anything," I said. "There are just things about the world we don't fully understand yet. To say the only explanation is God is a great jump. I also don't like the whole mentality that things exist merely for us to use; it's just that sort of attitude which makes people believe that abusing animals with cruel farming methods, and doing nothing to stop global warming is acceptable. Plenty of animals and plants have the ability to – and do – harm humans. We just happen to be the dominant species at this moment in time—"

"Wait," he interrupted me. "What do you mean dominant species *at this time*? As far as I know we have always been the dominant species."

I rolled my eyes. "There have been at least five major mass extinction events discovered in our world's recorded history, but there has almost certainly been more. The most famous being the one which wiped out the dinosaurs—"

"You're not going to tell me that dinosaurs were running around for thousands of years before us, and our ancestors were monkeys, are you?" he scoffed. A couple of his bible friends smiled at me like one does to a child who just told them a fairy tale.

"No. I am going to tell you dinosaurs roamed the world *millions* of years before our time... and, it's actually *apes* we share a more recent ancestry with."

"Evolution is a load of rubbish," he retorted. "Darwin's theory is full of missing links!"

I laughed and shook my head. "Oh 'missing links'. Are your family, or church, or whoever brainwashed you, *still* feeding you guys that little out-dated chestnut? Darwin admitted himself in the early days that his discoveries were incomplete but it was still the most comprehensive theory of the time. The whole 'missing links' argument is now invalid because, since it was made, they *have* found them. It's the twenty-first century now, dude, and the evidence is pretty conclusive. Get over it."

His jaw dropped, and I could see doubt in his eyes. His bible friends were rendered speechless and unsure – they turned to their leader.

Years of Christian repetition then recovered itself and Liam spoke again. "This is all a bunch of hocus pocus. Are you actually expecting us to believe this tosh? The world isn't even that old. In the bible it says—"

"Okay just hold it there," I interrupted, raising the palm of my hand. "Is this 'belief' in evolution you have logical, and based on actual research, or is it just a purely emotional reaction because religious beliefs that were indoctrinated into you when you were a child being contradicted scares you? Because I'm studying biology, and I really can't be bothered to debate a subject with someone who knows nothing about it. I think I would get more cerebral stimulation from banging my head against a wall."

"Please be civil, Frelia," Mr Harrison warned from his desk at the front.

I ignored him. "This is what I don't get about your kind," I said. "Plenty of passages from the bible are ignored and twisted to mean other things. What is it about this particular one you guys are so fixated on? You can believe in god *and* evolution, you know. In fact, many do, it's called 'Theistic Evolutionism'. It kind of makes sense, because there are many things about evolution which are mysterious, and beautiful. Like the eye. Did you know that they have traced multiple examples where the early species of this planet *independently* evolved eyes? Their DNAs somehow, *separately*, figured out a complex genetic code which gave them organs in their heads that could detect a phenomenon they had no way of even knowing existed before – light. And then you have creatures like chameleons, whose DNA learnt how to change their outer layer of skin so that it could shift its colour at will and camouflage them from predators. These things are the real magic of the universe, not some book of myths used to control people in medieval times. Why can't you open *your* eyes and see that? Because it is learning these things about the natural history of the world which sometimes makes me question my belief that there is *no* god."

"I've never have any doubts over my beliefs," said, lifted his head arrogantly. As if, by that short statement alone, he had contradicted everything I had just said.

"Well, maybe that is why you failed our mock exams last term," I said, flatly. "There really is *no* argument here, Liam. Creationism is *not* a credible theory – it is just a proclamation of collective ignorance. Maybe if you grew up in a repressive regime or in the sticks in Africa or somewhere then you would have a reasonable excuse, but as far as I am concerned, if you are from the first world and have been given access to proper education, and you *still* don't believe in evolution, then you're just a fucking moron."

Several people gasped.

"Frelia!" Mr Hammond rose from his chair. "Stop this now!"

"No!" I shook my head. "I will not. We need to *stop* humouring people like him, because they are dangerous and they are holding the world back. It's thanks to people denying scientific evidence just because it's inconvenient for them that the world is in so much trouble at the moment. Let me give you an example."

I turned back to Liam. "I bet you think global warming is a just a conspiracy, don't you?"

He hesitated. "Well, I did watch this thing—"

I slapped my forehead. "*See!*" I exclaimed, turning back to Mr Hammond. The rest of the class were all staring at me open-mouthed, but I didn't care. I was too riled by this point. "It's *ignorance* which is the biggest problem in this world. And do you know why? Because behind every psychopath who winds his way into becoming a religious leader or profiteer from the oil industry, there are millions of goons, like *Liam* here, who just follow what they say and never—"

"That's *enough*, Frelia!" Mr Harrison yelled.

"I just don't get what you're about," Mr Harrison said.

The classroom had swiftly emptied, and now it was just me and him. He was at the front of the room with his hand on his hip. He didn't seem angry, more wary, vexed and confused. I crossed my arms over the table in front of me and stared at him, unblinking.

"When you first sat in this room nine months ago I thought you were just one of those kids who saw Religious Studies as an easy option. You would just sit there silently; often I thought your mind wasn't even here. I have caught you sleeping, and on several occasions you have even left the room in tears. Your attendance has been barely within acceptable levels... but your test scores," he said, reaching for a folder on the desk and flipping through the pages until he found the right one. "They are... outstanding. You are far from what I picture as a model student, Frelia, but you achieve the best results."

"So why did you just blow up like that today?" he asked, looking at me earnestly. "Until now your occasional input into classroom discussions has been outlandish and obscure, to say the least, and now you suddenly turn into a raging bull!"

"I'm sorry, Sir," I said, looking at the clock and wondering how much longer he would be keeping me here. "Liam's been bugging me all year and I've been holding back and..."

"Well maybe if you were more assertive from the beginning it wouldn't have all exploded like it did today. As your teacher it is my job to ensure that my students, even when they disagree, all still treat each other with respect. Next year I want you to—"

"There isn't going to be a next year."

"What do you mean?"

"I'm quitting college."

His eyes widened. "Why on earth would you do that, Frelia?"

"I want to travel," I said, shrugging. "Truth is, I only enrolled this year because it was free, and I thought I might as well get some education while I had nothing else to do. And, well, now I do. I've met someone, and I think I love him and—"

"You're only *seventeen*," he cut-in, his eyebrows narrowing. "You can't just throw your future away over some – some crush."

"Spare it," I said, raising my hand. "This whole studying thing isn't my bag anyway. We're saving up to go travelling. I want to *see* the world, not read about it in books and talk about it with morons," I said, indicating the desk Liam had been sitting on a few minutes before. "You won't change my mind, Sir."

His shoulders fell resolutely and then he sighed. "You could go far if you wanted to, Frelia. Despite your ill delivery, what you said today was thought-provoking and full of passion. If you could just apply that into an academic context you—"

"But that's not *me*, Sir," I said, shaking my head. "I'll do the exam tomorrow, cause there's no point in me wasting this year – I'm not stupid. But earlier today I signed a form, terminating my studies when they asked me to re-enrol."

I got up from my seat, and placed my bag on my shoulder.

"Good luck, Frelia," he said as I made my way to the door.

"Thanks for everything, Sir," I said, waving as I walked out.

When I met up with Stephan at the park later that day he wasn't his usual self. He seemed distracted and aloof. He greeted me with an agitated smile and a brief nod. He did not look me in the eyes.

"Are you okay?" I asked as I sat next to him; he made no move to put his arm around me.

He faked a smile. "Yeah... sorry, just... first day at work... you know."

"How was it?"

"Oh, it was okay actually," he said. "Most of them were nice. Met lots of people."

"Cool. I got into an argument with Liam today," I groaned.

"Got a right bollocking off the teacher. This dude is so deluded, he is convinced—"

By the time I had explained it all, I realised that he wasn't even paying attention to me. He was gazing away at something else distractedly.

"Steph!" I said, nudging him on the shoulder. "Look – you're obviously tired, so how about I talk to you tomorrow."

"Okay," he said, running his hand through the stubble of hair that had begun to grow on his head. "Meet you here at the same time?"

I nodded. He raised himself from the bench and leaned forward to kiss me. It was brief, awkward.

"You forgot to wish me luck," I said as he walked away.

"Oh," he said. "Sorry... what for?"

"I have an exam tomorrow."

"Good luck, Frelia."

The next day I went to meet him after my exam and, although outwardly he was more cheerful, there was something a bit forced about it. Whatever it was, he was not ready to tell me yet. I had revision to do, so I told myself it must be stress from the new job and went home early.

I had more exams throughout the rest of the week for Biology and Physics. We didn't see much of each other but, when we did, things stayed roughly the same. He was awkward and distracted. I was focussed on my exams.

And then Friday came. It was the end of the week and I went to the park to meet Stephan after my last exam, planning to take him out with me to Janus to celebrate – but he wasn't there.

It was then that I realised that this whole week my mind had been so swarmed with all the information that I had been cramming in there for the exams, I had completely ignored all of the signs. All of it had been released in the halls of the exam room now, like a cloud of bees, and I was in a state of clarity. I finally let myself acknowledge that something was up with Stephan.

I stared at the bench. It was the place where we first met, and spent the majority of our bonding time together. I abruptly became aware of the fact that it wasn't that much time at all – not in the grand scheme of things.

I knew now in my gut that something was wrong with Stephan and me. A strange feeling crept into my stomach. The whole scene of the park around me felt odd – like I was seeing it for the first time. I felt a sense of turbulent motion even though I was standing still, and an understanding that locations are just a stage for events. It is the sequences that run through them which gave them significance. The memories I had entwined with this place, piled on top of it like a stack of tracing paper. I could *see* the individual leaves flipping through my mind. I could peel back the pages.

You've let me down Stephan... why? Have I ever let you down?

The setting around me abruptly dimmed, like summer afternoon had suddenly shifted into an early evening.

Stephan was sitting there, in orange robes, his head shiny and bald, like it was when I first met him. He had a bottle of liquor in his hand.

I stared and stared. Wondering what the hell was going on. He still hadn't noticed me. Would he notice me? This must be a dream, after all.

He was crying.

"Stephan," I called, as I walked over.

"Frelia!" he exclaimed through teary eyes. "I thought you'd left me! I've been waiting. I thought—"

I couldn't help but rush over and put my arms around him, even though this must all be a dream. He *felt* real when I touched him.

"I've been waiting for you!" I exclaimed. "What's wrong? You've been strange with me all week!"

He looked at me with blurry, confused eyes. "I left the monastery."

"I know you did! That was ages ago."

His head swayed and he closed his eyes, as though he was finding it hard to stay awake. I shook him by the shoulders and his eyes snapped open again. He looked at me.

"Why are you a ghost?" he asked, as his eye lids went heavy again. He rested his head on the back of the bench.

"What do you mean?"

"You... you're see-through..." he mumbled.

I looked down at my hands, and they *were* in fact, see-through. I was experiencing the same sensation I felt earlier. This knowingness that time was just lines of tracing paper over scenery.

I was just another layer, flittering across the setting.

And suddenly, I was back where I was before. Standing in the same place, and staring at the bench. The sky was lighter again, and I knew it was Friday afternoon and I had just finished my exams.

I stood there for a long time, just staring at my hands.

I knocked on Pandora's door. There was no response but I knew they were in there so I carried on knocking louder and faster, until I heard a clink and the door parted far enough from the frame for Pandora's disconcerted face to peer through the parting.

"I need to see Stephan!" I said.

"Frelia..." she answered, for some reason nervous. "Stephan is—"

I pushed the door open. Whatever she was being so weird about, I had neither the patience nor restraint to spare it time.

"Frelia!" she exclaimed as I strode past her into the house. "I—"

"Something really fucked up happened!" I exclaimed, almost in tears. "Where is Stephan? I need to see him."

I found him in the living room. He seemed somewhat defensive and alarmed.

"Frelia!" he said. "I'm sorry I've been... It's just that I got something—"

"I don't care about that!" I exclaimed. "Something happened. I went back to when I found you on the bench drunk—"

"Let's not dig up the past," he said. There was a strange blankness in his eyes. They weren't alive with excitement and enthusiasm as they had always been when they looked at me – something had gone.

"Listen!" I exclaimed. "It was like I travelled through time. It was really fucking weird. I—"

"What?" Pandora said, appearing beside us with her arms crossed over her chest. "Have you been taking drugs, again?"

"No!" I shook my head. "I'm clean. I swear. I—"

Pandora shook her head. I could tell she didn't believe a word I was saying.

"But Frelia, why something like this?" Stephan asked. "You're an atheist. You don't believe in—"

"I believe in what I experience," I said defensively. "And just now that includes all manner of things fucked up. Did I mention God? How is time travel proof of God? Anyway, please listen. I—"

"I think we've heard enough of your stories," Pandora said.

"What?" I said, looking at both of them and becoming aware of an air between them I had never noticed before.

I then noticed that Stephan was wearing a crucifix around his neck.

"What the fuck is that?" I exclaimed, pointing. "You're a Buddhist!"

Stephan looked at the floor, unable to meet my eyes.

"Stephan has seen the light and been born again," Pandora said, placing a hand on his shoulder. "It is a glorious thing."

I stepped away, remembering some of the deeper conversations I had had with Stephan about religion and spirituality. I had always said that organised religions such as Christianity were like those beaming lights you shine in people's faces during interrogation; blinding, oppressive, intrusive, and persistent. He had always been a bit more sympathetic, and held that religion can have both a positive and negative effect in people's lives, but ones with strict guidelines and rules sometimes blocked people from reaching true Enlightenment. It was in conversations like those that I really felt like we had connected on a deeper level, and I had believed I had found someone who was unyielding and insightful.

I suddenly realised that I did not know him at all.

"I'm not sorry, Frelia," Stephan said, looking at me, with his blank, lifeless eyes. "I experienced the force of Jesus, I had never felt anything so pure and—"

And then he looked at Pandora and his eyes changed.

Then I knew.

"Oh my God!" I exclaimed, turning my gaze between them in disbelief. "You're *screwing* her, aren't you?!"

There was a shocked silence and neither of them said anything. Pandora's expression was a mingling of guilt and shame.

"Don't... don't be absurd," Pandora mumbled. She opened her mouth to make some kind of denial, but I had heard enough. I ran out of the room, through the door, and into the street.

I didn't cry – I don't do the whole weeping thing (unless I want to get out of a boring lesson, that is) but it is fairly safe to say that I walked back home *very* angry; anyone I walked past must have felt a heat wave as I crossed their path.

I went straight to my bedroom, lay on my bed, and stared at the ceiling. I thought about everything that had just happened. How could I have been such a fool and been taken in by Stephan's charm? I had built an idea in my head of what he was and failed to see his true colours.

And what about that whole freaky experience at the park? Did I really just step through time and revisit the past? Could I do it again?

I stared at the ceiling, and recalled the state of mind I reached back then; the sense that the reality of space/time was layered like the leaves of a book. The white plaster above me drew closer, peeling back, revealing a scene. Two people were sitting opposite each other with a desk between them, as if they were conducting some kind of interview.

As I floated towards it, I became aware of the fact that, if I was really about to step into another space in time, the two people in it would be shocked to see me appear from nowhere, but I also somehow instinctively knew that I had the ability to cloak myself. I recalled the way my body went translucent the last time I travelled back in time and applied it in a different way.

"So, what makes you want to join this monastic order?" the robed man on one side of the desk asked.

The person he was interviewing was Stephan – though not as I have ever seen him. He had a green wave of hair raised from the centre of his head and silver rings in his eyebrow, lip, nose, and upper ears. He was dressed in a pair of torn jeans, and a red sleeveless top. The whole effect was quite cliché and it was a shock to see Stephan this way.

I was standing right beside them, but neither could see me.

That bright, enthusiastic and excited smile I recognised lit up his face, and he began to talk.

"I have always been fascinated by Buddhism, and I have been following the precepts of—"

I left that scene behind – I had seen enough. It was time to search deeper.

Four weeks before I met him he was a punk with enough piercings to kill a small mammal. Every time I went back further his appearance altered to whatever his latest fad was but his childish way of getting excited and swept away by things never changed. He had told all his friends he had cancer once, but I couldn't find a place or time where he was actually diagnosed. He got his parents to send him to rehab when he was seventeen, but I couldn't identify any signatures of a drink problem.

His religious pursuits began when he and one of his friends practiced 'satanism' in his room (this was in his goth stage, of course); they turned out the lights, sat opposite each other with a candle and an upside-down pentagram between them and chanted a prayer to Lucifer from some trashy book he had found in a shop. The whole effect was so juvenile and desperately histrionic that I had to stifle giggles behind my hand. He has since been a confirmed catholic, baptised protestant, high priest of a wiccan coven, initiated member of the Ordo Templi Orientis and, shortly *after* the terrorist attacks in America (when Islam was controversial), he became a Muallaf. He entered each progression with elated excitement, interest, and a disavowal of the previous religion he'd embraced.

How about his girlfriends before me? Well:

He ran away from his parents with a girl when he was fifteen and returned after a week. It was all a stunt to get his parents to notice him, and the next day he dumped her. He has been engaged five times. With one of them he even got as far as to arrange the whole wedding, but failed to appear at the altar.

I think you are starting to get the picture. But what I guess you are wondering is *why*? Why would someone develop such a flighty personality?

Cause and effect.

Upper-middle class family. His father was a cold and distant atheist who wasn't home much. He had four brothers, and he was the one in the middle, and received the least attention. The only time his parents paid him any heed was when he did something wild and crazy. Apart from that, his upbringing was prosaic, uneventful, and as boring as the awkward little boy who spent the first few years of school sitting alone during lunchtimes.

His father just ignores him now, as do the rest of his family. They have all grown weary and bored. Not to mention embarrassed.

My heart bleeds.

None of this is an excuse. Your past sets the foundations for where your life begins but most people of the western world are lucky enough to be the masters of their own destiny and can choose which direction they can take from there. Letting initial obstacles turn you into a flaky thespian that doesn't mind who they hurt in their efforts to be noticed is just the result of an innately weak character. By all accounts *I* should probably be either in prison or out on the streets selling my body for drugs, considering my upbringing. Hell, I know the state of my life is far from perfect, but I think I have reaped a pretty impressive harvest from my meagre sowings.

So what have I learned about my new-found powers by now?
- Well I can transport myself back in time (that much is obvious).
- It is for a limited period. If I stay too long my form begins to fade and I am pulled back.
- I can make myself unseen/unheard if I choose.
- While in the same state I can also walk through walls.

- I always go back to the same place, time and position I was in before I left.
- Considering the last four points, I think it is reasonable to conclude that it is not actually my body which goes back but more a corporeal manifestation (a 'projection' to put it more simply).
- But yet, for some reason even *I* do not know, I can take little souvenirs back and forth with me, as long as they are not too heavy. My clothes – for example.
- I suspect that I can never meet myself: whenever I try to go back to a time/place I have already been to, something blocks me.
- Often when I return I find that I have a set of memories for all the things which turned out differently due to my intervention. These memories sit alongside the old ones – it gets a little confusing sometimes, but I am always able to tell which one is the 'new' timeline.
- The whole time machine thing in the movies where you type in a date/time is a load of crap. Years, months, days and hours are human constructs, and the layers of the universe seem to be defined by events rather than the Gregorian calendar. When I choose to go back somewhere, I think of a certain occurrence that must have happened and I find myself there.

So... let's go back to the first time Stephan fucked Pandora...

It was night, and I found myself in Pandora's house. From the clothes scattered over the bedroom floor, I deduced that it was the night I took them out to Janus to celebrate Stephan's new career. It all made sense; they were drunk and it was the following day that Stephan changed.

They were on the bed with their bodies entwined like a pair of lusty pagans. Pandora turned Stephan around so that he was on his back and straddled him.

She let out a soft moan, and I cringed as I noticed a tensing of their bodies' that could only mean that he had just entered her. To be fair to Pandora, it must have been the first time for quite a while, judging from the ecstatic moan which escaped through her closed lips.

"Oh," she groaned. "Oh... Jesus!"

I decided that this was the right moment to make myself visible to them. I was standing at the foot of the bed and I began to clap my hands together in a slow, steady pace. They tore away from each other, gasping, as their eyes widened to the reality of my presence.

"That's it!" I exclaimed, flatly, still clapping. "Do it for Jesus, *Pandy*!"

She huddled the duvet over herself to cover her breasts and shuffled to the opposite end of the bed, terrified, ashamed, shocked and confused. Stephan was comparably stoic about the whole thing; he tried to make himself seem small by covering all but his face with the bed sheets, as if I would almost forget he was there if he remained inconspicuous.

"Oh my God!" she exclaimed, looking around the room. "Frelia! How did you get in? The doors and windows—"

"You always said I was special," I replied, grinning at her as I folded my arms across my chest.

"Oh my," she whispered, turning her head low and running her fingers along her forehead. "I'm... I don't know."

"It's ok, Pandy," I said, sneering at the figure of Stephan, still hiding himself under the duvet and unable to face me. "I think you've done me a favour. Anyway, I would love to spend some more quality time with you guys but I must dash, people to see, things to do, you know. Oh, and Pandy, I know it might be against your views and such, but I suggest a condom for next time."

"Wait! Frelia!" Pandora exclaimed, shuffling out of the bed and reaching for something to cover her modesty as I left the room. I slammed the door behind me and let myself be pulled back into the present again.

I opened my eyes and I was back in my room, staring at the ceiling. I laughed as I thought of Pandora and Stephan rummaging through the house almost a week ago now, checking every window, door and cranny to find out how I possibly got in and out.

A new set of memories came to me: Stephan never met me that day after I exploded in the classroom. In fact, I never saw him ever again. Pandora has been trying to call, and keeps sending me endless text messages. I never quit college.

The next visit I made was to see my mother.

She was sprawled out on a small couch at the end of her bed, watching TV. Some kind of brain-numbing soap opera. Her glassy eyes were fixed on the screen, empty and uninvolved. I watched her for a few minutes with spiders weaving webs of guilt around my stomach. This was an evening a few weeks ago, just a few hours after I shouted at her for telling me my father was a time traveller.

I drew a deep breath to prepare myself for this encounter and let it out slowly as I lifted my veil of invisibility.

My mother was so spaced out from all the drugs she was on that she didn't even notice me for a few moments. I stepped in front of the screen.

"Frelia!" she exclaimed, jumping from her seat into an upright position and clasping her knees. "What?" her head turned to the single window and door. "How did you get in?"

She then turned back to me and her eyes widened, as though she were seeing me for the first time. An unfamiliar clarity appeared in her usually forlorn expression. "Oh my!" she gasped. "It's like your—"

"Father," I finished for her as I turned the TV off. "Yeah, that's right. I've figured it out."

An expression of relief graced her features, I had never seen her so happy. Tears fell from her eyes and wet her cheeks as she clasped her face. "Oh my god!"

"God has nothing to do with this," I said.

"What?" she said. "Even after all this you still don't believe?"

"So I can travel through time," I said, shrugging. "I am exhibiting the same survival abilities and traits as my father. That's called DNA, mum. How is that proof of God? Anyway, why are you crying? Shouldn't you be happy someone finally believes you?"

"I am," she whispered, as she wiped another tear from her cheek. "It's just… I reached a point where even I began to question. I thought that maybe they were right and I was… well, you know…"

"Crazy," I supplied, as I walked over and sat myself next to her. "Well on that topic I have two things I would like to say, Mum." I put my hand on her shoulder. "And the first is that I am sorry. I am sorry for all of the crap I said to you, and all the times I called you a liar."

But I then withdrew my hand and stood up. "But I also want tell you that you are, in fact, a bit crazy. Though not enough to justify dumping you into this place. I've been on enough benders to know that if you coop anyone into a confined space and feed them drugs they eventually go a bit loopy. But Mum, you owe *me* an apology. You should have just lied, put a gay friend of yours as my father, or something. Just anything but the truth. Anyone sane would know that what you did was asking for it. Why couldn't you just *lie*?"

She looked down at her knees and sighed heavily. For a moment I thought she wasn't going to answer but she lifted her head back up and looked at me. "Because I shouldn't *need* to," she replied, more bold and sure of herself than I have ever seen her. "Why should I have to lie just so people don't think I am crazy?"

Her eyes became ignited with an idea. "You!" she exclaimed, grabbing my sleeve. "You can prove it. Show them what you can do! And then—"

"No," I said, pulling away. "Not over my dead body. I've just managed to create a somewhat stable life for myself, and you want to turn me into a spectacle? No!" I shook my head. "This is *my* secret, you understand?"

Her face fell and she nodded her head in resigned conviction. "Sorry," she said. "I wasn't thinking. Terrible idea. I want what's best for you, Frelia. I always have."

"Well you should have been there for me then!" I exclaimed. "Now, mother. Tell me, where do we go from here?"

She blinked a few times.

"If you want to make things right you need to bite the bullet and play by their rules," I said. "It's sad, I know, but it's just a fact. I know that it's not right you being in here, but what are you doing to help yourself or the world by just accepting that? If you want to be a part of my life and make the world a better place, you'll have much more opportunity to do that if you convince them you're not crazy."

She nodded her head. "Okay…" she whispered. "I will try. I can't promise anything though, Frelia. I have never been very good at… pretending. But I will try."

When I slipped back through the veils of space-time I landed back into my bed, back into my body. I clasped hold of the sides of my mattress for a few moments as I grounded myself.

When I opened my eyes there was a dark figure standing over me.

I jumped in terror and scrambled, pulling my legs towards my body and flattening myself against the wall.

"What the fuck!" I exclaimed as my eyes turned to the door. It was still locked, so was the window.

I dared myself to look back at him and he was still there, staring down at me, impassively, with a frown on his face. He looked familiar but I could not remember ever seeing him before.

"Who the fuck are you?!" I yelled.

In a flash he was beside me, with his hand over my mouth. "Sshhh," he hissed into my ear. "They'll hear you."

I tried to scream again because, let's face it, I'm a teenage girl, and some strange man has entered my room – if my guardians or any of my fellow housemates were there, getting their attention was a pretty wise course of action. But he held my mouth shut and I struggled against him.

"Stop it!" he urged, as he held back one of my wrists. "I *know* what you are Frelia! I know what you've been doing."

I looked at him again, and suddenly it all made sense.

He was my father. That was why he looked familiar. He had my eyes, and the outline of his face bore a resemblance to that which I saw in the mirror every day.

"What do you want?" I asked when he stepped away, finally giving me some room.

"I want you to stop!" he said firmly. "Stop going back. You shouldn't—"

"You think you could just come in here after all this time and try to tell *me* what I should do?" I spat, feeling angry. "Screw yourself. I'll do whatever—"

"You don't understand," he whispered, crossing his arms.

"It's for your own safety. You weren't even supposed to be born. If they find out—"

"They?" I repeated. "Who's this *they*?"

He hesitated and I could tell from his eyes that he was going to tell me as little as he possibly get away with. "My kind," he eventually said. "That's all I can tell you."

I massaged my forehead, feeling a headache coming on. This was all too much to take in at once. It was hard to think that I had only discovered this new ability a few hours ago – in passing time, that is, I had probably clocked almost a whole day of projecting by now.

"And what if I say no?"

"This is for *your* safety," he said. "Like I said; you're not supposed to exist. If they notice—"

"Why don't you just fuck off," I retorted. "Do you know where my mother has been all this time? Do you even care?"

For a moment an emotion close to guilt could be seen in his eyes, but he turned away and looked at the floor. "It was for her safety… look, your kind aren't supposed to know about us. If it ever became public knowledge you'd be in danger."

"This is the twenty-first century, dude," I said. "You could host a skirmish between a gang of goblins and unicorns outside St Pauls Cathedral and the next day all the journalists and academics would stand outside the bloody remains and rationalise it as a mass hallucination or some shit. I don't think you have much to worry about."

"You *will* stop!" he exclaimed, angrily banging his fist against my desk, making me jump in surprise. He glared at me for a while and then his face softened. "Please, Frelia, I know it's hard to understand, but you must! I am sorry about your mother but it was the only way I could keep you both safe."

After he left I didn't feel safe in my own bedroom anymore so I went to the only place I could think of: Janus. I went through the back entrance, as usual, and slipped into the maze of winding corridors. I searched the rooms, looking for Namda or any of my other friends who would listen to my story without thinking I was crazy. I needed to talk to someone.

It was busy that night. I then remembered it was Friday. The rooms were all crowded. Mostly with the bracelet-wearing, logo-flashing, black-makeup-smeared wannabes, who usually inhabited the main hall downstairs. It seemed that they had finally catapulted their way up to the top corridor and invaded the heart of Janus.

I scowled at them as I shifted my way through, looking for a friend, any friend, as I drowned in a sea of middle-class rebellion and pseudo-idiosyncrasy. I was lost.

I heard raised voices up ahead and became aware of a commotion going on. I scrambled forward, pushing and shuffling my way through pale shoulders, eventually seeing someone who wasn't a clone of everyone else around them. A girl with long brown hair, in a black trench coat and purple skirt. She was trying to reach the toilets but the black-clad swarm of teenagers around her were all pushing and pulling at her with cruel sneers on their faces.

"What's going on?" I exclaimed, grabbing one of the bullies by the shoulder.

"He's trying to use the toilet," one of them yelled.

I turned to the speaker. "I beg your pardon?"

"It's not really a she," he said, pointing a derisive finger at the victim. I took a second glance at her and saw that even though she was pretty, her jaw was a bit too angular and the shape of her body was somewhere in between. She was young as well, so I guessed she must have been somewhere in the middle of an HRT programme.

"So what?" I said, shrugging. "Why do you care what toilet she uses?"

"It's got a penis!" a girl explained. "It should use the boys."

"My name is *Tilly*," she said between gritted teeth.

I felt an overwhelming revulsion to this whole scenario. When I was growing up, Janus was my escape, a place I could go to and be accepted for who I was rather than ridiculed and judged, and now *this* is what it had come to? A place where the marginal are not even *safe*?

"I just want to use the toilet..." she said softly.

"Pervert!" one of them screamed.

She tried to make towards the door, but they blocked her

way and then all hell broke loose. The kids around her all pushed and shoved, knocking her over.

They formed a ring around her and starting kicking her with their big, heavy, designer boots. Tilly let out a scream and shuffled around, but the peltings came from all sides. I saw a flash of blood spurt from her nose as another boot sent her reeling across the floor.

They carried on kicking her. In the face, the head, the stomach. They stamped on her legs, and one of them even spared a moment to spit at her. I desperately tried to intervene, but there were too many and I couldn't reach them. They were killing her, but they carried on regardless. So long as the rest of them were doing it they seemed to feel it was okay, and none of them wanted to be the first to hesitate. Mob mentality.

I closed my eyes, remembering the warning my father had just given me but not caring. I had to stop this from happening.

Space-time flickered around me. It was time to go back.

Frelia is going back. It is time to change everything.

And I don't know about you, but I wasn't too keen on the way things finished between Tristan and Neal. So here is a new ending...

7
The Dog Man

Another morning.

Someone is breathing beside me. For a moment it is disconcerting, and I sit up to take a glance at the fray of brown hair spread across the pillow. A face with its mouth wide open.

My new lover, Danny.

I shake my head, suddenly feeling the urge to leave the comfort of the bed sheets. The dogs need feeding. The lawn needs mowing. I'm hungry.

I get to my feet but as I walk across the bedroom they become entangled in the clothes strewn across the floor. Memories of ripping a designer t-shirt off his body last night come into my mind. Designer. Everything was designer with him. Even his underwear has a Calvin Klein logo. Why would someone want to spend that much money on underwear?

Still, he presents himself well. Danny is nearer to my age. He is conventional. Respectable. He is someone I can take out for a meal without people staring at us because he has the young face of an angel and is sitting with someone twice his age.

He is also handsome, and very good in bed.

So...

Why is it that I can't get Tristan out of my mind?

I sigh.

Another morning without Tristan.

I enter the kitchen and the dogs are waiting at the door. They start jumping around me, demanding I put food into their bowls and yet getting in my way in every step of achieving it. After filling their bowls I pat them on their heads as they scoff down their breakfast, then I head over to the counter to make some for myself.

As I turn the kettle on, I hear Danny walking down the

stairs. I force myself to smile, hoping that one day it will be genuine.

But he never enters the room.

"Hello?" I call.

"Hi..." he utters through the doorway.

"You can come in..."

He nervously pokes his head through the door and fixes his eyes on the dogs.

"I don't like dogs," he reminds me.

I am just about to make a clever reply about how they won't bite when Missy starts growling.

"Missy! Stop that!"

Why didn't I see it before?

Making you feel insecure made me feel good about myself. It made me feel stronger. I am an ageing man and someone as young as you wanting me made me feel special. I took you for granted.

You were genuine and open. I thought it was a weakness and exploited it. I thought that by being erratic and evasive, by making you feel like you needed me more than I needed you, it would make me stronger, and that way I could hold you in my arms forever.

You ventured into our journey together with your arms wide open, I dressed myself from head to toe in a suit of armour. But you didn't need a sword to get under my skin. You just did it with your eyes, your face, your lips, your body. You.

In the end it turned out that you were the stronger one: I needed you just as much as you needed me, but only you were brave enough to show it.

You were brave enough to admit what both of us knew from the first time we woke up next to each other. We are meant to be together.

Why didn't I see it before? It was always you.

"You want to go outside?" I ask Danny as I look to the window – the sun is shining; it looks like a beautiful day.

I've just finished breakfast. Danny didn't eat anything because I only have white bread which he refuses to eat because he is worried about his waistline.

"With the dogs?" he asks, casting a nervous glance at the door they have been shut on the other side of.

"Oh don't worry," I sigh. "I will put them on leads, they'll leave you alone."

"But my shoes might get muddy..."

We have never been far apart.

It has been almost ten weeks since I last touched you. Since I told you that you could never have me. I was lying. I was too proud to admit that I belong to you.

We have never been far apart, because you have always been on my mind.

I just pray I never left yours.

"Call me if you want to meet again, maybe we can sort something out."

He says something like this every time we part. I usually don't mean to call him but I get lonely and hope that he can distract me from the images of Tristan in my head. Every time I ring he sounds so enthusiastic. It is obvious he's been waiting for me to call.

This is what the old me would have done:

Smile. Nod. Wave while he leaves. Go back into my house and resist the urge to ring him for as long as possible to keep him on his toes and wanting more. If he breaks first and dials me up, it will make me feel good about myself.

If I wasn't interested in meeting again, the old me would have done the same – but been smug in the thought of them pining over me.

That was the old me. It was the behaviour I adopted because it was safer.

Not anymore, it is time for the real me. For honesty.

"I'm sorry, but I think we should stop seeing each other."

His head hangs low. The contrast between the forlorn expression on his face and his pseudo-apathy a few moments ago almost makes me laugh. But I don't.

"There is someone else, isn't there..." he says.

A silence. I think we both knew it all along. He has always been my distraction. I guess he hoped he would become more than that over time. I hoped he would too.

I nod.

He turns away and gets into his car.

I am coming for you, my love.

Once I made you feel like you had to earn me when you already had me. I made you feel like you had to show me how much you cared, while I pretended not to care because it made me feel special. I no longer care for self-aggrandisement, I care about you. I want you to be happy.

Once you made me feel special, and I abused that gesture. Now it's your turn. I am going to make you feel as special as you are.

I am coming for you, my love. I just hope it is not too late.

I jump into the shower and wash away the slimy layer of excess pride which I have armoured my skin with over the last few months. Next up, a dollop of shampoo on my hand. I rub it into my hair to cleanse the dusty dandruff of old indulgent habits I've let myself get into. I massage the suds into my scalp, it is time to go back to my roots. I love Tristan, and I think Tristan loved me. I wanted to spend time with him, but avoided him as much as I could make myself. I wanted to talk to him, but my precious ego held me back from picking up the phone. It is time to scrub my hands clean. I want Tristan, it's as simple as that. Why did I let it become so complicated?

The water washes away my vanity. My selfish ways are sucked down the plughole.

I towel myself dry and study my reflection in the mirror. I am a new man. I am naked, exposed. Liberated.

I plant a line of toothpaste onto my brush. It is time to wash the poison from my mouth.

I jump into the car and rev the engine. I am a man on fire. My feet against the pedals, my hands on the wheel – I am steering myself into a new destiny. The car pulls out of the driveway and I begin my journey into the city.

First stop: his flat. I step inside but he isn't there.

A few items of clothing, which are too smart and pristine to be Tristan's, are balanced on the armrest of his couch. Who left them? Possibly a new man in his life?

I pick up the jacket. It looks costly and new, and smells of some kind of fancy cologne.

I smell a yuppie.

I growl under my breath, throw the jacket on the floor, and go back to my car. It is time to claim my territory.

I go to the shop for provisions. If I am up against a yuppie I need to arm myself.

He is probably treating Tristan with lots of money and wealth; how can I defeat him when all I have given him is mind games and grief. What can I offer Tristan apart from my heart and soul?

First of all I need something to distract a yuppie with, so I pick up a copy of the Financial Times – that should do the trick. A groin guard for in case things get nasty – because we all know some of these faggots fight like girls. Finally, on my way to the counter, I pick up a bottle of champagne to celebrate with if I bring Tristan home. If I fail I can easily just whack the yuppie over the head with it.

Next stop: Janus. I pull up outside, swing the door open and stroll up the bar. My eyes search the tables.

When I recognise his face, my body freezes. I stand there for a moment and stare.

Tristan. He looks up, our eyes meet, and time seems to stop. He opens his mouth in surprise. I feel a knot in my heart but the sight of his face brings a smile to my lips. He never fails to take my breath away.

Someone is with him. His back is turned, all I can see is a cowboy hat on top of a brown coat. He carries on talking to Tristan as I meander over to their table, completely oblivious to the fact that Tristan's attention has been drawn elsewhere.

I stand at the head of the table and we stare at each other for a few moments.

The man in the cowboy hat stinks of that yuppie aftershave.

"Hello, Tristan," I interrupt them.

The cowboy hat turns around. He is broad shouldered and,

I have to admit, handsome. A bit too plain for my tastes, though. I like someone with more character.

"Hi," he says, while Tristan remains still and silent. "You a friend of Tristan's?"

"I suppose you could call me that..." I said.

"Well, sit down then," he offers, motioning to one of the chairs. "I'm Harry. We were just talking about setting Tristan up with a shop to sell his paintings so he can stop getting scammed by that damned gallery—"

"Fascinating," I interrupt him, dryly, as I reach into the pocket of my jacket. "Hey, have you seen this week's issue of the Financial Times—"

"Read it," he shrugs. "It came in the post yesterday, I have a subscription."

Damn.

"Can I just have a moment to talk to Tristan, please?"

"Yeah, sure," he says. "Go ahead."

"Alone."

He raises an eyebrow. "What do you need to say that I can't—"

"It's okay," Tristan suddenly butts in, turning to Harry. "Just give us a moment."

"If he has something to say to you, I want to hear it."

I ignore him. I don't care anymore. This can't wait any longer.

I kneel down in front of Tristan and, as I place my hand on his arm, memories of his bare flesh underneath that shirt come into my mind. Two months ago, his body was mine to touch, caress, and make love to. Just a few words from my mouth and I lost that right.

I want him back.

"Tristan, I need you."

"Don't, Neal," Tristan says, casting his eyes around the bar involuntarily. "It's—"

"I don't care, Tristan. I don't care if everyone is staring at me. I don't care about those silly little games anymore. I just want you."

"Hey man, take it easy," the yuppie interrupts us. "Me and Tristan are—"

I look into Tristan's eyes. He is sceptical. I can see him

doubting my honesty.

"I love you, Tristan. The way I treated you was unforgiveable but I promise I will never do it again. Two months and all I could think about was you!"

His eyes are glistening but I can see confusion and conflict in them. A tear rolls down his cheek, I reach out, and tenderly brush it away with my finger.

"Come with me, Tristan. Now. Please."

"You're that guy he told me about, aren't you!" Harry butts in. "He said you were a complete asshole!"

"Yes," Tristan turns back to his new lover and nods his head. "He is an asshole."

I feel my heart sinking.

"But unfortunately, I love him."

Harry opens his mouth to make another objection but I no longer hear his voice. All I can see is Tristan's face as he turns back to me and faintly smiles. The whole bar of people staring at us disappears. The walls melt away. All that exists is Tristan and me. I reach for his hand and we both get onto our feet.

Just as we make our way out of the bar Harry appears in front of us, blocking our way. He narrows his eyes.

"You bastard!" he yells as he raises his leg and swiftly brings the toe of his boot against my crotch, only to meet the hard shell of my groin guard.

"Stay away from them," I advise. "These balls are Tristan's now."

"I'm sorry, Harry," Tristan says. "But this is something I have to do."

In the end it all came down to the power of words. Words we said to each other but never meant. Words which lived silently in our hearts, never expressed until now.

I wind down the window and feel the breeze against my face. One hand on the steering wheel, the other entwined around his fingers. The world flashes past us in a blur. I turn and look at his face, feeling my heart beating against my chest at the thought that he is in *my* car.

This is our moment, and no one else's.

8
Blisters

"I need to tell you something. I have been trying to tell you for a while… but it's hard…"

The words felt like glass marbles in my throat. They had been there for a long time, needing to be choked out.

"I am not a boy."

I was expecting a violent reaction but all I received was a cold, confused, silent stare at first. Which I could only guess meant she did not understand.

"I mean… I know I was born… like one. But I never felt… right. You must have noticed that something wasn't right, didn't you?"

No answer.

"I think I am a girl… I think I have always been. I tried to be a boy. I tried really hard, but I can't do it anymore. My body is changing… and I *hate* it. It doesn't feel… right…"

My tears were cut-off by the sting of my Grandmother slapping me across the face. She had never done that before. I cried harder, turning away, losing the small amount of courage I had managed to piece together for this.

"You! Silly! Little!" she hit me again with each syllable, her voice cracking with each breath. I cried. Shuffled away. "You're a boy! *Charlie!*"

"No! You don't understand. I don't *feel*—"

"Go to your room!" she exclaimed, pointing towards the stairs. "Go to your room! And don't speak of this *ever* again! Now!"

I think on some level I have always known.

I was an only child. I had no siblings to compare with, but I remember a time of confusion when I was first sent to school and my existence became gendered. We were separated for toilets, PE lessons, even where we sat in the classroom sometimes. By then I knew enough about the world to know that I was, technically, a 'boy', but nothing ever felt right from that day and my life became a silent struggle. I think the other kids knew something wasn't quite right as well. I tried so hard to be normal and blend in but the more I tried, the more it became obvious that I did not belong. I was weedy, wimpy, and soft, but that didn't stop people being tough with me. I was always getting bruised and blistered.

It was when we had sex education classes when I was twelve that I really began to become conscious that something was terribly wrong. I had to sit at the back of the classroom for an hour every week and be told about how hair would grow from my face; and maybe even my chest; my voice would break and drone; and that thing between my legs, which had always felt alien to me, would grow. It made we want to scream. One day I even ran out of the room, crying. Everyone laughed.

In one of the later lessons our teacher delved into the topic of sexuality and half-heartedly recited to us from a book about how some-people-are-different-but-it-is-okay. Other kids giggled and whispered to each other as boys-who-like-boys and girls-who-like-girls were explained, and I waited with creeping anticipation for an explanation for *me*, for what *I* was. It never came; the bell rang and the lesson ended.

That week a turbulent storm played out in my mind and I hardly slept. I had by then begun to realise, on some subconscious level, that I found boys physically attractive but I still had not met one who was nice enough to me for me to like them. I didn't feel like I was gay. Me as a boy, with another boy, somehow felt wrong.

I went to the following lesson a week later with apprehension, hoping that an explanation would come, but the teacher went straight to the topic of contraception, and I was left adrift.

I guess in one way I am lucky because in this day and age people like me have access to the world of the internet. I predictably began with online encyclopaedias and from there I went on to scientific and medical journals. I even found a forum called *Trans-Connect*, where other people who felt the same as me held open discussions and talked to each other.

The string of emotions I felt for finally finding clarification for what was wrong weaved me through a terrifying but liberating journey, an entwining of ominous terror and illumination. It was frightening, but I no longer felt like I was alone. I even signed up with a user account for that forum, though I couldn't bring myself to make any posts because it was all still too raw.

And with it all came the revelation that there were solutions: hormonal treatment could save me from a repulsive biology that was soon to riddle my body.

But this solution was fraught with obstacles. I was still three years, two months, and five days away from being able to go through such treatment without the consent of my parent or guardian.

And that person is my Grandmother.

My Grandmother is a stubborn and traditional woman. I could still remember the last battle I'd had with her a year before. It was after I watched a stomach-turning and enlightening documentary about the meat industry.

"What's the matter?" she asked later that evening, as she carved through the skin of the battery farmed chicken resting on the table. I narrowed my eyes as she drove a greasy carving knife back and forth through its flesh. Throughout our childhoods, a romantic idea of chickens and pigs roaming around farmyards is planted into our minds through misleading books, songs, and cartoons. I had just realised that adults lie too. The idyllic homestead pastures had mostly been replaced by faded, industrial buildings where millions of birds are held in cages, so tightly packed together that their beaks and claws are mutilated to stop them harming each other. *This* was the modern, enlightened world of the 21st century.

"I just want vegetables. Please," I said as I spooned myself some of the carrots and greens she had warmed from the tin. My hand wavered over the gravy jug for a moment, but then I remembered her habit of pouring the left over grease from the baking tray into it.

She stared at me, perplexed, as I helped myself to some boiled potatoes and then tucked into a very plain dinner.

"You think too much. Thinking too much will make people think you are funny."

"It is just wrong. It is wrong, and it needs to be changed."

I don't think any less of her. My Grandmother raised me as if I was her own child. She is full of love and cares for me, but she is simple and from a different time. Back in her day the world was at war. It was a time where the main moral concern was what humans were doing to each other, not to other species and the world. Food was rationed, scarce, and something to be thankful for, not to worry about.

But I am from a different time and I do worry.

For a few weeks *we* were at war, and every day she put a new carcass upon the table and tried to tempt me to eat it. At first I thought she was just doing it to make a point but, after a while, I realised that this was the way it had always been. We had been eating meat every day, and it was something I had taken for granted.

Peace was only reached when both sides had drawn up treaties and concessions were made. We eventually went to the supermarket together and bought vegetarian sausages, gravy, free-range eggs, and responsibly-farmed milk. She later examined the receipt and complained that they were too expensive, so I got myself a paper round to chip in towards the costs.

But despite the fact that I won that round, I knew it was going to be much trickier this time. How could I convince a woman like my Grandmother that I needed to be taken to the doctors and given hormones which would put me through the opposite puberty to what her god intended? That her little grandson Charlie just wanted to grow her hair and fantasised about wearing skirts?

I hate myself for it, but this is how.

"Gran," I said, finally breaking the silence a week later. We had hardly uttered a word to each other since she sent me to my room that day.

I placed a stack of papers on the table in front of her. It was a collection of my research. Explanations by experts and academics for what was wrong with me. I had been carefully choosing which ones to show her for days.

"What is this, Charlie?" she said, leafing through some of the pages with increasingly widening eyes. She looked up at me. Tears were already sopping down my cheeks, and my lower lip was trembling.

"Remember when I had to come live with you..." I whispered. "Because... because I found Mum..."

Swinging from the ceiling. That is how I found Mum, that day, when I came home from school. There has always been an unspoken agreement between us that we don't use the 'S' word. It makes it too real.

Her face went white. I hated myself for that. I hated myself even more for what I said next.

"And you said—" Tears again. I tried to stop them but it was useless. "You said that... if... if only you could go back. That if she told you... and you knew... you would have done anything to stop her from... from—"

"What do you want from me?" she whispered.

"Do you care the same for me?"

"Of course I do!"

"Please Gran. Just read it. It's not something I made up in my head. There are others. And there are things that can be done to help. Please help me. I need help."

I went straight to my room, lay on my bed, and cried for most of the night. I was sure that I would not get any sleep but I must have because at some point I opened my eyes and it was light again. I got ready for school and crept downstairs silently, dreading what I would be up against if I encountered my Grandmother on my way out of the house.

She was waiting for me in the living room.

"You're not going to school today," she said. She was still sitting there, staring at the table – it was like she had not even gone to bed.

"What?" I asked. "Why?"

I didn't go to school for two whole weeks.

The first day I was taken to my doctor. She was fairly understanding but said I could not be diagnosed until I had seen a specialist.

The second day I was taken shopping for clothes. My Grandmother was acting like an automaton, she had not looked me in the eyes once since this whole thing began and she only spoke to me when it was necessary. It made me feel terrible that my emotional blackmail was forcing her to do something she hated. It was like I was holding her hostage but it was really my own head that I had pointed the gun at. She waited outside while I tried on the clothes. I could tell she was embarrassed – I was as well. I received some very peculiar looks when I came out of the changing rooms with a new wardrobe of clothes draped over my shoulder and the whole shop watched us when my Grandmother came back inside to pay.

On the third day we changed my name by Deed Poll. I know that Charlie is technically gender neutral, and that was the exact reason why it had to be changed. I had already decided weeks ago that I wanted to be called Tilly – it means "mighty in battle", and I knew I had much strife ahead of me.

On the fourth day my grandmother rang up my school and finally confessed to them what my 'sickness' was. It took a fifth day, a weekend ceasefire, and then another week of heated debates, requests for detailed reports from my doctor, interventions from the school board, and my assignment for bi-monthly meetings with the school counsellor before suitable terms for my reintroduction were agreed upon.

The following Monday I was back in school, but I was absent from class often throughout the next few months. I went back to see my doctor twice because I was horrified to find out that the waiting list for the specialist was four months. She was, once again, very understanding, but told me that, as being transgendered is still officially classed as a 'mental illness', she could not officially diagnose me until she got a report from a mental health professional, and suggested I pay a bit of money to see a general psychiatrist privately. Even then, it took weeks of harassment until I got my appointment, and, all the while, my body was, still, slowly changing. When I did eventually manage to see a psychiatrist I was forced to answer some very personal questions, but that part was surprisingly easy, and I left the room two hours later feeling lighter. Gran, who was waiting outside, looked like she had just attended a funeral.

Shortly after that I went back to my GP, who confirmed that the psychiatrist had diagnosed me with gender dysphoria and told me what I already knew: that, with my grandmother's consent, I could be prescribed 'puberty blockers' to stop my body from changing. And if, when I am sixteen, my 'symptoms' still persist, and the doctors, psychologists and specialists still agree on my condition, then I could start going through hormone replacement therapy to put my body through female puberty. I was more versed in the legalities, bureaucracies, dangers, possible side-effects, and statistics than any of them. I also knew what she left out: that when I am eighteen I will be legally viable for sexual reassignment surgery.

My Grandmother signed her consent like it was a death warrant – which is not far from the truth. I wanted to comfort her but I couldn't. She still could not look me in the eyes.

But none of this was anything compared to what I went through at school.

I am a weak person. When confronted my instinct is to curl up into a ball, but I have no shell or spines so I am the easiest of prey. I try to hide and keep my head low, but there is something about me that draws predators.

These things have always made me the perfect target in the schoolyard, so you can imagine the effect of throwing me back into the habitat of wolves and sheep with a new name, new skirt, new blouse, and heeled shoes. It was not armour, it was flashing lights and a siren. I was effluvious with the scent of blood.

I think the faculty must have had a stern talk with my classmates about the situation before I was first reintroduced though because, for a while, it was like I was diseased. People stared at me all the time but no one said anything. Even the ones who had been hounding me *before* the change left me alone.

For a while.

It wore off. I began to hear people muttering to each other as I walked down the hallway, and this gradually progressed to more blatant and public displays. Physical attacks were limited to odd occasions when I was caught in an enclosed space and there were no teachers around but verbal abuse was a score-based sport and the mentality of the playground meant that almost everyone had to take a nip once in a while or risk being pulled from the pack. With most of them it was half-hearted and done only under the coaxing of others. Some notably took pleasure in it though.

Ladyboy. Fag. Chick-with-a-dick. Nancy. Freak. Tilly-with-a-willy. Pervert. Boy George. Tranny. No tits. The list goes on and on. Screamed at me down the corridors and always followed by laughter. Muttered in the classroom or whispered into my ear, as I was shoved into the lockers, had my books thrown across the hallway, or was punched in the arms, shoulders, stomach, thigh, chest, or back. Never the face.

The first officially institutionalised attack against me was over my use of the female toilets. I had known from the beginning that it was going to be a possible issue so I had always tried to be quiet and discreet and became a master at holding my bladder so I could only use them at the quietest of times. I was frequently late for lessons because I would often catch my chance while the others were engaged in the post-bell rush.

But no matter how careful I was there would occasionally be other girls there. Some of them would glare at me as I walked in, or even yell abuse at me from outside the cubicle.

But none of them turned it into an official problem until Clarissa, a girl from my own tutor group, encountered me one afternoon. She tried to bar my way but I ran past her, then she and her friends kicked at the door while I was trying to relieve myself.

When I turned up at class a few minutes later, she and her two friends were not there and a sinking feeling crept into my guts. Something was about to go terribly wrong.

Twenty minutes later I was summoned to the headmaster's office

Three weeks after that the GNs were installed. "Gender

Neutral Toilets" are the latest hype in the world of political correctness, and you should have seen the light in the headmaster's eyes when he presented to me and my Grandmother his resolution. He even bragged that they were to be the second school in the whole county to have them. He actually thought that it made the school a progressive forerunner in equality.

It was barbarism in its purest form.

The thing that the teachers did not understand is that most girls of Clarissa's age and temperament lack integrity and conviction. The occasional objections they make about the world around them are fleeting, fickle, and usually more about giving them a brief moment of distinction in a society that constantly pushes kids down and makes them feel ineffectual. The handful of headstrong teenagers who actually have the energy and persistence to bring about change tend to concern themselves with much more global and venerable issues than who is daring to use a (partitioned) cubicle, which just so happens to be next to another (partitioned) cubicle they (may) want to use in the restroom. If the faculty had just paid her little heed she would have soon grown tired and found a new distraction.

My use of the female toilets was a situation that occasionally caused tension, true, but it was one I could live with, whereas the corridor outside the GNs became a feeding ground. It wasn't long until wimpy younger boys were dragged there by bullies, kicking and screaming; and outed homosexuals in the upper years were pressured into taking the detour. Militant feminists fuelled the fire by using them just to make a point, thinking they were helping the situation but, in fact, escalating it. Life became prosperous and easy for predators because cattle in various shapes and sizes were being reared up and penned behind a fence. Clarissa and her friends were the most frequent prowlers, and took upon themselves the duty of sitting on the bench opposite it daily so they could taunt the passers-by as they ate their lunch.

It got to the point where every day I woke up with a sense of dread at the thought of going to school and, after a few months, I was even beginning to contemplate suicide. It was just a stroke of fortune that at that point two things happened which gave me the strength to carry on.

The first thing was that I found something that belonged to my mother, and it changed my life forever.

I was scouring the attic, one day, while my grandmother was at church. I guess I was just bored, more than anything. I was a bit curious about my grandmother because she never really told me much about her life before I came to live with her. I had long given up on finding out anything about my mother because the mere mention of her brought my grandmother to tears, and she hadn't left many things to remember her by, as she had sold anything of value by the time she died.

I found some of her toys, which surprised me, but then I realised that it shouldn't have; my mother was a child too, once, and she grew up in this house, just like me. It was a strange thought. Apart from that, most of it was out-dated junk I guessed was my grandfather's.

I was just going through a suitcase filled with magazines when I found a little box at the bottom which caught my eye and made me gasp because it had my former name on it, in my mother's handwriting,

Charlie.

My heart jumped, and I just stared at it for a while. Eventually, my surprise was overcome by curiosity and I opened it.

Inside it were a pack of cards and a note.

Dearest Charlie,
If you are meant to find this, you will. I will let fate decide
if this path is meant for you.
I am so sorry,
Mother

The cards were faded with age, and each one had its own beautiful watercolour design depicting a scene. It took me a while to realise what they were – tarot cards. This arcane legacy contradicted everything I thought I knew about the pitiful drunk I used to find passed out on the living room floor when I came home from school. I should have guessed she was probably a very different woman before my Dad did... well... what he did to her. My father was nothing more than another bully, and my mother let him break her. I was determined to not let the same thing happen to me.

Throughout the following week, I spent most of my spare moments rifling through them, examining each and every card in detail. They made me consider a whole new side to my mother and feel a connection to her I had never felt before.

I went through the whole pack several times, inventing narratives and scenarios in my mind for each image. The stories often changed a little between viewings, depending upon my mood, which I found fascinating. I began to build a relationship with them.

The second thing happened a week later.

I received a surprise personal message from someone on *Trans-Connect*.

> *Hello,*
> *Feeling a bit shy? Sorry, I have just seen you online a few times, and realised you've never posted. I understand... it took me a while to open up on here as well. BTW I couldn't help but notice on your details that you're from the same town as me!*
> *PM me if you ever want to chat.*

I was wary at first. All these months of being harried at school had made me paranoid about everyone and everything. I worried that it was someone from school lining themselves up to make a cruel joke on me, but then I saw that his particular user was a frequent poster on the discussions, so it seemed to be legitimate.

I replied and we ended up chatting all evening. His name was Ben; he was twenty-three, born female, at the end of his HRT program, and on a waiting list for state-funded surgery. It was a thrill to talk to somebody who was nearing the end of a long journey I had barely started, and it instilled me with hope.

He asked me if I was being hassled at school so I told him about some of it but not the full extent because I was too ashamed.

Eventually we ended up on the topic of the cards I found.

Are you sure she never said anything to you that somehow led you to find that box?

Not that I can remember, I typed back.

Have you used them yet?

I have been looking at them a lot, I replied. *I think they are quite old… I wonder where she got them from…*

What I meant, is have you used them on someone yet? Like, predictions and stuff?

No…

Why not?

I don't have any friends.

You could try them on me if you like?

I don't really believe in stuff like that… I said, making the first excuse I could find. The thought of testing myself on another person made me feel nervous.

I'm not sure if I do either, he replied. *But there is something… weird about your story that interests me. Go on, flip some cards over and let's see what happens.*

I turned some cards over and put them in line. The Hierophant, The Fool, The Ten of Wands, The Chariot, and The Ace of Wands. The Hierophant bestows a hat upon someone who much resembles The Fool; who naively ventures off into the mountains. In the Ten of Wands someone was trapped between impending spears, struggling to maintain their ground. The Chariot, depicts someone being raised upon the shoulders of two strong women. The Ace of Wands, an empowering conclusion, presents the final prize: a glowing rod wrapped in cloth.

I think someone has deceived you, and because of this you will soon find yourself in a difficult situation. You can trust in the aid of two women who will appear out of the woodwork. You will emerge from this challenge in a better position than you were before.

My occasional exchanges with Ben in the evening made life a little more bearable and he soon managed to coax me into making posts on the forum, and other people on it began chatting to me. The next thing I knew I was an active member of an online community with people I shared an understanding with.

School remained more or less the same but finally having a handful of people I could almost call friends, even if it was just over the internet, made me cope with it better.

We all had to do a short presentation on an ethical issue a couple of weeks later. It was a task most of the students did half-heartedly but my confidence had recently been boosted by my contacts online so I was happy to have a chance to try and spread awareness about the hidden side to our meat industry.

I was laughed at and people soon had another thing to tease me about. Kids who were not even in that lesson goaded me for weeks after with jokes about how far my love for animals extended.

I got a message from Ben a while later. He was a bit freaked out because it appeared that everything I predicted for him in that tarot card reading had come true: an ambitious and sly colleague who had been jealous of his growing position in the office had been misleading him about his workload and then lying to the managers about it in an attempt to get him fired, but eventually two of his female peers had stepped in to help him expose the truth. The colleague was fired, which opened up an opportunity for Ben's promotion.

I was not quite sure what to make of all of that, but he eventually managed to convince me to offer readings to other people. I got more and more positive feedback and started giving readings to people online on a regular basis.

This transitioned into the real life a couple of months later when a girl in the year above me caught me playing with my cards in a corner of the library. When I saw her coming over I made to hide them away because the last thing I wanted was to draw any more unwanted attention to myself, but she was surprisingly intrigued and not in a mean way. She begged me to try them out on her. I caved in, and two days later she returned, squealing about how some of the things I foretold had already come true. I soon had a hoard of her friends harassing me to have their futures' told as well.

Somehow, after only giving readings to a few kids in the senior years, word of my new found "hobby" spread across the school like wildfire, and a few days later it was a regular addition to the ever-growing list of things my classmates harassed me over. My change of gender, the animal rights presentation, and their reaction to this new one fell into an escalating pattern. It vexed me because any other kid who dabbled in Tarot or spoke out against animal cruelty would have received little heed but it seemed that being the only transgendered person in my school had imposed upon me the status of an infamous celebrity – I drew unwanted attention by just existing.

I tried to keep my head down and even stopped bringing my cards to school but the ones who appreciated my readings nagged me and I soon realised that, no matter how hard I tried to fade into the background, they were now always finding *something* to talk about. My school year were fascinated by me, and activities which were fairly standard for a girl of my age, such as experimenting with makeup, getting my ears pierced, and even the slightest alterations to my hair, were immediately noticed and drew wolves who had heard the whispers to come and howl at me.

One lunchtime, a boy called Jarvis blocked my path by slamming his arm against the wall. I tried to skirt around him but he just stood there, staring at me with a peculiar expression on his face.

"Can you really do it?" he asked.

"Do what?" I replied, guardedly. I looked around, realising

that he was alone. Which was unusual; people usually only gave me bother when they had an audience to impress upon.

"The cards," he uttered. "The future stuff."

"Err, well I don't really…" I began to make an excuse; something about the vibe I was getting from him was making me uneasy.

"Can you read for me?" he asked.

He pulled me into a classroom, and cast a wary glance down the corridor before shutting the door. I sensed his need for secrecy so I sat at a table in the far corner of the room.

"So… what do I do?" he asked, uncharacteristically nervous as he ambled towards me.

"Just split the pack," I said, gesturing him to sit on the other side. He sat down and tepidly picked up half the cards, then turned to me questioningly.

"Put them down," I said.

I shuffled the two halves together, and as soon as I turned them over I knew something was deeply wrong. A heavy silence hung between us for a few moments.

"Something has upset the stability in your life at home," I began, eyeing up The World card. It was upside down.

He didn't say anything but I took the way he shifted uncomfortably and looked down at the table as a confirmation.

"I think it's your parents… there is a… friction," I said, choosing my words carefully. The cards were hinting that there was much more than mere friction going on, but I could see that Jarvis was unsettled.

"Is it going to get better?" he asked.

I turned to the last few cards for the resolution. The Tower, The Lovers – also reversed –, the Hanged Man.

"Only when your father leaves," I said. "You need to help your mother get—"

"No!" he exclaimed, shaking his head violently. "I asked if it is going to get better! The way it was before!"

I paused, cautiously deliberating my next words.

"It will get better," I said. "But first he has to leave. *He* is what is wrong, Jarvis. Not you or—"

He seemed close to tears.

"Jarvis," I whispered, not quite knowing how to respond to a boy who had spent the last year giving me regular bruises and was now sitting before me teary-eyed and looking so vulnerable. "What has your father been doing?"

"What the hell do you know!" he snapped, jumping up from the table. His face turned red. "You're just a freak! You don't know shit!"

"It's the cards," I whispered, suddenly feeling scared. "I can't change them. Jarvis… you can talk to me. Or someone. You need help."

"No! Forget it!" he yelled, as he stomped towards the door. "If you tell *anyone* about this you're dead!"

The whole incident shook me a little, and a nervous feeling crept into my stomach when I remembered he was in the same class as me for my next lesson. After the bell rang I went to line up outside the classroom, trying to be inconspicuous. I thought that if I just did that then Jarvis would avoid me.

I had never been so wrong in my life.

He snatched my bag from my shoulder as he came up behind me. I tried to grab it back but one of the other boys pushed me away.

"Oh, look what we have here…" Jarvis sneered as he reached into the opening. "What does the tranny carry with her?" He pulled out a stick of mascara and tossed it over his shoulder. "Makeup! Oh – that's a pretty pencil case…"

By now he had caught everyone's attention and they were all laughing. "What's this, Tilly?"

He pulled out my tarot cards. They were wrapped in purple silk, but he soon had that unravelled and floating to the floor.

"Nancyboy has decided he's a gyppo now as well!" he exclaimed as he began to rifle through them.

In desperation I tried to push my way past the boy who was holding me back but it was hopeless, he just shoved me aside.

"Oh look," he said. "Tilly's fighting back. His balls must be growing."

He then kicked my bag, sending it skidding up the corridor. I barely noticed. I was more concerned with what Jarvis was doing to my mother's tarot cards. He was now tossing them into the air, sending them drifting down like little white feathers.

I ran over to catch them but the other boy just pushed me back again, this time so hard my head struck the wall and I cried out.

"I shouldn't fight you, really," said the boy who had been landing me with punches for months. "You think you're a girl now? Well, maybe you should fight one." He turned to one of the girls standing a few yards away, Gemma. She was a quiet member of our year group, more like a timid sheep than a wolf – I had never really had much bother from her before.

"Gemma," he said. "I bet even *you* could beat up Tilly… go on."

"But…" she said, looking at me and then turning back to Jarvis, searching for an excuse. "I—"

"Oh, don't worry," he grinned as he kicked my bag against the wall again. "He's a wimp. Go on! *Do* it!"

Jarvis had now finished scattering my cards and was now busy scuffing them against the murky floor with the soles of his shoes. I was almost blind with rage. My mother's cards!

I ran over to save them but Gemma kicked me. It appeared that even sheep had hooves when they were pressured by the herd. I tried to push her aside but she came bouncing back, kicking me in the shins over and over again. I just wanted my cards back. I kicked her back, to serve as a warning, but she wouldn't stop. Jarvis was still stamping on my mother's cards and she was in the way.

I slapped her across the face and her head rolled to the side. She looked at me in shock and placed a hand to her reddening cheek. Suddenly the laughter stopped and the corridor went silent. Clarissa stepped between us, grabbing Gemma's hand and pulling her away.

Jarvis and the other boys must have realised that this time they had taken it way too far, because they cleared the area. I went down on my knees and began gathering my cards and everything else they had tipped from my bag.

The headmaster was out that day, so it was Ms Hodgeson, the deputy headmistress, who I was sent to see. She was a broad woman with thick, sturdy legs like tree-trunks. I had never spoken to her before because she was primarily a PE teacher for the girls.

"Sit down," she said when I entered the room.

It was a shock for me to be here; I wasn't expecting the incident to be reported to the teachers at all – wouldn't bringing it all out in the open, and get them in even more trouble than myself?

In a way I was elated because I had never had the courage to come to the teachers about all the stuff that had been going on but now that it had been done for me, things could only change for the better. Maybe—

"You are suspended for three days."

"Wh-at?!" I gasped.

"You hit a *girl*, Tilly."

"But she was kicking me and—" I began to explain.

She silenced me by shaking her head. "She and Clarissa have already told me what happened," she said with finality.

"She attacked *me*!" I exclaimed. "Jarvis and Gary stole my cards. They were my mother's, and—"

"I don't want to hear any of it," she said, calmly. "I have been teaching Gemma for two years, and she is a very sweet girl. She told me about how you got yourself into a disagreement with the other boys but, Tilly, she was only trying to intervene! I will have a word with them but—"

I didn't even listen to the rest of what she said because all I felt was shock coupled with despair. I had never felt so trapped and isolated in my whole entire life. I stared at the carpet and, in that moment, the last shred of any childish naïvety I had about the world being fair died.

That incident taught me not to trust the system, and it taught the wolves that teachers were gullible and would side with the majority, no matter how implausible their story was, so they carried on testing my limits. I kept my head down and took it all without making a noise. I just didn't care about anything anymore. My grades dropped. I never took my tarot cards or anything of value back to school. I withdrew more and more into myself.

I squirmed through it all until the summer finally came, but it passed by way too fast. When I came back in September, the boys were wider of frame and the girls were fuller in the chest. The tablets I was taking were keeping my body in a developmental stasis while everyone else was going through puberty. Even though I had a prepubescent figure, I had learned ways of wearing clothes to disguise it; also, I had the high voice of a child while the boys were all beginning to sound like men. Reluctantly, they were finally starting to think of me as a girl, which is probably why they fought back so hard with verbal abuse and the fabrication of weekly rumours, mostly involving my penis.

The truth is, I don't need them to remind me of my penis. It is always there, waiting for me, every time I use the bathroom or take a shower, and in those unbearable moments when I wake up in the morning to it raising the bed sheets. I wear girls' clothes, apply makeup, my hair is long now. All of these things make me feel happy and nearer to finding myself, but it also lures people around me into feeling like they should try to make my life miserable. I feel like Tilly in my heart, and I am adamant when it comes under discussion that I am a girl, but the truth is that I am deeply insecure about it. I always will be until the day that I am old enough for them to cut that last piece of Charlie away…

By Christmas I was in despair again. I needed something in life to look forward to.

It was time to take matters into my own hands.

"What have you been doing?" my grandmother asked me one day when I walked into the living room a few months later. She had just returned from church and was staring at me shrewdly, as if she had just noticed something.

"What?" I asked, innocently. I was genuinely confused.

"You're changing," she said, looking me up and down.

"Changing?"

"You… your… body," she said.

My stomach turned over and I knew that my face must have already given me away so there was no point in lying to her.

"What have you been doing, Tilly?" she asked, her

widened eyes looking me up and down. "You've been taking something else, haven't you?"

I nodded.

"Hormones?" she exclaimed. "Where did you get them from, Tilly? You're not supposed to have them for another two years yet!"

"One year and nine months," I corrected. "I ordered them online."

Her hand went to her chest and, for a horrible moment, I thought she was going to have a heart attack. I studied the carpet.

"You must stop," she said.

"It doesn't matter anyway!" I exclaimed. "It's useless. I've been taking them for months, and look! Hardly anything has changed!"

"Tilly," my grandmother said, her voice now softer. "Come with me for a moment."

She got out her digital camera and told me to stand in the middle of the living room so she could take a photo. Afterwards she got me to help her upload the picture onto her computer and brought it up on the screen.

"Can't you see?" she said, bringing out another photograph of me, taken a year ago, and holding it up.

I looked at it again. The proportion between my hips and shoulders had swayed, and even the shape of my face had altered a little. My skin was thinning and becoming softer and the fat was being redistributed, just as I read it would.

And even though the buddings on my chest could hardly be called breasts yet, seeing the whole picture of what had happened to me over a space of time made me appreciate that it was still a beginning. I stared at the screen for a long time.

"You know... I haven't seen you smile for a long time, Tilly," she said.

She also looked happy, and I realised that I had not really seen that for a while, either. She was happy because I was happy. It was a moment I would always remember because it marked a transition not just for myself, but for her too: she had finally let go of her grandson and learned to love her granddaughter.

I think it must be the boys at school who are really psychic, or maybe my happiness was too obvious and I had too much of a spring in my step, because it was the very next day that they brought me crashing back down again.

It was lunchtime. I was on the green outside the humanities' building. It was spring and the sun had just come out so I was sitting on the grass reading a book.

And then Jarvis and three of his friends walked over to me.

"What'yer reading, Tilly," he said cheerily as they closed in.

He tried to grab the book from me but I jammed it into my bag and ducked away from him. I was practised at making a hasty retreat by then.

"We were talking to you, Tilly!" one of his friends said, pulling me back. "There's no need to be rude."

"Leave me alone!" I said, shrugging him off. I started to walk away but a foot appeared between my legs and tripped me over, sending me rolling down the bank.

By now others had noticed something was going on and I heard laughter all around me.

"Clumsy!" Jarvis yelled sardonically, and then he turned to the gathering crowd of spectators. "*Charlie* is still not used to those heels. I'm not surprised though, with those massive feet!"

"And that swinging thing between his legs! It's bad for balance!" another added, dangling an emphatic finger from his crotch.

"My name is *Tilly*!" my voice cracked.

"Oh, really?" he said. "A girl are you? Why don't we check?"

They came for me. I tried to run but by now there was a ring of people around me and they blocked my path. One of them grabbed my legs, another grabbed my arms. They turned me over so my face was in the grass. I kicked and thrashed but they were all bigger and stronger than me.

"Let's see what Tilly really is!" Jarvis howled, as he reached for my waist and pulled down my skirt.

"No!" I screamed. "No! Stop it! Stop!"

But he and the other members of the pack carried on

laughing as they tore open my tights.

With shaking fingers, I finally came clean to Ben that night and told him about what had been happening at school. He was mortified and shocked at the extent of it all and plied me with endless questions until I ended up telling him about everything that had been happening over the last couple of years.

You can't go back there.

I have to, I typed back. *If my grandmother finds out how bad it is she might blame it on me being a girl and try to make me be a boy again. I can't do that. It is the only thing I have keeping me going.*

Have you ever heard of a place called Janus? he eventually asked, after a long silence. *I used to go there when I was younger.*

Janus? What is that?

It's a club. I made a lot of friends there. It's a place where people are accepted, even if they are a bit different. I always felt safe there.

I don't know if I can, I replied.

Why?

I am… nervous. About going to places.

Tilly, you are one of the bravest people I have ever met.

I frowned.

You don't know me, I eventually typed back. *I am weak. That is why they pick on me.*

Tilly, I only dared to admit to the world I was transgender when I was seventeen years old. You came out in a school that was already bullying you when you were thirteen. Don't you realise how outstanding that is?

No, I replied. *I did it because the thought of*

turning into a boy scared me. There was nothing brave about it.

You think that turning into a girl didn't scare me? Tilly, I felt the same but the difference is that the reaction it would cause from others scared me more.

I have just never been able to... pretend I am something I'm not. I admitted.

And you think that is a weakness? Tilly, you let them get away with murder because you are too timid to stick up for yourself, but you have something that none of them will ever have. Integrity.

I stared at the screen for a while and different kind of tears came to my eyes. They were because I knew what Ben was saying was true and I finally felt the beginning of something I had never felt before: self-worth.

Thank you for talking to me, Ben. I then typed. *You are my only friend, and I don't know what I would do without you.*

It is always a pleasure chatting to you, Tilly. Be brave, and whatever you do, don't let them break you. You are worth a hundred of every one of them.

I am just scared that something bad is going to happen, I admitted.

Why?

I just have this feeling... I have lost faith in everything. The school. The kids. The teachers. I have no respect for them anymore. I'm afraid of what I might do.

"You just want attention," Alexander said. He was one of those kids who are always trying to get in with the cool crowd but never quite achieve their ranks. One of his favourite methods for his repeated attempts was to ridicule me while they were around. On this particular day both he and I were sitting in our Art lesson within earshot of Jarvis and some of his friends, so he was exploiting the situation. I kept my eyes glued to the paper, carried on scraping the pastel across the page until the curve went completely black. Hoping that maybe, if I pressed harder, it would drown out the sound of his voice.

"I mean, first it was that animal rights crap," he said. Some of the others around him sniggered. "That presentation you did in RE about how you don't eat meat because the poor little chickens can't flap their wings. I mean, come on, who actually cares about that shit?"

"Then it was the whole, 'I'm a girl really'," he pitched his voice high and flapped his arms around. "And then when we got bored of that one—"

If only, I thought to myself as the temperature of my blood rose. *If only you and the rest of you sad kids got bored of me. If only you had something else to—*

"You came in with those little cards, pretending to be all witchy and supernatural. You're not even a real girl, *Charlie*."

A lump twisted in my throat. No matter how much armour I gathered around myself to try to stop them hurting me, there was always their endless supply of that particular ammunition. My piercing weakness.

More cackling laughter.

"Where the hell did you get them from, anyway?" he said, once the laughter had died down. He was obviously missing the adulation. "Is there a special website where sad little attention seekers like you buy that shit from?"

"My mother," I whispered, a flashing memory of the way she swung from the ceiling flashed before my eyes. I tried to blot it out, but it lingered. "They were my mother's."

"I bet she's a freak too. She must be."

"She's dead."

There was a flicker of guilt for a moment, and his friends must have felt it too, because they all stopped laughing and turned their faces down to the table. But Alexander carried on staring at me, his face going red.

Typical, I thought, the hatred in me simmering. *He just*

overstepped the mark and all he cares about is that he lost face in front of his friends.

"I think you're just making that up as well," he eventually said. By now his friends had acquired shreds of decency and were no longer backing up his starlight show. "It's all just a load of bullshit. Come on, just admit it."

I turned away, looked back at the picture I was creating. Tried to think of what else needed to be done to complete it. All I could see was red. I clenched my fists under the table. Tried to ignore him.

"How did she supposedly die then?" he asked. I made the mistake of peeking up at him and saw that he was grinning. "Did you choke her with your cock?"

And then something snapped within me.

I pushed the table over, and the whole class jumped as it toppled, skidding across the floor.

"Why don't you just *fuck off*!" I screamed as I ran across the room and grabbed him by the hair, yanking his head back. His eyes went wide.

"Listen to me you little cunt! When I was a child I saw shit that would make your skin crawl! I am sorry, I am so *fucking* sorry if my pain and the way I deal with it is inconvenient for you! I am sorry that your life has been so fucking perfect you can't understand the way I am. But just do me a favour and stay the fuck away from me, you little fucking *maggot*." I growled, slamming his face onto the desk.

I turned to the others. Clarissa, and the other girls who instigated my ban on the female toilets. Jarvis, and the boys who yanked my skirt down on the green. "Why don't you *all* just fuck off? If I am such a fucking attention seeker then why don't you all just rise above it and leave me alone?"

I slammed my palm on the desk of one of the boys, not remembering why, but just knowing that I *hated* him. "Can't you see that all I want is to be left alone?" My eyes circled the room. All of them. "Just *fuck off*! If I was so fucking desperate for you all to notice me, then why is it that sometimes I just want to fucking die!" I kicked the supply cupboard. "What is it which is so sad about your lives and makes you all so fucking *fascinated* by me?" I grabbed the nearest jar someone had been swilling their paintbrush in and flung it at the window. "And then you have the fucking nerve to tell me that I want this shit? Tell me, retards, if I really wanted this shit, why is it that I would quite happily never see any of your fucking faces ever again? Just fuck off. Fuck off! Fuck Off! FUCK OFF!" I grabbed a chair and threw it at the door. "Fuck off!" It skidded across the floor and two boys had to jump from their seats to avoid it. "Just fuck off!"

And then I caught my breath and realised where I was.

Alexander had a hand cupped to his face; he was bleeding from the nose. A line of kids had dirty paint water splashed over their shirts. A window was broken. My pastels were scattered everywhere. A cupboard was dented and hanging by a single hinge. A table was upturned. A chair was on its side. Everyone was staring at me. Everyone was silent.

I ran. I knew my grandmother was at a WI gathering that day so I went straight home. I had no idea what I was going to do next. Within five minutes the phone started ringing. I tried to ignore it but it just carried on and on. Eventually I picked it up.

"Is a Mrs Harper there?" I heard my headmaster's voice on the other end.

"No, she isn't," I said.

"Tilly?" he said, swiftly sounding flustered. "Is that you?"

I didn't say anything.

"Look, Tilly… what has happened is very serious. We need you back here. With your Grandmother."

"I'm not going back."

"Well… er… I am sorry you feel that way, Tilly… but you are enrolled at this school, and unfortunately there are going to be consequences for—"

"Oh will you just *fuck. Off*!" I cried. "Listen to me. I am not going anywhere near your shitty school ever again. So forget about suspensions or whatever you want to do. I quit—"

"It is not as simple as that, I'm afraid. You have abused a

fellow student and vandalised school property."

"*I've* been abusive?" I exclaimed, and shockingly, I started laughing. After everything that had just happened I was *laughing*. It was like I had finally snapped and gone crazy. "I've been abused by those little shits of yours for years and you've done *nothing* to stop it!"

"We have been more than… accommodating to your… needs."

"I'm not coming back. So you can take your meetings and your procedures and your stupid, bloody gender-neutral toilets, and shove them up your ass!"

He gasped and then I heard some scuffling noises. I was just about to hang up when another voice came on the line.

"Tilly, this is Mrs Hodgeson, deputy headmistress, here," she said (as if I was going to forget who that silly little bitch was). "Please report to the headmaster's office *now*, or I will have to call the police."

"Do it!" I exclaimed. "I could tell them some *very* interesting stories."

I ran straight upstairs to my room and hurriedly got ready for a swift exit. I didn't actually want to be there if the police came round because I didn't trust them either. I ripped off my uniform and got changed into a skirt, corset and black coat. I let my hair down, gave it a quick brush and coated my mouth in lipstick.

I remembered that place Ben told me about – Janus – and did a quick search for it online to find directions. This was the push I needed to go there. There was nowhere else left for me to go. I was on the edge. If I didn't find *something* there to turn my life around, I didn't want to carry on living.

I turned over some tarot cards before I left, asking if I should go. The answer I got was a definite "yes", but it included The Death card and The World card – which inflated the nervous bubbles which were already burbling in my stomach: whatever was about to happen to me there would be life changing and dramatic.

Just before I left, I piled up all my school uniforms into an old bin we had rusting in the yard, poured methylated spirit over them, and set it alight. It was cathartic, and would serve as a message to anyone the school sent over.

Janus was a little flashier than I was expecting. It had a shiny new sign above the door and the walls looked like they had been painted very recently. When I first entered the main bar downstairs it was more or less deserted, which was not surprising for that time of day. I got a glass of cola and sat in the corner, waiting for something to happen.

It stayed this way for a couple of hours, which gave me more than enough time to brood over everything that had just happened, everything which had led to me being here, and then, suddenly, in the early evening there was an explosion of people filing in through the door. Most of them were dressed in black and didn't seem much older than me. Angry rock music thundered from the speakers, making the floor tremble.

I began to feel nervous.

I was also confused. Didn't Ben say this was a place where people were free to be different? Everyone seemed very much the same to me. Eventually someone caught my eye, not just because they stood out from the others in the fisherman's pants which ballooned from around their legs and the black netted top they were wearing over their t-shirt, but also because those figure-hiding garments combined with their wavy hair made me realise that I could not tell if they were male or female. They walked straight up to the bar like they owned the place and, after a brief chat, the barman handed over to them a bindle stuffed with possessions.

I was intrigued by this person and ready for a refill so I went over to the bar only to find that when I got there I didn't have enough courage to start a conversation. I stood there nervously, not knowing how to introduce myself. I didn't need to in the end because they waved at me.

"Hi…" I said.

"What's your name?"

"Tilly," I replied. "What's yours?"

"Sam," they said, which of course gave no further clues to their gender. Their voice was no indication either, because I couldn't figure out if it was a low alto or high tenor.

"You new here then?" they asked.

I nodded. "A friend told me about this place…"

Sam studied me. "This place has seen better days," he/she then said, turning their gaze to the newest horde of people making their way to the bar. They were all dressed in black. "I don't come here so much anymore… the vibe has gone a bit sour."

"Why are you here then?" I asked.

"Frelia – a friend of mine – told me to come here tonight. I hope it's bloody important… I also had to collect this," they said, tapping the stuffed cloth tied to the end of the stick. "I left it here a while ago… crazy night…"

Just then I heard a snigger behind me and turned around. My heart skipped a beat when I caught sight of a face I recognised. It was one of the girls from school. I couldn't remember her name, but she laughed at me and then whispered into the ear of someone next to her.

"Are you okay?" Sam asked, his/her eyes going from me, to the girl from my school. The whole gang of people she was with were now staring at me.

I shook my head.

"Come with me," Sam said, taking my hand and pulling me away from them. I didn't look back but I could still hear them sniggering.

Ben told me this was a place I would be safe, where people wouldn't care, but it was all a lie. There were wolves here. There were always wolves.

I felt a degree of safety with Sam around though, and he/she fascinated me. Everything about this stranger I had just met conveyed an aura of bold indifference. I could feel those kids watching us as we walked up the stairs and it made me nervous, but Sam maintained a care-free grace and the laughing seemed to fall to deaf ears.

At the top of the staircase we had to skirt around a guy in a big coat who was staring at faces of everyone who walked past. The odd thing about him was that he was dressed so plainly that it actually made him stand out.

"Is this better?" Sam asked, as he/she led me down the upper corridor.

"Yes," I said. "Thank you."

"What's the deal with those kids? Do you know them?"

I nodded. "Well, one of them… she goes to my school.

They aren't nice there... and I am... in trouble..."

Sam opened a door and pulled me into a room. We stood there in silence for a few moments. I looked at Sam again and still couldn't figure out whether Sam was male or female. I was tempted to ask but it seemed inappropriate. Who was *I* to grill someone about gender specifications, and what exactly would it change if I did find out?

"What kind of trouble?"

We were cut off by the door opening. An odd looking boy with a large mouth and one of his front teeth missing entered the room and turned straight to Sam.

"Hey dude. You're back..." he said, somewhat awkwardly. Sam's eyebrows narrowed and it became clear there was some kind of animosity between them.

"I thought you'd be here," Sam said, dryly.

"Look, I'm sorry about what happened. I—"

"Pag, this isn't the time," Sam interrupted, flatly. "Do me a favour and look after this girl for a while. I need to find Frelia."

"Errr... yeah. Sure," Pag said, turning to me for the first time. "Hey dude, I'm Pag. What's your name?"

"Tilly."

When Sam first left the room all Pag did was stand gawkily by the door but then, after a few moments of stilted silence, he pulled up a chair and sat opposite me.

"Are you okay, dude?" he asked. "You look upset."

"I'm *not* a dude!" I yelled.

Pag's eyes widened at my outburst. "Oh shit, look du – oh shit, I mean – look, I'm sorry. I just call everyone dude. I know you're a girl."

"No," I shook my head. "You don't understand. I was born a boy..."

"Is that why those people down there were laughing at you?" he asked.

"You saw that?"

He nodded. "I saw Sam taking you up the stairs. They were following you, so I. Oh shit!" he exclaimed, slamming his palm on his head. "I didn't mean to worry you. Look, just stay here, and you'll be fine."

I looked at the door nervously. They were looking for me,

and worse, I was starting to need the toilet. I was trapped. This was even *worse* than school. At least there the corridors have a degree of safety because they couldn't beat you when the teachers were around.

"I shouldn't have to stay here!" I screamed. My blood was turning hot again; it had been in a tepid state all day so it didn't take much to bring me back to boiling fury. It had been building up for a long time.

"I know…" he said. "I know…"

"And I need the bloody toilet!" I roared. I just didn't care anymore. They could even kill me if they wanted to. I was sick of running away.

"No!" Pag yelled, coming after me. "Tilly!"

I burst out of the room and found the corridor swarming with people. I spotted the girls' bathroom. It was only a few feet away.

"That's her!" someone yelled and then suddenly everyone's attention was drawn to me. I tried to ignore them but they ringed around me and blocked my path.

"Where are you going?" that girl from school said, appearing in front of me with an exhilarated gleam on her face. "You've already been banned from the ladies'!" she proclaimed, pushing me back. Another pair of hands behind me then pushed me forward and it started a pattern. I was flung back and forth while people laughed.

"Stop it!" Pag swiftly appeared, stepping into the ring and grabbing my shoulders. "Just leave her alone!"

"It's not a 'her'!" someone proclaimed. "She's not a real girl!"

There was a disturbance in the crowd, and another girl shoved her way through the hordes of gathered people. She was dressed in torn jeans, and had three rings hanging from her eyebrow. She was making her way towards me.

"It worked! It worked!" she said, joyfully, as she grabbed my hands, as if I was an old friend, and looked me in the eyes. "You're going to be okay now," she whispered.

"Who are you?" I whispered.

"I'm Frelia," she greeted. "It's a long story!"

Her attention then turned to the crowd of people around us, and her face went from warm and welcoming, to a cold and stony expression. The crowd all abruptly went quiet: somehow they already knew that this was a girl to avoid being reckoned with.

"You can all bugger off now! The show is over!" she announced.

"She – I mean *he* – is trying to use our toilet!" a girl protested.

"So what?" Frelia said, shrugging. "Why do you care?"

"It's got a penis!" she retorted. "It should use the boys'!"

"My name is Tilly," I said between gritted teeth.

"I don't want it using ours either!" a boy declared. "He might look at my junk."

My temperature was rising again. So was my need for the toilet. I exploded, scrambling my way towards the door. I made it a few feet before I was pushed and shoved and sent reeling to the floor. I yelled out in fury but a blow caught the side of my face and made me dizzy. I curled up into a ball to protect myself. I had been here before, and I knew a long sequence of kicks and blows were to come.

But they didn't. Something changed. I heard loud thuds and other sounds of disturbance from a few feet away.

I dared myself to look up. Pag and Frelia were brawling with a crowd of kids behind me, while the ones in front were being fought off by a pair of young men I didn't recognise. Sam suddenly materialised from nowhere, swinging his/her bindle to clear the area around them and then lunging it into a boy's gut, sending him falling back. Another boy and girl emerged from the woodwork and called out Frelia's name. It was chaos and people were fighting everywhere, but it was easy for them to figure out which side they were on because the enemy were all clad in black.

I got to my feet. By this point Sam and the two guys had managed to fight their way over, and they all formed a circle around me.

"Frelia!" one of them said. "I'm here."

"Thanks, Pikel," she said over her shoulder.

"So *this* is the really important thing I had to be here for," Sam said drily. "You really know how to organise a party these days, Frelia. How the hell did you know *this* was going to happen?"

"If I told you I'd have to kill you."

The kids were all clustered at the end of the corridor, none of them daring to get into the range of Sam's broomstick handle.

"Are you okay?" a girl in a patchwork dress said, putting an arm around me. "I'm Namda."

I nodded, almost in tears because I was so overwhelmed by the fact that so many strangers had come to my aid. Not one person had ever done such a thing for me in my entire life, and now I was being protected by numerous people I didn't even know.

"Go use the toilet, Tilly," Frelia said; this caused an uproar of protests, but Sam, Pikel, and Pag held their ground.

I pushed the door open and found the lavatory was completely empty. I could hear shouting coming from outside so I knew I should try to be quick.

I climbed up onto the counter where the sinks were, crouched, pulled down my tights, lifted up my skirt, and urinated, spreading a pool over the floor – to show Janus just how much I appreciated the venue and the clientele.

"You done?" Frelia yelled over the racket of voices when I ventured back to the corridor.

I nodded.

"Okay, time to leave," Frelia decided.

"I couldn't agree with you more," Namda muttered.

"I know a way around the back," Frelia said.

Some of the kids tried to follow us but a few swings of Sam's stick kept them at bay. We rushed down the dimly lit corridor and Frelia guided us through a network of cluttered rooms and hallways, into the labyrinth of Janus.

"Hello!" a voice called out, making me jump. We all turned our heads, and a group of teenagers carrying musical instruments in plastic cases emerged from the shadows.

"Who the fuck are you?" Frelia asked, suspiciously.

"We are Sunset Haze," a petite girl in a grey dress said.

"I know you! You guys played last week!" one of Frelia's friends exclaimed. "You were really good! I—"

"This isn't the time, Kev!" Pikel interrupted him.

"What makes you think you should come with us?" Frelia

asked. "I don't even know who you are."

"You're not the only one who's special here," the girl replied, knowingly.

"Fair enough," Frelia said, one side of her mouth curving into a half-smile.

"I'm Ellen," she said, and then presented the rest of her band. "This is Patrick, Jack, Faye, Amelia, and Steve."

"Well, Ellen, I have news for you," Frelia said, once the introductions were over. "I don't have a damn clue where we are going, yet…"

"Neal's opened a new bar," a young man with blonde hair suggested. "I think it's pretty empty right now."

"Good idea, Tristan. We'll head there," Frelia decided.

"Can we make a little detour?" Ellen cut in gently. "There are two more people we are meant to find…"

We ventured outside and I felt giddy and liberated. One of the girls from Ellen's band introduced herself to me. Her name was Faye. She was about my age and had a warm smile. She pulled out a flute and began to play a song that lightened the mood a little as we made our way through this offbeat part of town. I looked around me, surprised at how large a crowd we had become. It felt like together we had created an energy, and it was intoxicating. We were on an adventure and I didn't even know what its purpose was or where it was headed but that didn't matter.

Ellen led the way and eventually we stopped outside an abandoned shack. After some coaxing, a girl with dishevelled hair and torn, dirty clothes crawled out from underneath the wreckage. Sam and Pag rushed over to embrace her, and the three had a touching, teary reunion. Her name was Halann.

With our number increased by one, we carried on making our way and I joined Ellen at the head of the crowd for a while. Her enigmatic eyes appeared to be following something that I couldn't see, and occasionally her lips moved silently as if she was whispering to someone that was not really there. The other members of her band weren't perturbed by this at all and seemed to accept it as normal.

The second stop she made was by a lane in some neighbourhood. She signalled for us all to halt and motioned a finger to her lips.

"You and you," she whispered, pointing to Frelia and me. "Come with me. The rest of you wait here."

We silently followed her down a dim alleyway and, after we turned a few corners, we heard something scuffling in the darkness. I caught sight of a girl. She was clearly scared, and she backed up against the wall of a shed like a terrified kitten.

"Leave me alone!" she screamed between panted breaths. "Just go! Go! Pretend you didn't see me!"

"Don't worry, Elaine," Ellen called out to her softly. "We're here to help."

"How do you know my name? Oh my god! Look, I didn't do it!" she cried, shaking her head frantically. "I didn't do it!"

"I know you didn't," Ellen whispered, slowing edging closer. It was only then that I realised that this girl was covered in blood and was holding a large kitchen knife in her hand. "My sister – you can see her, can't you. Just like you can see the other girls. They guided me to you. I am here to help. He's gone now, Elaine. And I promise that from now things are going to get better for you. Drop the knife!"

Elaine stared at Ellen for a long time. And then she let the knife fall from her hand and it clattered across the ground.

Ellen then turned to Frelia. "Find a place in time no one will ever find it," she said.

Frelia grabbed the blade and turned away for a few moments. I never quite found out exactly what it was that she did with it, but a few moments later she turned back around and it was gone.

"Tilly, give Elaine your coat," was Ellen's next instruction.

I pulled it free from my shoulders and helped her wrap it around Elaine, to hide the sight of her red-splattered clothes.

It became my duty to look after Elaine, because she was still in a state of shock from whatever ordeal she had been through; she didn't say much and remained glued to my side.

Tristan led us the rest of the way to Neal's bar, which was a large building with a small lamp shining above the door. Neal himself was a middle-aged man, and he could not hide his surprise when the whole gang of us showed up, though

Tristan took him aside and gave him a brief explanation. It soon became clear to me that they were a couple, but what was even more surprising was that nobody seemed fazed at all when they kissed each other openly. They were all busy claiming seats from the jumbled tables, chairs and benches scattered around the room. I sat myself between Elaine and Faye.

"I'm sorry about the state of the place," Neal eventually said, walking over a few minutes later bearing a tray filled with glasses of beer. "I haven't had the chance to do it up yet."

"I like it," Kev said.

"You would, mess-head," Pikel grinned. He was sitting next to Frelia, and couldn't keep his eyes off her.

"I've already told you I'll paint the walls for you," Tristan said.

"I would love you to," Neal said as he handed him a drink. "But I'm not quite sure what I want yet... I have to think of the clientele. Do you want a beer?" he asked when the tray came to me. He gave me a smile that made me understand what Tristan saw in him.

"Um..." I mumbled, feeling a bit ruffled. I had never been offered alcohol before and my grandmother never kept it in the house. "I... don't know..."

"Do you drink?"

I shook my head.

"Never?" Neal said, barely veiling his surprise when I shook my head again. "My Gods. Do you want to try?"

"I'm not sure..." I mumbled. "What's it like?"

He laughed. "You're adorable! I don't want to ruin that. How about lemonade?"

I nodded and he nipped over to the bar.

"Do you own the whole building?" I asked when he returned.

He nodded. "Yeah but it's all a bit ramshackle, I'm afraid. So I'm not sure what to do with it... the rent's cheap though... anyway, what happened? Some of you look a little roughed up."

"They attacked Tilly," Frelia said.

"Why would anyone want to attack *you*?" Neal said.

"You're only a little one. That place is a bloody disgrace these days. Just stop going!"

"You should all just come here instead," Pikel said simply.

"Oh, I didn't mean—" Neal began.

"No, I know you didn't," Pikel said. "But I do. Listen, I have been going to that damn place every week for months and I think I understand it now. Janus was once this great place where nobody gave a fuck and you could just have fun, but then some bloody kids who don't have a clue tried to steal your vibe."

By now everyone had gone quiet. Their attention was devoted to Pikel, and what he was trying to say. It felt important.

"You just need to move on," he declared. "Look around you – *this*, what we have here tonight – isn't it that feeling, that craziness you were looking for? *You* are Janus. Let those kids keep the empty shell. You can make a new one!"

"But what if they follow us?" Frelia asked.

"They will," Pikel said, shrugging. "Slowly. And then, so what? Neal will have a packed out bar of consuming morons, and you can just move on again. It's just human nature or whatever you call it. To keep yourselves free you just need to move every now and then."

"Sounds good to me," Neal said, beaming.

"Me too," Frelia said, leaning over and kissing Pikel on the cheek. His face went red. "Just do us a favour Neal, and don't bloody do it up. Kev's right, this place is perfect as it is."

"Could we use one of your rooms upstairs to practice?" Ellen asked. "We don't mind paying some rent."

"If you're good enough you can have it for free!" Neal said. "As long as you play down here occasionally. Nothing draws punters better than some music."

"Lots of us are creative by nature," Namda said. "You wouldn't need to worry about decorating, Neal. People who come here will add their own bits and bobs."

"And I will destroy it after!" Halann exclaimed with a grin on her face. I got the feeling she was only half joking.

Within moments everyone was talking and laughing again. Neil brought around more free beer and it gradually spiralled into a party. It was fun to watch everyone become drunk and giggly as the night went on, but I stuck to just drinking lemonade.

It wasn't until I saw daylight peeping through the blinds that I realised a whole night had gone. By that time some of them had crashed out on the floor; Namda and Halann had taken Elaine away to get her a change of clothes and give her a makeover; Pag and Kev were engaged in some peculiar discussion about quantum mechanics which the rest of us didn't understand; Frelia and Pikel had long ago disappeared together; Jack was playing his guitar; Ellen and Patrick were singing; and Faye and I were the best of friends, already discussing the possibility of me transferring to her school.

I knew I had a whole series of hells to go through when I went home to my grandmother, but I was ready for them. I was ready for the world.

~

Acknowledgements

Foremost I need to thank Roy Gilham, who from the day we met has read and critiqued pretty much everything I have ever written. Your feedback isn't always kind, but it is honest and often constructive.

, The teachers at Trinity College St David. Throughout the course of two degrees they managed to sharpen my writing skills to a level where I could finally begin to express some of those crazy things going on in my head in a manner where other people could, also, begin to enjoy them. That is a very precious gift to give to someone. Dic Edwards and Paul Wright are two names I feel a particular need to mention.

Simon Llewellyn, for being the second person to ever read the entire manuscript. When someone like you says good things... well... that *is* a good sign.

Iris Mansfield, who read one of the stories to check for accuracy and gave me lots of useful comments.

Douglas Thompson, for recommending I try submitting to Elsewhen Press – that was definitely a good shout.

My editors, Dan and Sofia, who, with much patience, brought vast improvements to this novel and taught me how to use a comma.

And finally, Pete and Al, for your enthusiasm, hard work, and taking a chance on me.

Elsewhen Press

an independent publisher specialising in Speculative Fiction

Visit the Elsewhen Press website at elsewhen.co.uk for the latest information on all of our titles, authors and events; to read our blog; find out where to buy our books and ebooks; or to place an order.

Elsewhen Press

an independent publisher specialising in Speculative Fiction

THE RHYMER

an Heredyssey

DOUGLAS THOMPSON

The Rhymer, an Heredyssey defies classification in any one literary genre. A satire on contemporary society, particularly the art world, it is also a comic-poetic meditation on the nature of life, death and morality.

A mysterious tramp wanders from town to town, taking a new name and identity from whoever he encounters first. Apparently amnesiac or even brain-damaged, Nadith Learmot nonetheless has other means to access the past and perhaps even the future: upon his chest a dial, down his sleeves wires that he can connect to the walls of old buildings from which he believes he can read their ghosts like imprints on tape. Haunting him constantly is the resemblance he apparently bears to his supposed brother, a successful artist called Zenir. Setting out to pursue Zenir and denounce or blackmail him out of spite, in his travels around the satellite towns and suburbs surrounding a city called Urbis, Nadith finds he is always two steps behind a figure as enigmatic and polyfaceted as himself. But through second hand snippets of news he increasingly learns of how his brother's fortunes are waning, while his own, to his surprise, are on the rise. Along the way, he encounters unexpected clues to his own true identity, how he came to lose his memory and acquire his strange 'contraption'. When Nadith finally catches up with Zenir, what will they make of each other?

Told entirely in the first person in a rhythmic stream of lyricism, Nadith's story reads like Shakespeare on acid, leaving the reader to guess at the truth that lies behind his madness. Is Nadith a mental health patient or a conman? ... Or as he himself comes to believe, the reincarnation of the thirteenth century Scottish seer True Thomas The Rhymer, a man who never lied nor died but disappeared one day to return to the realm of the faeries who had first given him his clairvoyant gifts?

Douglas Thompson's short stories have appeared in a wide range of magazines and anthologies. He won the Grolsch/Herald Question of Style Award in 1989 and second prize in the Neil Gunn Writing Competition in 2007. His first book, *Ultrameta*, published in 2009, was nominated for the Edge Hill Prize, and shortlisted for the BFS Best Newcomer Award. Since then he has published more novels, including *Entanglement* published by Elsewhen Press. *The Rhymer* is his eighth novel.

ISBN: 9781908168511 (epub, kindle)
ISBN: 9781908168412 (192pp paperback)

Visit bit.ly/TheRhymer-Heredyssey

Elsewhen Press

an independent publisher specialising in Speculative Fiction

BOOK 1 OF THE BLUEPRINT TRILOGY

FUTURE PERFECT

KATRINA MOUNTFORT

The *Blueprint* trilogy takes us to a future in which men and women are almost identical, and personal relationships are forbidden. Following a bio-terrorist attack, the population now lives within comfortable Citidomes. MindValues advocate acceptance and non-attachment. The BodyPerfect cult encourages a tall thin androgynous appearance, and looks are everything.

This first book, *Future Perfect*, tells the story of Caia, an intelligent and highly educated young woman. In spite of severe governmental and societal strictures, Caia finds herself becoming attracted to her co-worker, Mac, a rebel whose questioning of their so-called utopian society both adds to his allure and encourages her own questioning of the status quo. As Mac introduces her to illegal and subversive information she is drawn into a forbidden, dangerous world, becoming alienated from her other co-workers and resmates, the companions with whom she shares her residence. In a society where every thought and action are controlled, informers are everywhere; whom can she trust?

When she and Mac are sent on an outdoor research mission, Caia's life changes irreversibly.

A dark undercurrent runs through this story; the enforcement of conformity through fear, the fostering of distorted and damaging attitudes towards forbidden love, manipulation of appearance and even the definition of beauty, will appeal to both an adult and young adult audience.

Katrina Mountfort was born in Leeds. After a degree in Biochemistry and a PhD in Food Science, she started work as a scientist. Since then, she's had a varied career. Her philosophy of life is that we only regret the things we don't try, and she's been a homeopath, performed forensic science research and currently works as a freelance medical writer. She now lives in Saffron Walden with her husband and two dogs. When she hit forty, she decided it was time to fulfil her childhood dream of writing a novel. *Future Perfect* is her debut novel and is the first in the *Blueprint* trilogy.

ISBN: 9781908168559 (epub, kindle)
ISBN: 9781908168450 (288pp paperback)

Visit bit.ly/Blueprint-FuturePerfect

About the author

Tej Turner has just begun branching out as a writer and been published in anthologies, including *Impossible Spaces* (Hic Dragones Press) and *The Bestiarum Vocabulum* (Western Legends).

His parents moved around a bit while he was growing up so he doesn't have any particular place he calls "home", but most of his developing years were spent in the West country of England. He went on to Trinity College in Carmarthen to study Film and Creative Writing, and then later to complete an MA at The University of Wales, Lampeter, where he minored in ancient history but mostly focused on sharpening his writing skills.

Tej has just returned from backpacking his way across Asia and keeping a travelblog (http://tejturner.wordpress.com) to let his friends and fans follow him on his adventures as he gallivanted around Burma, Indonesia, the Philippines, and Nepal. When he is not trekking through jungles or exploring temples, reefs, and caves he is usually based in Cardiff, where he works by day, writes by moonlight, and squeezes in the occasional trip to roam around megalithic sites and the British countryside. The next time he has enough money he will be flying off on another adventure.

The Janus Cycle is his first published novel. He is currently engaged in writing an epic fantasy series.